C000133129

THE 9th HOUR

Claire Stibbe

United States of America

THE 9TH HOUR

Copyright © Claire Stibbe 2016

Noble Lizard Publishing

This is a work of fiction. Names, characters, places and incidents either are the product of the author's imagination or are used fictitiously, and any resemblance to any actual persons, living or dead, events, or locales is entirely coincidental.

All rights reserved. No part of this book may be reproduced or transmitted in any form or by any means, electronic or mechanical, including photocopying, recording, or by any information storage and retrieval system, without prior permission in writing of Noble Lizard Publishing.

Alternatively, the author can be contacted at her website.

www.cmtstibbe.com

ISBN-10: 0-9906004-4-0
ISBN-13: 978-0-9906004-4-2

Printed in the United States of America

Artwork: Author Design Studio
Editing: Kingdom Writing Solutions

Acknowledgements

My thanks to New Mexico for providing the inspiration for my books. To my parents for such an incredible upbringing and to Jeff and Jamie for their loving support.

Special thanks to officers and detectives of the Albuquerque Police Department, to Detective Brian Crafton, to the Citizen's Police Academy and to Officer Michael King whose compassion and humor will never be forgotten.

I would also like to thank Twisted Ink Publishing, The 13th Sign, An Tig Beag Press, Famelton Publishing, Miriam Drori, Teri Pickering and Wood & Gibson Literary Discussion Group.

Claire Stibbe
Albuquerque, New Mexico
September 2015

Other Books by Claire Stibbe

The Detective Temeke Crime Series
Night Eyes
Past Rites

Historical Fiction Series
Chasing Pharaohs
The Fowler's Snare

ONE

The man walked to the edge of the wood swinging a steel forged axe. Blood dripped from the blade and left a sticky trail in the dead brown leaves.

He whispered as he walked, hardly feeling the wind against his naked flesh or the snow between his toes, oblivious to the wolf that waited in the shadows, tongue lolling through the gap in its teeth.

"Freedom or life?" the man murmured. He waited for a rise in the wind. "Freedom *is* life."

He stopped in front of a stand of trees, peering up through the branches at a dark blue sky. Night. His favorite time of day. That's when he last saw his precious brother, Morgan, all those years ago. Calm blue eyes flickering as he lay on his back in a bed of leaves.

"I'm immortal." Those were his last words.

Sometimes the man would hear things like the rune poems they used to sing, sometimes he liked to run naked through the trees feeling the leaves and branches slapping against his thighs, delighting in the pain. Delighting in the scars.

Delighting in the memory of his mother's clear angelic voice singing the tributes to Odin.

Sometimes he heard the sound of a truck powering down the track in the morning. At first he thought it was Morgan reborn, until the memories came flooding back.

Dead. Morgan was *dead*.

Well, not quite.

If he listened hard enough he could hear a little boy's laughter.

"No more games," he said out loud. "It's time for bed."

He let the fiberglass handle slip through his hands, let the axe fall. *Thud.*

The sound reminded him of summer rain and the blur of voices that were once his family. He couldn't remember their faces. It was so long ago. But they did have faces once, didn't they?

Sometimes he thought he could see Morgan in the bathroom mirror or on the staircase. Sometimes he saw him running between the trees, turning suddenly and laughing. Morgan liked being chased. He liked being caught. He was only nine.

The man closed his eyes for a moment, hearing the hollow breeze in the pine trees and the young girl's whispers rattling into the night. What luck for him that such a beautiful head had appeared in such a place. She was young. Too young. He would have searched the universe to snap her up, and tonight the pleasure was all his.

When Odin had all nine, Morgan would walk again. That was the promise.

The man had the seventh head but not the eighth and the ninth. That was the worst of it. Thinking about numbers made his brain hurt, as if his mind was a series of grooved tracks where one had somehow become scratched.

"Odin doesn't need to know," he whispered, trying to ground himself.

No, Odin didn't need to know about the mistake. Everyone makes mistakes. One head's just as good as another.

Yes, he was good at keeping secrets. He was good at almost anything. Defense was his greatest gift. He'd always defended his brother from the bullies in the playground and he demanded the same in return. And now here he was, alone in the woods in a dark moonlit world.

He was dreaming more and more, and that bothered him. Dreams of pine trees and frozen lakes, dreams of sledges and laughing children. Dreams of going home, things he couldn't have. To replay childhood memories over and over again in the hope that the ending would somehow change.

He wasn't sad. Not all the time.

When he took life, it was only to resurrect that which was cruelly taken from him. It was a power he secretly loathed, as if someone had thrown a switch that could never be turned off.

There were no witnesses, no first-hand accounts. That was the beauty of it.

No one to tell him to take deep breaths as they tied him to the bed. No one to flip the switch that released all the barbiturates, the paralytic, and whatever else they pumped into a prisoner's veins. That was his dream, his longing.

It would stop then. All of it.

He would take his last breath and become immortal. Just like his brother. The battle of good against evil was almost finished. He'd done the right thing.

Only, not in the right way.

TWO

Detective David Temeke parked his 1962 Hotchkiss round the back of the Northwest Area Command building where, hopefully, Unit Commander Hackett wouldn't see it. He had been teased enough about the rattling exhaust and the squeaky horn, but the thing still flew like a phantom. At least in his mind.

He tensed as he turned off the ignition, thinking about his latest case. Former homicide detective, Jack Reynolds, was found dead in his car last Wednesday night with a decapitated cat on the passenger seat. What a bummer, and three weeks before Christmas.

There was a note attached to its back leg with the words *until the ninth hour* written in perfect cursive. Temeke's jaw tightened just thinking about it. No bastard was going to leave a bloody feline in his car.

There had been other victims of this deranged serial killer. A seventeen-year-old senior at Cibola High. Patti Lucero. It was all over the news and highway billboards and if they didn't hurry up and find her, there would be candlelight vigils in every town.

Temeke zipped up his jacket and looked up at a gray brick building dedicated to two fallen cops. It was recently built, light and bright, holding an Impact Team of three detectives, one unit sergeant and eight additional teams of sworn officers and admin staff. Very lucky boys and girls, some of whom were still in their beds snoring like chainsaws. It was five-thirty in the morning.

He shivered as he walked toward the front door, rasping a match on the wall to light a cigarette. Two long hard drags later and he noticed a patrol wagon parked nearby with a crime-stopper sticker on the rear window. It was a picture of Bullet, the friendly coyote wearing a Kevlar vest. The heading read *Be alert! Crimes hurt.* Kids liked Bullet. If they were lost or in trouble they could always find a safe-house with the familiar sticker on the front door.

Temeke ran a hand over his bald head. It was powdered with a light dusting of snow, the first flakes of December. The passenger window was heavily tinted and the rubber seal in the door was cracked and peeling. Somehow the wagon no longer looked like the model of security the public was led to believe.

He dropped the remains of his cigarette on the ground and watched it sizzle in a pile of gray slush before the faint orange glow died altogether. He couldn't believe he'd been relegated to Northwest Area Command, all because he couldn't get along with the nine detectives and two sergeants assigned to the Homicide Unit. Eight, now Jack was dead. The Chief of Police wasn't partial to Temeke's crude humor or his tendency to cut corners and he was beginning to feel like he was being put out to grass.

The doors of the building swung open and Lt. Luis Alvarez, his brother-in-law, burst forth like a big gut from a tight shirt. He was the only friend Temeke had.

"Blimey Luis, got enough gel on that hair?" Each bristle stood to attention with beads of pomade glistening in the sun.

Luis grinned and pointed back at the lobby. "Stinks of bleach in there. Fergus has been mooning Sarge through the window. Left a nasty stain on the glass."

Temeke remembered the vagrant, all covered in dirt

and flashing more of his credentials through an open fly. He leaned towards the window and screwed up his face. "Looks like two puffy clouds with a crack down the middle. And that crack, my friend, was packed with a bit of Aunt Nora two weeks ago."

Luis shook his head. "Hackett's mourning Detective Reynolds. Hardly ate the burrito I brought him."

Temeke tried to picture the scene. "When you found Jack what did you see?"

"I found his car under the bridge on exit 230 to San Mateo. He was hunched over the steering wheel, driver's window open. There was a gunshot wound to his temple."

Temeke couldn't understand why Jack Reynolds would have stopped under the bridge in the first place. Unless he was picking up someone he knew.

"Just after the murder of the Williams kid, I took a phone call from a young woman. She claimed to have been shot near the Shelby ranch," Luis said, looking around the parking lot. "She said the little one had been killed. Said it was a mistake. Phone went dead after that. We found Morgan Eriksen. He was disoriented, drugged like he didn't know what had happened. Trouble was, he had the victim's blood all over him."

"Stroke of luck he was sitting there waiting for you."

Luis grinned. "Lunch? Fat Jacks?"

Temeke shrugged. "Depends what Hackett's got up his sleeve. It's the 9th Hour. Every hour."

Luis bounced down the steps and along the sidewalk towards his parked car, hand tugging at his ear lobe. "I've been thinking. The victim was a lot younger than the others. All child and no makeup. Unless he was some kind of pedo, I think he took the wrong one. She wasn't tagged like the others."

Temeke knew Luis' mind had that uncanny way of unraveling faster than a wind-up toy. The victims in their case ranged from fourteen to eighteen; each had been found wearing a silver earing engraved with a number. The Williams girl was only nine and all she had were two diamond studs in her ears. "We don't know he wasn't a pedophile. We only have their heads."

"Who was she with when she was taken?"

Temeke walloped his forehead with a palm. "Her sister. Her fourteen-year-old sister."

"It's just a thought," Luis said, standing beside his car. "But we think he took the wrong girl."

Cursing loudly, Temeke waved goodbye and stomped into the lobby. The door slammed shut behind him and he stood there for a moment, agonizing on how they were going to keep that bit of news from leaking to the press.

He stiffened suddenly and lifted his chin. "Hello... that's not bleach," he said, catching the scent of perfume before a draft snatched away even the faintest whisper of it.

Hispanic, he decided. One hundred and twenty-five pounds of muscle and shiny brown skin. Malin Santiago, the squad's newest recruit. He craned his neck towards the stairs. Too many cigarettes had put a stop to leaping up two flights of them and he decided to use the elevator.

Commander Hackett hogged it whenever he could, insisting the stairs were his. Hackett was his preferred name and he was a bad-tempered old sod at the best of times.

Temeke punched the button and heard a familiar grinding sound from somewhere up there in that dusty shaft. One of these days he would see a blur of faces in that tiny window as the thing zipped downward before crashing to the ground floor. Life was always a gamble.

He was met with the smell of burning rubber as the elevator clawed up one floor, stopping on the second.

The walls had a new line of graffiti he hadn't seen before. The first line read, *Jesus Saves* and underneath someone had written *Pink Car Edition Hot Wheels*.

It reminded him of his childhood. Life in Brixton, London, had never been easy. He had been beaten up twice for having immigrant parents and a school uniform. There was gang graffiti under bridges and the constant reek of death in the public toilets. That's where the gangs beat you up. That's where they left you to die. And that's where bodies frequently turned up. In the lavatories. Where gangs had been peeing all over the evidence since eight o'clock the night before.

England was a wet green place he'd never forget. Too damn cold to go back and there was no family left to speak of now his parents were dead. He moved to New Mexico ten years ago. Better food, better climate. Until the summer months when the heat made the sweat drip between your buttocks.

He was jolted back to the present as the elevator reached the second floor. Hackett stood in the corridor tapping his wrist and hugging a buff file under one arm. "Anything wrong with the stairs?" he asked.

"Stairs? What stairs?" Temeke saw the roll of the eyes and grinned. "Am I late?"

It was his day off and he was already working a double shift. He'd had no sleep last night and if it hadn't been for those pesky teenagers bumping and grinding in his driveway to a round of *Let's Play House* by Elvis Presley, he might have got a lot more.

"You're always late." Hackett peered at his watch and sneezed. "Twenty-two minutes late if you must know. And I've got an allergy in case you were wondering."

Temeke was wondering. If it was flu he would have told Hackett to push off. Worse than Hackett's wittering was the frightening fact that he hadn't been able to see

Luis Alvarez for lunch in nearly two weeks. Come to think of it, he hadn't seen much of his wife either.

"You know why you're here?" Hackett said.

"No one told me. No one ever does."

"I expect you saw the paddy wagon." Hackett combed a thatch of gray hair through his fingers. "They brought Eriksen here this morning. Looks like he wants coffee and a chat. With *you*."

"Me? Why me?"

"He knows you took that phone call last Friday afternoon from his delectable girlfriend. I think he'd like to know where she is."

"I'd like to know where she is. Said she was in a house surrounded by trees. Said she was chained to a bed. Then the line went dead. Now why would a nice young girl chain herself to a bed?"

"If I were you, I'd call the psychic. He's bound to know something."

"How much are we paying him, sir? Because according to him, the Duke City Police Department is full of murderers and we lucky detectives are too dumb to see it."

Hackett pursed his lips and sniffed. "We pinged the location of the number she used. Came up stolen. Trouble is, they keep changing."

"So tell me, if Morgan Eriksen's inside, whose holding his girlfriend?"

Hackett walked down the corridor alongside Temeke, one hand in his pocket. "She called Lt. Alvarez two weeks ago, told him about the barn, about the Williams girl. She hung up before he could get anything else out of her. Whoever this man is, he calls himself The 9th Hour Killer."

"And the public thinks it's Morgan Eriksen."

Hackett barely nodded, face reddening. "I won't let DCPD go down for this one, Temeke. We've got to find the real killer before the police look like a bunch of idiots. And it won't be the first time."

"Probably got a little truncheon, sir."

"Night stick, Temeke, *night stick*. And it may have escaped our killer's notice but these nine hours are turning into a few days."

"Gives us a bit more time then."

Hackett patted a large belly which gaped through the missing button on his shirt. "This might come as a complete surprise, but you're not exactly the flavor of the month downtown. That's why they sent you up here. The Chief's not ready to get rid of you yet. I'm embarrassed to tell Judge Matthews you've been picked for the case. But the fact is, no one else wants it. Not when there's a cop killer out there."

"Very commendable, sir."

"Sarge said you were chatting up his daughter yesterday."

"Becky's just a kid. She squeezed my butt when I was leaning over the water fountain. Took the handcuffs right out of my belt and tied herself up. It's true, sir. Wriggled out all by herself. Double-jointed she told me."

"Listen, I don't care about her joints. Keep your fingerprints out of the system." Hackett sneezed and wiped his nose on a square of toilet paper. "You've got a new partner. Malin Santiago. Speaks Norwegian like a native. I want you both out in the field."

"Trying to get rid of me?"

"To make things easier, Sergeant Moran will locate the witnesses, download any surveillance footage and manage the database. How's your wife?"

The question took Temeke by surprise. Hackett hardly ever asked officers about their spouses. "Complaining. Said the fairy on the Christmas tree's packed on a few pounds since last year."

Hackett stopped in front of a black and white poster

of a young woman, seventeen years old with pale blue eyes. "Patti Lucero. Missing for over a week," he said, sucking in air and shaking his head. "Listen, I know you're pushing forty and fed up but this could be our lucky break. Eriksen won't speak to me. He won't speak to Homicide. See if he knows who did it."

"Maybe he doesn't know."

"Of course he knows."

"I hope you're right. I wouldn't want you making a prat of yourself in front of the judge, sir."

"You'll have a few good men," Hackett said, sighing. "You and your partner are the few good men. No need to meet with the usual squad members and you needn't worry about their investigative plans. I've got it covered. This case is top priority. Why? Because it's getting out of hand. Every month a girl goes missing, gets a nice silver earring, and the public are starting to panic."

Temeke nodded. "Witness interviews, search warrants, reports?"

"Like I said, I want you both out in the field. But if you don't mind keeping me updated, I'd be grateful." Hackett lowered his voice. "There's been a few complaints about Darryl Williams, you know, the father of the nine-year-old. Neighbors heard some gun shots last night. I hope nobody told him the killer made a mistake. A father could go over the top if he found out his youngest daughter was mistaken for the eldest. And I don't want him using that gun on the killer."

Temeke shrugged. "Not before he's answered a few questions that is."

"I want you to take him this." Hackett handed him a small red notebook. "Let him know she would have wanted him to have it."

"And he's going to be okay with the fact that the field investigators didn't find it all those weeks ago when they were clearing for evidence. He's going to be okay with the fact that a dog found it instead."

"Dogs are just as intelligent as man. Only a little more thorough I should say. Eriksen leaves for the Pen this morning. If you guys hit it off, better pin Highway 14 in your GPS. You've got three hours before he leaves." Hackett handed over the buff file and jerked a thumb towards the end of the corridor. "Interview room 3, last on the left."

"Is his face in the papers yet? Because if not I'd like to keep it that way."

"Your case, your choice."

Temeke had hoped he'd seen the last of dead bodies for a while, only recently they were becoming as common as weed. It was the faces he couldn't stand. Granted, the eyes were closed unless you found one in a back alley all pale and staring. Drunks and the elderly who had seen something of life were bad enough, but it was the kids that tore him apart.

He nodded at an agent and stared through the security glass at the man sitting at the table. Blond hair braided in a rope from the forehead to the nape of the neck. There was the hint of a tattoo above one ear, barely visible behind the stubble.

Two officers peered through the glass. Captain Fowler, straight-faced and coldly efficient, whose humor never rose higher than sarcasm, and officer Jarvis, fleshy and a little overweight, jaw working over a wad of gum.

"Morgan Eriksen," Fowler said, folding arms corded with muscle. "Half Norwegian. Apparently. Can't see why he'd want to talk to you."

"Has he been read his rights?" Temeke asked.

"Yeah, only he's too frozen to speak."

"Frozen with fear, amusement? What?"

Fowler shrugged and shook his head. "Who knows."

"Lucky he's hobbled at the ankle and wrists, sir." Jarvis chimed in, jabbing a pudgy finger at the window and winking a pale blue eye. "There's no way he can escape. But he could spit."

Temeke felt the nudge at his elbow, saw Fowler's thin lips making a beeline for his ear. "Really gets under your skin, doesn't he?"

THREE

Temeke knew the best way to craft an interview was to allow the prisoner to plead his case, to be comfortable enough for the tougher questions. This one looked nervous and he didn't look much like a pleader.

Temeke nodded at Agent Stu Anderson, tried to restrain a snort at his blue-gray hair and matching tie. His throat tightened as he leafed through the top file. There were pictures of several female victims and his eyes froze on little Kizzy Williams, a nine-year-old African American girl. "How long was Eriksen in processing?"

"Two weeks," Stu said. "First orientation didn't go too well. Tried to slice the finger off a prison guard with a plastic knife. He's smart though. *Very* smart."

"Doesn't sound smart to me."

"He tucked that knife in his cuff when no one was looking." Stu folded his arms and rocked back on his heels. "He's from California, an athlete."

So that's why the Fabulous But Incompetent had been called in, Temeke thought. Eriksen had crossed several state lines.

"Been in the Westwood Journal a few times. Won the Josiah Royce award for swimming at college. Looks like a good all-rounder. Recent medical showed dissociative personality."

"Not sure how you'd tell," Temeke said, scratching

his chin, "because he was drugged up to the eyeballs when he was found. Who in their right mind would give an overdose of Nembutal to a little girl and then turn the bottle on himself? They both should have died peacefully."

Stu frowned. "What do you mean?"

"The girl was devoid of a head in an area where you'd normally find one. Morgan couldn't have given her the old chop. Not in his state of mind."

Stu stopped rocking. "You've got a heart as warm as the Sandia Crematorium."

"So when's Hackett holding a press conference?"

"Hasn't said."

"Probably not advisable. Don't want the public knowing what the suspect looks like. Don't want the suspect knowing what the suspect looks like." Temeke frowned and held up the earpiece. "You leading?"

"I'll prompt if you need me. Give him regular breaks. He works better that way."

"Oh, and by the way, when he gets to PNM, make sure he's allowed a few calls. I'd like to listen to the tapes."

Temeke knew Eriksen's world would be different once he was locked in the Penitentiary of New Mexico. Guards yelling, the echoing clang of metal gates and the constant reek of cleaning fluids. It would be a cacophony of sounds and smells, and bright-ass lights on at seven o'clock in the morning. A few months of dominoes slamming against metal tables and he might be itching to tell the truth.

Temeke entered the small cell and slapped the file down on the desk. He had a weird feeling in the pit of his stomach and if he could put a name to it, *fear* was the first thing that came to mind.

"I'm Detective Temeke—"

"I know who you are." Morgan Eriksen scuffed the

floor with one foot. "Word gets out."

"Oh really," Temeke said, sitting. "And what did you hear?"

"Your mother's British. Lived in Brixton. So you moved to the US in, what, 2001? Just after your father died. He was from Ethiopia. That's something you and I have in common. Immigrants. Now you're a big shot in the department, only you had to crawl your way to the top because you're black. They don't like blacks, do they?"

"They don't? I hadn't noticed."

"You're married to Serena, double vision, hates the heat. Oh, and you have a very big secret." Morgan lifted his thumb and index finger to his lips as if he was smoking a joint. "That's what I found."

"Looks like you know all about me." The constant clink of the cuffs reminded Temeke that his prisoner was restless but well-shackled. As for the spitting, Jarvis was in for a kicking.

"I suppose you're wondering why I wouldn't talk to anyone else. There was no one else. At least nobody I could trust." Morgan inclined his head and smiled. "I like you. But don't think I'm going to plead my case because I won't. I'll be walking out of here in a week or two."

Temeke pursed his lips and flicked an eye over the cuffs. "You won't be *walking* anywhere, son. You'll be in the Pen this afternoon under lock and key."

"I'm not your son, detective."

"No, you're quite right. Lucky me." Temeke glanced briefly at the file.

"What do you see?" Morgan said, tapping his chest.

Temeke stared at Morgan long and hard. "When I look at you?"

"Yes, when you look at me."

Maniac, Temeke wanted to say and shrugged.

"Player."

"Ah, you've studied my file. You've studied me. You've no idea how special that makes us feel."

"Us?"

"Him and me," Morgan said, eyeing the empty chair beside him.

"Oh him." Temeke looked at the chair, wondering what ghosts the poor boy saw. "And who's *him*?"

"My brother."

"What's his name?"

Morgan lifted his chin and sneered. "You can't see him can you?"

"Neither can you." Temeke heard a snarky remark in his earpiece and decided to move on. "Know anything about the recent disappearance of Patti Lucero?"

"Know about it? It's all over the news." Morgan chuckled. "I'm a celebrity now."

"It may have escaped your tiny little mind, Morgan, but you've been inside longer than that. So we really can't assume you did it. And the public aren't privy to a recent picture. We decided to spare them that horror." Temeke noticed how the smile twitched off. "So who's been snatching these high school girls in your absence?"

Morgan bowed his head and studied his feet. "There's two of me and only one of you. Good luck with that."

"So you keep telling me," Temeke said, thinking of another bullet to fire. He wanted to know how Morgan got involved, how he did it all those months ago. "Let's talk about something else, shall we? On the night of Monday, October 27th at around eleven o'clock, did you take Kizzy Williams from a tent in Cimarron State Park?"

"Yeah."

"When you took her from the tent was she asleep?"

Morgan's mouth twitched slightly. "She was."

Temeke was relieved. There was no way the little girl would have gone willingly with a man like Morgan Erikson. His arms were covered in Celtic knots and on one side of his head were tattoos of the sun, moon and stars peeking out between the stubble.

"Where did you take her?"

"About fifty yards downriver there's a ranch," Morgan said slowly, staring at Temeke's bald head as if he could see his face in it. "That's where I parked my pickup."

"Shelby's ranch, right?"

"Yes."

"Did you talk to her?"

Morgan looked down at his hands and clenched his jaw. "I asked her about her dad, her sisters."

"Tell me about her sisters."

"One sings, the other's an athlete. What's to tell?"

"The athlete's tall for a fourteen year old. Looks about sixteen, doesn't she? Girls can do that... you know... look older."

Temeke watched Morgan lean back in his chair as if distancing himself from the comment. His eyes seemed to dance around the room, lips pressed into a thin white line.

"Have you always got along with your brother?"

Morgan shrugged. "We've had our moments."

"Bad moments? You know, when you make a mistake... mistaken identity."

Morgan's open mouth began blowing out short breaths and he bounced a curled knuckle against the desk.

"When did you realize she was the wrong girl?" Temeke watched Morgan's eyes, saw the eyebrows hitch upwards almost to his hairline. "Because she was the wrong girl, wasn't she? I expect you found out when you pulled her out of the tent. She was half the size of the older one. Underage and all. That must have been a big disappointment. Did you hurt her?"

"When she woke up I had to choke her. She was making too much noise."

Temeke listened to the Nordic accent fading in and out. "Did she die when you choked her?"

"No."

"When did she die, Morgan?" Temeke gritted his teeth. This was the part he dreaded the most.

"Not until the ninth hour."

"According to this, your girlfriend spent her time getting a bit of the old heave-ho with another man. Who was this other man? Because you didn't kill Kizzy Williams, did you? No, someone smarter than you did."

Morgan gave Temeke a pitying shake of the head. "Why am I here?"

"Because you were *there*."

That's how it was with Morgan, taking his sweet time with everything. It took the next half an hour to describe the ranch and the stupid trees he cared so much about. His slate-gray eyes were dull as if he was already dead and sometimes he would look up and sniff the air, flexing his hands. Big choking hands.

"We like the dark ones. Brown eyes, china doll faces. This one did everything we asked."

Temeke felt his chin come up sharply. "What did you ask her to do?"

Morgan frowned and gave a scoffing laugh. "It's isolated out by the farm. Mountains, trees, so many trees. They'll do anything for me because there's no one there to help them. I asked her to be my friend. She was happy then, chirpy, you know."

Couldn't have been that chirpy, Temeke thought, not if the rest of her remains had never been found even after a pack of sniffer dogs had swept the entire countryside with volunteers from the County Sheriff's department.

They found the statue of a dwarf with an eye in the middle of its forehead and nine human faces carved in tree trunks. There were four areas where upright stones marked some kind of ritual ceremony, only they were mostly grown over with grass.

The shadows gave a man that feeling, that keen instinct that something wasn't right. Even the dragonflies with their membranous wings that wafted just above the surface of a small pond were no longer beautiful. There was a jaundiced blush about the place as if the sun would never set.

"Tell me about the barn," Temeke said, studying Morgan's sallow face.

"A barn's a barn. Straw, stalls… what do you want to know?"

"I want to know about the fridge."

The report showed photographs of a tired old barn on the property and a commercial fridge against one wall. It was wrapped in chains and padlocked and quite out of place with its hideous display. Inside were four shelves filled with partial human remains, all girls.

"He kept all kinds of things in there, things I wasn't supposed to see," Morgan whispered.

"But you did see something."

Morgan nodded, eyes flicking sideways to an empty chair beside him. "There's no way I can tell you that."

Temeke knew what happened to Kizzy. She survived just long enough to write one line and to hide a little red notebook between two planks in the wall. She was only nine years old and her head was one of the seven found in the barn.

"I put her to bed." Morgan half-smiled then.

"Whose bed?"

"The caretaker's. He comes midweek to empty the traps."

Temeke remembered the day they drove in to

examine the ranch. The caretaker was walking up the hill towards them and gave a wave and a smile, the kind that lingered long after the car had gone past. Hunchbacked and weighing in at about a hundred and fifty pounds, he was not a man Temeke would call threatening. Come to think of it, he had a walking stick and all.

"Did she go willingly?" *No, of course she didn't go willingly.* She was likely dragged kicking and screaming by a half-wit three times her size.

"She asked for her dad." Morgan said with a prick of irritation. "I told her he would come for her in a day or two. I told her he knew where she was."

Darryl Williams had no clue where his daughter was. He was fifty yards upriver, wide awake and rousing half the campsite. Temeke had stewed for a night or two just thinking about it. "Did she believe you?"

"No. She bit me. She always bit me." The bow of Morgan's lips stretched in a generous curve.

"Where did she bite you?"

"Here mostly," Morgan said, turning his wrist just enough for Temeke to see the underside of his arm.

There was only a slight blemish now, so tiny anyone would have thought it was a birthmark. But the scar would have been different then, deeper, redder. They arrested Morgan soon after Kizzy's head was found. There was enough DNA on those teeth to incriminate him.

"Did you have occasion to hit her?"

"Yes."

"Can you tell me what happened?"

"Uh, I told her to be quiet and she kept talking. So I backhanded her."

"Pardon?"

"I backhanded her."

"That would have shut her up."

"You have no empathy for what I did." Morgan's

eyes slid to the empty chair. "Isn't that right? He has no empathy."

"Who are you talking to?" Temeke said gently, ignoring the time's up prompt from his earpiece. Morgan didn't need a break. Not while he was hot and talking. "Why don't you tell me about him?"

FOUR

Malin Santiago had been waiting for this day. After years of back-aching work, she had returned to Albuquerque to work for the DCPD and for a detective trained in violent crimes against children. But he wasn't just any detective.

Detective Temeke was unmatched at solving cases, cases that baffled his more traditional peers. Sleepless nights never bothered him. In fact, they only served to fuel the lewd humor that she enjoyed and nobody else understood.

He drove a jeep with a horn that sounded like a dog's squeaky toy and he was British with an accent to die for. Drank coffee not tea, and he was one of the few men in the department that hated heights. It was the only weakness she knew of.

Sarge's daughter had the biggest crush on him, strutting around in clothes that treated men to a glorious display of butt and bust, both bursting with enthusiasm. There was a rumor that Detective Temeke had explored those acres of creamy flesh in the bathrooms one afternoon. But Malin didn't believe it. They were jealous, that was all.

One of the admins said he had a pink china pig in his drawer, something to put his spare change in. It just didn't seem to complement the butch image that sat in front of her, fingers tapping the keyboard at a phenomenal rate.

He was a striking man, darker than a coffee bean. He reminded her of one of those greywacke statues in the National History Museum, the ones with prominent cheekbones and perfect lips, the ones with a muscular body she tried hard not to stare at.

"Hackett tells me you speak Norwegian," Temeke said at last, fingers still tapping the keyboard and chewing a half-eaten sandwich.

"My mom was Norwegian."

"Fluent?"

"Pretty much."

Detective Temeke looked at her through narrowed eyes and then carried on typing. "How long were you dating Sgt. Hollister?

"I wasn't dating him," Malin said, feeling the heat in her cheeks. "He had no business ringing my doorbell at two-thirty in the morning and telling everyone I was his girlfriend. *Girlfriend*? I never said I'd go out with him."

"What was he like, this Hollister?"

"Someone you wouldn't approve of."

"I'm beginning to like him already. Lucky you weren't fired."

"Sir?" Malin felt the pain in the back of her throat and tried to swallow.

"Why did you ask for a transfer," he said, speaking in tones that conveyed little emotion.

"I wanted to come home after my mother died."

He was silent for a time, as if mulling over her response. "Your name," he said, chin slightly raised. "It's pronounced Ma*h*lin… right?"

"Yes," she said, glad someone knew how to pronounce it. "Of Magdala. It's Hebrew for *tower*."

His face twisted, giving her the impression he was thinking deeply. "You're not one of those bloody Christians are you?"

"As a matter of fact I am. Does that bother you?" Malin knew it did just by the look on his face.

"Why do you want to work for me?" he said, rattling an empty coke can and hurling it into the bin.

"You're not like the others," she said, regretting the hackneyed comment.

It got his attention though. He wheeled his chair to the center of his desk and stared, eyes blacker than moon shadow. "What am I like?"

"Humane, fair. But then you know what it's like to be on the other side of the tracks, to be hated for the color of your skin. You know what it's like to be one of them."

"One of *them*?"

"The scum of the earth."

"I wouldn't describe myself as scum. I wouldn't describe you as scum. The people out there are the same as you and me, scrabbling for a place, desperate to survive."

"See, it's not like you and I do things differently."

"I don't know what you mean."

"I think you do."

His eyes narrowed again for a moment and then relaxed, chin tilted sideways a little, just enough to make her smile.

"You've rolled a few in your time," she pressed, warm sweat trickling down her back. "Probably got a stash under the kitchen sink. I don't smoke pot myself but I—"

"Work for an escort agency," he murmured. "Minerva, I believe it's called, after the Greek goddess. A slight contradiction in terms since she was a virgin."

"Worked," Malin corrected, sucking in breath, gut swirling like a bad meal. She thought she had meticulously preserved that sad piece of her life.

"You wasted no time since you arrived. Here you are

nearly suspended and now you have friends in high places." Detective Temeke leaned forward, lips widening a little. "I could question you, book you and thank you for your cooperation. Or I could send you running back where you came from. But you wouldn't like that would you?"

"No, sir, I wouldn't."

"Good. So don't go gripping that greasy pole late at night. You'd get just as much attention in the post office."

"I don't pole dance, sir." Malin felt her voice shift up an octave and winced.

"You'd get paid more if you did overtime with the squad. Better get your dimply ass behind that desk tomorrow and read the Eriksen file. From cover to cover, you understand?"

"It's not dimply."

"It is dimply. *Sunbeam.*"

Malin felt her eyebrows lurch upwards, threating to overtake her hairline. Sunbeam had been her escort name and it was a stupid name at that.

"Read that file," he said. "You'll find there's a love triangle. I don't want Patti Lucero turning up dead. There's much more to our man than bloodthirsty lecher. He tries not to yawn when you yawn, tries to play the no empathy card. Something you might be able to help me with."

"Sir, I—"

"Wrap it up, Santiago. You needn't have got all gussied up to see me. Any old suit would do."

Malin felt her cheeks balloon with anger and before she could get a word out he silenced her with a rigid finger. "Don't hide in the lobby stinking up the place with perfume and don't make waves. And no rubbing shoulders with those lunatic cops. They'll be the first to dance around your empty desk like gypsies if you get fired. You'll drive me to Darryl Williams' house tomorrow. I've got something to give him."

"Yes, sir." Malin felt the prickle of tears behind her eyelids.

"And we'll be taking that nice Explorer of yours," he said, shooting a glance out of the window. "Rather get that dinged than mine."

It suddenly seemed a long way from the chair to the window. She couldn't have stood up even if she'd wanted to. Instead she just watched him flicking through the pages of a small red book, sighing occasionally.

Seven girls killed over the span of seven months, taken from shopping malls, school parking lots, tents. Pretty girls. Dark girls. Friendly girls. What was it that connected them? she thought. Accessibility out there alone? Or a buzzing nightlife in the local clubs?

The lucky break came only hours before, a phone call from a young woman. Morgan's girlfriend, Patti, was also scared out of her wits, yacking on about a barn on the Shelby Ranch and a fridge full of grotesque things.

The Shelby Ranch was high up in the hills and bordered by a trickling stream. Half a mile to the west were the remnants of three cabins, one still standing and nestled beneath the palisade cliffs. The others were merely ruins.

The caretaker, a Mr. Bonner Levinson, reported the shiny new truck on the property with a crime-stopper's sticker in the window. It was the Police badge on the door panel, a custom car magnet that got his attention.

He also tried to shoot a lone wolf that kept hanging around the cabins. He swore it wasn't a coyote. Too big for that.

"You're familiar with the Eriksen case, I hope," he said, eyes flicking to the gun in her belt. "Any shared traits?"

"Yes, sir. The girls were either Hispanic or African

American, ranging from age nine to nineteen. And all we have are their heads. Commonalities, attractive high school students vanished in broad daylight, all between the hours of four o'clock in the afternoon and six o'clock, and in a public location."

"What does that tell you?"

"No obvious motivation. So we're dealing with a single killer."

"Not quite. He has an accomplice. A killer whose last victim was nine years old. Different from the others. Looks like he's changing his pattern."

"Looks like he'll have to, sir, ever since we've found his lair."

"Good observation, Marl. I'd never have thought of that myself."

She watched the crossed arms, the harsh squint. He would have given her a quick disgusted snort if she hadn't started talking. "I think we're dealing with a mythopath, sir."

"You made that up."

"Whatever they call someone who believes in mythology, although in his case, talking heads. And he's a sociopath."

"Why a sociopath?" Temeke said, raising an eyebrow and tilting his head. He scrabbled about in a drawer before shining an apple along the leg of his pants.

"Because you said he has no empathy." She sensed him looking at her, sensed his amusement. He should have given her some kudos. She had been listening after all.

"I *said*, he plays that card."

"He doesn't like women, short ones that is, cuts off their heads as trophies, pierces their ears, and hides the torso so we can't read the stomach contents. Probably covers his head with a hairnet and strips naked to do it because we've never found any fingerprints. Have we?"

"No, we haven't."

"Nine is a significant number in Norse mythology, sir. Odin was hanged from the world tree for nine days and nights. There were nine worlds, eighteen magical songs and eighteen magical runes. Interesting don't you think?"

"Perhaps." He gave her a flat gaze before studying the notebook.

"What's it say?" she asked.

Temeke sunk his teeth into the apple and began to read between chews.

When I am afraid, I put my trust in you.

Temeke tapped his lips with the apple and began talking to himself. "It's a song, isn't it?"

"A Psalm, sir. When I was a kid, I learned to recite and write Bible verse from memory."

"So what's the next line?"

Malin stared at drawn brows and a smile that appeared tight. "In God, whose word I praise. In God I trust—and am not afraid."

She saw him cock his head and raise his eyebrows, heard the deep, weighted sigh as she looked out of the window. Reading the last words of a nine-year-old girl brought a fresh wave a bile into her throat. She would have chucked her breakfast in the trash can if it had been any closer.

Nine. Kizzy Williams was *nine*. That made her different. That made her special.

"You'll be working split shifts with me, Santiago, so you'll be on again tonight. I hope that doesn't interfere with your private life—"

"No, sir."

"One wonders how you ever had the time."

"You can call me Malin, sir."

"And you can call me *sir*," he said, hurling the remains of the apple core into the bin.

She almost flinched at the order. No one ever called their partner *sir*, at least no one she could name.

"Did Hackett's assistant find you an apartment?" he asked.

"Puerta de Corrales, sir. Where Sgt. Moran lives."

"I'd like to meet this Hollister when he comes to Albuquerque... the very minute. Is he big?"

"Built like a Sumo." Malin restrained a smile.

"There's something that doesn't quite fit. Something that keeps bothering me," he said.

Malin bristled. "About Hollister?"

"No. Not about Hollister. About Morgan Eriksen. He's got no priors, no record until now. Cleanest slate I ever saw."

FIVE

The man stood under a hot shower, eyes tapering at the swirl of blood between his toes. Water only reminded him he was swimming in grief, a river of it, flowing from north to south, east to west. They said he would learn to live with it. But there were the night terrors, the visions. It was always the first thing in his head when he woke up.

He dried himself off and padded naked into his bedroom. There were two photographs of Morgan on the dresser, one young, one old. There was something odd about them, like a piece missing from a jigsaw. He had noticed it one night, noticed the crooked incisor on Morgan the younger. He had never had his teeth straightened. Hadn't lived long enough for that. But Morgan the elder had the straightest teeth he ever saw.

He knew why. He just couldn't face the truth.

Abandoned. First by his mother. Then his brother. Mamma just got up one morning, packed a bag and left. That was after his brother died, after the funeral. They all knew where she went. To the arms of the hunter in the woods.

Photographs refueled the old memory. But they never took away the pain. It was like an old friend knocking on the door, keeping his heart from ever feeling light again. There was something safe in the familiar. It was where all the old ghosts were.

The killings didn't start until he came to the United States. So drunk on that fishing boat, so much money. It was easy to get a driving license in Maine, easier still to pick up women who offered him a bed to sleep in and a computer to use. They also had cell phones.

But there was only one he really loved.

The rattle of the dog chain made him turn to the king-sized bed. Patti looked at him, face ashen, lips trembling. He had always assumed she was happy, but it was her whimpering that distracted him, her flinching when he tried to touch her. It wasn't the Patti he remembered, the Patti that ran to him one night, arms outstretched, the Patti who once dated his brother.

She couldn't resist him then. She couldn't resist him now. He could tell by the way her eyes kept flicking down his naked body and then up again to his face.

"Give me the number," he said softly, holding out the banker's check.

She rattled it off faster than a social security number. He was impressed. "Wells Fargo. The money's all there," she said. "We never spent any of it."

"Be a good girl and sign it."

She held the pen over the check. The signature was elongated and spidery. A clever forgery of Morgan's. Ole would have all his money back now and Morgan would never know.

Patti was a crier. She cried when he killed the little girl she tried to save. If she hadn't run away through the trees dragging the little one behind her he might have been more merciful. Instead he tied her up, kept her indoors, kept her close just in case she did it again.

She was young and fresh, except for that gunshot wound in her thigh. It was putrefying, stinking up a storm, but he couldn't let her go to the hospital – not with a mouth like hers. He often heard her pitiful moans in the night, slapping them quiet with the flat of his hand. She was dying anyway.

It was time.

"Odin must have heads," he said, sitting on the bed beside her. "Must, must, must."

She reached out for him then, fingers touching his arm. "Don't do it, Ole. They'll kill you if you do."

There was something in the way she said his name. A mingling of sounds more beautiful than a church choir. He wound his arms around her waist, laid his head on her breast. The soft clank of the chain soothed him as he closed his eyes for a moment, smelling the denim of her jeans and the scent in her long dark hair.

"How much do you love me?" he said, lifting his head suddenly, running a finger down her cheek, down her neck. "You do love me, don't you?"

Patti nodded, sucking in breath. She kept her eyes on him, only her fingers were gripping the quilt now, wrists white behind those tight little shackles. "I love you," she whispered. "You promised you'd let me go if I signed it. Untie me?"

He took a deep breath and listened to the crowing in his mind. *I am immortal, I am immortal.*

Patti knew it too. That's what she was afraid of. Her eyes were damp and overly bright, and he could hear the tremors in her voice.

"You mustn't worry," he said. "I'll take you somewhere nice. I promise."

"They'll find you and lock you away. Just like Morgan."

How strange she should be so concerned. "No one will ever find me," he said, kissing those soft pink lips, tasting the salt of her tears. "Tell me something. Your mother's house, what's it like?" He saw the frown and two blinking eyes.

"One story."

"Does she have a dog?" he asked.

"Yes."

"What's its name?"

"Buster."

"A cat?"

"No."

"That'll do for now."

He watched her while he dressed, studied the bindings at her ankles and wrists. There was something exciting about the beads of sweat on her upper lip, the flickering muscles along her arms, a body ready to run. Only he'd slice off those pretty legs if she tried.

There was something exciting about the house too, an exquisite Tuscan estate with sensational views of the golf course. At least that's what the red-headed realtor said. She also pointed out the barreled hallways, timber trusses, 35 foot ceilings, Canterra fireplaces. He didn't need to look any further. It was perfect.

She also pointed out how unusually handsome he was. It was the accent, he told himself. Women were suckers for accents. But he didn't like her fawning tone, nor did he want to be enticed into the furnished master bedroom.

She stared at him with those dazzling eyes, quirking an eyebrow and running one finger along her bottom lip. She told him she liked his cologne, wanted to guess the name of it. He couldn't remember what else he said, but by the look of her face it must have been bad. She became flustered then as if she'd lost all traction, smile fading from those red painted lips.

That's when he blacked out.

And when he came to he found the body floating face-down in the swimming pool. A sad looking thing, arms and legs splayed out in the water like an abandoned doll. He dumped her in next door's dumpster which had been filled with tree branches and compost. With any luck she was now at the bottom of the Cerro Colorado

Landfill.

Scratches on his arms and thighs reminded him the young realtor had fought well. Fought with every last breath. Almost as impressive as Patti, only she had been a real little lady and not some painted skank.

He would call Morgan when he could. He would tell him about the new house, how he had to leave the woods, the barn and the trees. And he would make sure there were nine heads for Odin, even if he had to do it all by himself.

No one knew his name. It was Ole, short for Olafr. Or Morgan. Or both.

When he needed to be Morgan, he conjured up the boy in him. And when he was Ole, well… that was another story.

He saw every text Darryl Williams sent, heard every phone call he made. He could even access the code to the front door.

He combed his fingers through his recently cut hair. It looked better short. It looked better brown. A crucial metamorphosis, especially after the photograph of Morgan he kindly faxed to the Journal last night. Morgan had long blond hair. It would never do to look alike now.

"How do I look?" he said, turning back to Patti's tearstained face.

"So very handsome."

He cocked his head and smiled. She always looked good in a white shirt. So simple. So classy. "How long have we known each other, Patti? A few months? And in those months have you ever known me to steal?"

She shook her head.

"But you took something from me. You took the girl, remember? And the cops took Morgan all because of that nosy caretaker. Did you tell him too?"

Her eyes were hazy with fresh tears and she didn't

answer. Couldn't because she was guilty. She had told the police about the cabin, about the barn, about the girls. That's how they knew where to find them.

The mere sound of her voice set him on edge, the sniveling, the whining. And then, "It was so wrong, Ole. All those things you did."

"You have no idea what I did."

"I saw it. All of it."

"So you called old Mr. Levinson and then you called the cops. Lucky I didn't bring Loki. He would have taken your leg off."

"I couldn't bear it." She began crying again.

All day he meditated on the death of the nine-year-old, how his life had been turned upside down since Morgan's arrest. Morgan was a fool. He'd taken the wrong one.

Ole had found another girl a week ago, a girl to replace Patti. A girl on a bright red bike, a girl he couldn't get out of his mind. He wanted to listen to the wind, to daydream, but matters were closing in on him, especially the matter of the cell phone. It was foolish to leave it behind.

"You've been using the phone again, haven't you? You called that detective. How did you do that, Patti, all tied up? Show me how you did that?"

Patti furrowed her brow and swallowed. She was too thirsty to talk, too frightened. He knew, of course. The pin in those shackles was tight enough. But with a day or two of twisting and straining, she could have freed one hand at least.

"Couldn't exactly tell him anything. You don't know where you are, do you? This phone," he said, holding it up as if she couldn't see it, "is registered under a stolen name. They'll never find you."

"They will, Ole," she said in a scratchy voice. "They'll put a trace on it. And they'll find all those girls in the woods."

His eyes fell on the digital clock on the nightstand. It was ten minutes to six. He snapped on a pair of latex gloves and plucked the earring from his t-shirt pocket. It was a silver disk engraved with the number 8.

"Well then, we better get a move on."

SIX

Darryl Williams slipped the gun from his waistband and checked the ambidextrous safety. It felt good in his hand. Too good. Sometimes he would do this two or three times a day, pointing it at the tree in his backyard, pretending it was *him*.

He had only just cleaned it, always marveling at the small springs for such a big gun although it was a bear to put back together. When he finally fired a round at the tree yesterday, he could almost see those gases porting through a small hole in the barrel.

He stared at the picture on the wall, a patchwork of blues and greens so intense, it made his eyes water. Bluebells in a wood, a painting Kizzy had done at school. It still hung in her bedroom, proof that she had once been there.

He had accepted many things in his life but never forgiveness and he had hated a whole life-time's worth in those first few months until he was completely burnt out.

The phone call came thirty-four days ago. He remembered it vividly. It was the same day he was promoted to a loan officer at Wellington Capital Bank on Southern.

Detective Temeke called to confirm they had a body, if you could call it a body. Darryl couldn't feel his legs after he'd seen it and he couldn't feel them now.

He sat on the bed and stared at the gun in his lap. He could either top himself, or someone else, and the someone else option seemed to be the most practical. He had two surviving daughters to take care of. It wouldn't do to abandon them.

He felt soft cotton beneath one hand, fingers caressing the quilt his late wife had made. There were little hexagonal boxes and perfect stitching, and then the colors all melded into a teary haze, worse than when he was drunk.

He had tried to stop drinking, tried to stop buying the stuff when his kids were around. He brewed dandelions with ginger, cloves and orange peel. It went much further when you mixed it with wine and you got a whole lot drunker too.

He wiped his eyes and looked outside the window at the back yard and the arroyo beyond. On the horizon he could see the west mesa and the remnants of five cinder cone volcanoes. They had erupted long ago, leaving behind a lava flow of fine black dust.

All dead and forgotten, he thought. Like the dad he once had. He missed the tall lean figure that towered over him as a child, missed his soothing voice. He knew that voice more than anyone else. That was the pain for him.

He gazed at the fir tree in the corner of the yard covered in snow, a reminder that Christmas was near. He began to wonder how many times Kizzy had seen the same view, what thoughts had gone through her head. This was her bedroom, after all.

The detective had called again this morning about a journal they had only just found. A journal they should have found thirty-four days ago when the scene was first combed by a pack of field investigators. Now Darryl would relive Kizzy's nightmare through her own words.

There can't be any more hate in me, he thought, until

a new day came bringing a fresh portion of it.

Kizzy was good at writing diaries. She was good at writing stories. He remembered her doing cartwheels in the sun and he could still smell the scent of her hair. Only he couldn't quite see her face. It was a shadow now, unless he found a recent picture of her, and he was tired of slipping the small photo from his wallet and crying over it if he was honest.

There was a knot of pressure in his chest when he recalled a recurring dream, a face with milky eyes like the one on the autopsy table. It was always without a body and he would wake suddenly and be cruelly reminded he was the one that had survived. There wasn't even the barest threshold of life in that face and thinking of it made him dizzy, disjointed. He tried to tell himself it was just a painted doll's head, something a child would make in sixth grade. But it wasn't. The nightmares were always the same and a scream would catch in the back of his throat choking him awake.

Pastor Razz said *hate* makes a man sick. Forgiveness means letting go, lessening the grip of bitterness and pain.

I won't forget. I'll never forget, Darryl thought, brushing one hand over his close-cut hair and squeezing the gun with the other.

There had been no funeral because forensics only had her head. Who in their right mind buries a head without a body?

Carmel had died nine years ago from an asthma attack and he could never bring himself to spend her life insurance. It stayed in his bank for seven long years until he bought the new house. So she could share it with him.

As for the murdered, there were men out there preying on the innocent, men still at large and men so evil their very faces were enough to keep a child indoors. One murder every month. Someone had to find him.

Kizzy was baptized in September, a month before she was taken. Darryl wondered if that was a fluke or if it was a God thing.

"Up is better than down," Kizzy used to say. "That's where the bluebells are."

"*Heaven*, Kizzy," Darryl corrected. "Where there's no more crying or pain."

"But Dad, there are bluebells there. I've seen them."

Kizzy was determined there were carpets of them in the mountains spreading beneath the giant pines. Only bluebells thrived in English woodlands, not the sandy loam of New Mexico. Still, they went camping to look for them, the summer she died.

Kizzy was like him, big eyes and a big nose. Darryl began to laugh at that for the first time in thirty-four torturous days. Deep in his throat the sound came like rain beating on the roof tiles and he almost lurched forward in his chair.

His mind was suddenly a blur of memories, fishing, hiking, horse-riding as he looked out of that window at the old wooden swing set he had bought for Kizzy's birthday. The seat was powdered with snow now and there were large flakes in the air like the molt of a cottonwood tree.

Best not think about what that man did to her. Best not think of her last moments.

A small part of him always did – especially the last moments. He wished he could have been there if not to save her then to hold her while she died. During his darkest times, he would hesitate in his thoughts, pausing to wonder. Why her?

Did that man have a swing when he was a child?

The thought took him by surprise. What did he care? The man was a monster. He was never a little boy with rosy cheeks and a swing to sit on. Was he?

He's someone's son. He's someone's brother. He's.

45

Some. One.

Darryl batted the air with his hand. He felt no pity. Not an ounce of it. Not when a homicide detective showed him Kizzy's little green blazer all covered in blood. She was proud of that blazer and the gold embroidered bird on the pocket. It had the words *Clemency Christian School, Home of the Doves* written beneath it.

The doorbell sputtered and then gave a peevish ring, breaking the longest silence he had ever heard. He left his gun on the bed and staggered toward the front of the house, dreading what he might find. Through the spyhole he could just make out a man darker than tar. Temeke, he thought. With the notebook.

He had an Hispanic woman with him this time, petite, pretty, probably in her early thirties. Why did warning buzzers whisper in his ear each time he saw an attractive woman?

"How have you been?" Temeke said, eyes shining like two wet pebbles.

"So, so, Detective," Darryl whispered as he sat down on a wooden chair. He waved them over to the couch and noticed a whiff of cigarette smoke.

"Temeke. Call me *Temeke*." He introduced his partner as Malin.

"That's a type of fish isn't it?" Darryl said, noting the slight shake of the head, the tiny smile.

"It's not spelled the same," she said.

Her face was freckled, unusual for an Hispanic woman, and she looked just as uncomfortable as he was.

The detective stared long and hard. "Had a few phone calls from concerned neighbors. Haven't been using that tree for target practice, have you?"

"A few times," Darryl said, nodding.

"How many times?"

"There's four slugs in the bark."

"This is a caution. Next time you use that gun in this neighborhood, it's mine. Understand?"

The detective's words hung in the air and Darryl merely nodded again. He could have confiscated the weapon there and then. But he didn't.

"I'm right in thinking you're a widower?"

"Yes," Darryl said, watching the detective's eyes as they wandered around the room, pausing at a ball of knitting in a wicker basket. "My sister lives here. She looks after the girls."

Temeke nodded and placed a scuffed red notebook on the coffee table. "We thought you might want to look at this. I'm sure she would have wanted you to have it."

They all looked at it like it was a strange archaeological relic until Darryl broke the silence with a choked *thank you*. He opened it and saw a dried flower pressed to one page, a desert primrose if he could give it a name.

"She liked flowers," he murmured, knuckling away a tear and wondering how many more would streak down his cheeks like an open tap. "How did you find it?"

"One of the field investigators found it in the barn last Friday," Temeke said, biting his lip, "behind a brick in the wall."

Darryl felt a slight chill and wondered if he had left a window open in the kitchen. There was a time last week when he thought he saw something through the lashing rain. He was overreacting of course, always thinking he was being watched.

Was it the wind shaking Kizzy's little swing or did he see someone standing beside the fir tree? He'd been more sensitive to sights and smells since the *thing* happened. He could never call it a murder. It just didn't seem right. "I wonder why they didn't find it sooner."

Temeke cleared his throat. He seemed to be watching him intently. "It can take hours, days to photograph and collect evidence. In this instance, months because of the monsoons. The most we've had in one hundred years, so they say."

Darryl drew his mouth into a straight line and pondered that for a moment. "Even with cadaver dogs?"

"Well it's funny now you mention it. A dog did find it. But not in the nick of time, sadly. Maybe it was all that rain. Maybe his sniffer was on the blink."

Darryl felt a surge of laughter in his chest, bubbling out into the open. It was louder than he expected. Genuine. It felt good to laugh again. "I appreciate you coming over," he said. And he meant it. "Do you have any suspects?"

"We've got one inside at the moment. Can't tell you his name. I don't think he did it. But I think he knows who did."

"I hear the police use psychics. Are they any good?"

"Well that's the thing. We know a psychic, well he's a nut-case really. Said he saw it in a dream. Most of the time he claims the president's been shot and by the time you turn on the TV there he is in the White House, sipping a cup of Darjeeling. On this occasion the lying sod hit the jackpot."

"What did he see?"

"Trees with faces. They were carved on the trunks. He was very accurate."

"Do you use psychics for every case?"

"I won't use them in any case, stanky-ass waste of time."

Darryl saw Malin give the detective a wide-eyed look.

"What I meant was," Temeke said, lowering his voice, "they're usually after a fast buck. But I had a hunch this time. He took us right there, to the farm and all."

"Where are you from?" Darryl asked, hearing an

accent. It was Australian or something similar.

"Albuquerque."

"No, that's Australian."

"England actually."

"Do you miss it?"

"I don't miss the rain and it's bloody freezing even in the summer."

Darryl felt himself brighten. "Kizzy always wanted to go to England. She wanted to see the bluebells."

"My brother and I used to take the bus to St. Matthew's Church in the spring. We'd find a few under the trees and pick them for my mum. They had a scent you'd never forget. That and furniture polish in the living room."

Darryl liked Temeke. He was somehow misplaced between one world and the next.

"Talking of churches," Temeke said, "have you seen your pastor recently?"

"Last week as a matter of fact," Darryl muttered. "He keeps talking about forgiveness. I can just about forgive the man that flipped me off in Smith's last Saturday night but not a killer. Not the man that took my little girl and locked her in his house. There was no reason – no reason at all."

"It was her stories that kept her alive," Temeke reminded, eyes floating to the floor. "And her optimism. You know that."

Darryl watched an army of dust motes drifting lazily in a beam of sunlight. He could hear the creak of his chair and the chimes from the clock in the hall. He wondered what Kizzy heard during those last hours. Rain possibly, pattering against the windows and the bark of a dog somewhere in the distance. Had she thought of him? Had she cried out for him?

Kizzy was in heaven where the bluebells are. And that's all that mattered.

"Darryl," Temeke said, leaning a little closer. "The man we've got is being transported to the Penitentiary of New Mexico. He's admitted to being there. But not to killing her. I promise you, I'll find this man. And when I do I'll squeeze him so hard he'll be screaming for me to stop. We'll let ourselves out."

Darryl watched them go from the living room window, studying their footprints in the snow. Flakes fell in tight clusters now, fast and thick, and he could hardly see the Ford Explorer through the haze.

He didn't much care that a prisoner would be shackled to the inside of a prison van and on his way to PNM. What bothered him more was the gun on Kizzy's bed.

There would be a day when that monster would come outside. And when he did, Darryl would be waiting for him.

SEVEN

Temeke shifted his weight in the car seat and adjusted his shoulder holster. The drive-through of the local café was thick with exhaust fumes, most of which was up his nose by the time he tried to order a double espresso. Apart from an occasional gust of wind that blew in under the canvas roof of his jeep, he sensed something in the air, something that made his heart drop into the pit of his belly.

It was the newspaper on the passenger seat. Morgan Eriksen had made front page news, color photograph included. It wasn't a mugshot. He was sitting on a deckchair by a swimming pool with a beer in one hand a burger in the other. Nobody knew how it got there and if they did, nobody was talking.

He hardly listened to the droning voice of the car radio, a pastor with a message about fathers. The bitter smell of coffee made his throat tighten and he couldn't drink another cup. Strange memories began to swirl though his mind and he saw himself as a boy, cowering at his father's raised hand.

Temeke never cried after that, at least not that he could remember. He went through life protected by a thick wall of indifference. It was safer that way.

At forty-three, he was recognized as one of the most persuasive negotiators the police had, a man with whom the prisoner could relate. According to his boss, there was one thing the department disliked and that was his unique quietness, the irrefutable feeling that he was hiding something. No one really knew him. But that's how Temeke liked it.

They can never build a case against me, he thought.

Only they did, of course. They disliked him for being quirky, for his reserve, for his deprecating sense of humor. He was an unusual dog in the fight. All this was before Morgan Eriksen insisted he would talk to no one else. It shook the department up a bit.

It was late afternoon when he turned west on Ellison and north into the station parking lot. He parked the jeep behind the building and clamped a cigarette between his lips, flame flaring and dying with every drag. He sat there for a while, sucking the nicotine into his lungs, wondering why he ever started smoking in the first place.

Looking east, he studied the rugged slopes of the Sandia Mountains rising almost to the clouds. On sultry nights a large full moon could be seen hanging like a happy face in the sky and if he listened, he could often hear the warbling of a Navajo flute in the distance. To the west, adobe houses stretched as far as the eye could see, spilling into a rose-colored desert of piñon and sagebrush. It was a sacred place, a magical place.

He hated it today.

The phone vibrated on the console revealing Luis Alvarez's number. Temeke could imagine his brother-in-law copping a wide-legged stance, duty belt sagging from the weight of his hardware.

"I called the Journal, bro," Luis said. "Spoke to Jennifer Danes about that article. She said it was you she spoke to. Said you sent that photograph over last night."

Temeke began to feel a wave of dizziness. "Me?"

"That's what she said."

"I did no such thing. Must have been bloody Fowler

with a fake British accent."

"I doubt he could pull that one off."

Temeke could hear the laugh in Luis' voice. He could also hear the doubt. "Sounds like someone's trying to give DCPD a bad name."

"Here's some good news," Luis continued. "Got a call from one of my buddies at the Press Club, a guy called Midge Toledo. Works behind the bar. Said someone came in a couple of days ago asking for a driver. Had a ton of money. And an accent. The reason Midge remembered him was because two of the waitresses were giving him the eye. Got a good description."

"What did he look like."

"Blond hair in a braid. Foreign."

"Did he pay with a credit card?"

"Cash. But get this. Toledo bagged his wine glass."

Temeke punched the air with one hand. "I owe you one."

"You stood me up again," Luis said. "Anyone would think you were seeing someone else."

"How was Fat Jacks?"

"Heaving."

Temeke chuckled. Too many kids drank shots of Tequila like juicy juice and then wondered why they spent the next half hour throwing up an entire paycheck.

"I'll be offline for ten days. Going fishing with the wife at Cochiti Lake," Luis said.

"Do they have any fish in Cochiti Lake?"

Temeke heard Luis laugh, heard the click and the dial tone. Lucky sod, he thought, flicking his cigarette under Hackett's car and making for the warmth of the lobby.

Sergeant Moran straightened up wearily from behind the Journal and mumbled a greeting. Becky, his daughter, stood by his side, amber eyes sweeping with eyeliner and lips pursed around a lollipop.

"Are you sure that's a skirt?" Temeke said, pointing at a garment no bigger than a man's handkerchief.

"Course it's a skirt, silly," she said, rolling that lollipop along her bottom lip. "All the girls are wearing them."

Not for long, he thought. It would be up round her waist before the day was out, especially with baby-face Jarvis on his hands and knees pretending to hunt for his pencil. He was partial to high school seniors. Dirty old sod.

"I've got a new boyfriend," she said, lips drawn back over white teeth. "Older than the last one."

"Not too old I hope." Temeke saw the red bike leaning against the wall. She'd likely pedaled over from Cibola High to see her dad to tell him the good news.

In that skirt.

"Looks like a movie star," she said, lifting her chin a little higher.

"I hope he's got the salary to go with it."

"I need to talk to you," she said, eyes flicking toward the drinking fountain.

"What about?" He followed her. It wasn't the first time. He'd begun to dread that drinking fountain. Didn't like bending over it for too long in case a hand found its way around his buttocks.

Fingers brushed against his arm, and then two flat hands cupped his chest. He found himself backing up against the wall, eyes flicking at the duty desk in case Sarge was looking.

"I've got a date," she whispered, "after work."

"I'm glad to hear it."

"You think that's OK?"

"Of course it's OK. Girl like you should have a boyfriend. Your dad's met him, right?"

"Well that's the thing." She sucked in her bottom lip, eyes dreamy, far away. "That's what I wanted to talk to you about. He's older than me. Much older. I like older men. Is it wrong to like older men?"

Temeke looked down at two amber eyes, oddly attractive against olive skin. He felt that unmistakable vibration in his gut, the one that told him she wasn't telling him everything. "Depends how much older."

"Thirty or so."

"What's a thirty year old man want with a teenage girl?"

"I'm an adult."

"Only just," he said. "You might want to find out what his intentions are."

Temeke saw the pinched lips, saw her hand go up to her neck and rub it distractedly. Saw two breasts straining against her shirt. It reminded him of an inflated sex doll he'd found in Hackett's murder book closet.

She drew in breath. "That's such a fatherly question."

"That's because I'm old enough to be one."

"You look younger than my dad," she said, moving closer. "I thought you were about thirty-five, younger even. I've never seen a man as dark as you."

Temeke checked himself. Had to. Moved three steps away from the scent of her perfume, almost sickened by it. He saw the riot of color on her fresh young face, saw the restless stance. She kept soothing that thin cotton blouse, touching it to keep her hands busy. If he could bet on it, she had mixed feelings about this man.

He could still hear Becky's light-hearted chatter all the way up the stairs, something about a Scandinavian movie she'd seen on TV. When he got to his desk he thought of those finely chiseled cheekbones and the petite frame, similar to the photographs on his cork board.

The victim profiles were laid out across his desk, each smiling back at him like seven exhumed corpses. *Jaelyn Gains, 16 / Lavonne Jackson, 14 / Mikaela May*

Ortega, 15 / Lyana Durgins, 16 / Elizabeth Moya, 15 / Mandy Guzman, 13 / Kizzy Williams, 9.

His fingers tapped out a staccato rhythm on the desk. It had taken the police months to find Morgan Eriksen and the bloodstained shirt. Kizzy's blood. The poor boy had been beside himself, all trembling and muttering as Luis had told it.

Temeke had used up most of his lunch hour wading through records and listening to a phone message from Andrew Knife Wing at the Romero Street post office. It was a lead he couldn't pass up.

A psychic lead.

Stu Anderson poked his head around the door. "Are you ready?"

"Ready for what?"

"Round two."

"You mean, Eriksen hasn't left yet?"

"He wanted a word before he left. Something on his mind. I thought we were keeping his face out of the papers for now."

"So did I, Stu. So did I."

"Another thing. He's been receiving postcards from an Aunt Hedda. They're written in some kind of code, map coordinates, cell phone numbers, that kind of thing."

"What's the zip code?"

"Albuquerque." Stu handed Temeke a scrunched up piece of paper that smelled like soap. "He must have known the phones were tapped when he was in the detention center. Passed this to another inmate in the toilets. Midge Collins. In for rape."

"I hope he didn't bend over." Temeke studied the letter, blue ink bleeding between the lines and a partial address.

He sighed all the way to the interview room.

EIGHT

"You wanted to say goodbye?" Temeke asked, sitting at the table.

Morgan craned his neck at the mirror on the opposite wall. "I had hoped my attorney was coming today."

"I had hoped you'd had a nasty accident with a carving knife, but we can't all have what we want."

Morgan gave Temeke a scowl. "Have you heard from Patti?"

That was the problem. Temeke had and he wasn't about to endanger her life by admitting to it. "Do you think she's still alive?"

Eriksen cocked his head to one side. "You'd tell me if you heard from her."

"So you can continue passing love letters to Collins?" Temeke scooted the scrap of paper toward Morgan, watched the sudden twitch of his eyebrows. "Collins is a bit forgetful. Fried his brain before he came here. It was all those pills he took, uppers, downers, twisters, benders. Forgot you'd given it to him. Alerted the warden because he thought he'd found the toy in the cereal packet."

Morgan lowered his voice. "I gave it to Collins to give to his wife. I didn't think he'd screech like a little girl."

"Collins doesn't have an ounce of intellect, son. Not a vestige. You're not planning an escape, are you? It's a good lunch today. Ravioli."

Morgan wiped his nose on his fist, chains rattling between his wrists. "I wanted to know if Patti was OK."

"The address is a bit smeared, son. You might want to elaborate on the number so I can find out."

Morgan held up both hands, cuffs rattling. "7034... something like that." He was quiet for a moment, dragging out the silence, and then, "What part of Africa are you from?"

"Dar es Salaam. On my father's side." What that had to do with a bar of soap, Temeke couldn't imagine.

"Tanzania," Morgan said, giving a superior sneer. "You've never been there have you?"

"No, I have never been there."

"What kind of African are you if you haven't been to your country?"

"My country is the US," Temeke corrected. "Same as you."

"Norway is beautiful. So many trees..."

Temeke wondered if Morgan had been consummately evil since childhood. That's when the weird stuff usually happened, like hurting cats and throwing lighted clods of dung into the next-door neighbor's open window. There was nothing in the database on Morgan. It was like he had never existed.

Temeke adjusted his ear-piece and glanced at the two-way mirror. It was the third time Morgan had spoken to anyone, once to the judge and twice to Temeke. Now he sat in an interview room where three agents and a doctor in psychology listened behind a sheet of glass. And none of them could make head or tail of it.

"So what made you decide to come to America?" Temeke said, feeling like he was looking down the barrel of a shotgun.

"It's where everyone goes. Everyone that doesn't

belong, that is. Like me. Like you."

Temeke couldn't resist a smile. "You're from Westwood Village. Went to Ralph Waldo Emerson Middle School and Alexander Hamilton High. Sounds like you belong. Where did you go to college? Don't tell me. UCLA."

Morgan splayed his fingers out on the desk and gave Temeke a sideways glower. "Fiat Lux."

"*Let there be light.* That's quite a résumé. So what did you study... acting?"

Morgan looked down at his hands and wrapped his fingers together in a tight grip. "Psychology."

"Ah, the study of the human mind. Tell me something, you've started getting a few phone calls. Seems someone's got you twisted right round their little pinky. I'm surprised you fell for it. Trouble is, it's not safe in here, Morgan. Maybe in your cell, but not in the showers. Who is this new friend?"

Temeke saw the slackened mouth and then the frown. He knew Morgan would close down if he didn't change tack. "So let's talk about Patti's state of mind. Not like she comes here, is it? Not like anyone comes here. What would your psychology degree tell you about that then?"

"We're separated."

"By a barbed wire fence and a very thick wall. Did you love her?"

"Yes, only she tried to sell me off. Left me for someone else."

"Didn't get very far now, did she? By all accounts she's banging your best friend if that last tremor was anything to go by. Registered 7.0 on the Richter scale."

"I spy with my little eye... someone trying to provoke me." Morgan drummed his fist on the table and pointed a finger. "Did you know your wife gets it somewhere else?"

"Blimey, Morgan, that's the oldest trick in the book.

Get a copper jealous and jumpy and out of his gourd. Let's get back to Patti, shall we?"

Temeke visualized Patti Lucero's smooth white face and pale blue eyes. Her picture stared down at him from the cork board by his desk. She was happy back then.

"Patti wanted him," Morgan said. "I could see it in her eyes. The way she watched him, the way she listened to every word."

"Who?"

"She had no idea what he was. It was all a game. A poker game. I lost. She was the stake."

"That was a bit rash wasn't it?"

"He threatened to kill her if I called the cops."

"It was your blood and prints all over the shop. Not his."

"He took samples when I was asleep."

"When you were *drugged* you mean. Don't want us thinking you took part in all of this."

"Patti knew what he was. That night she went down to the barn and untied the kid. Took her into the woods, to the hunter's cabin. They nearly reached the road before the first shot."

"Who was shot?"

"Patti. In her leg. She shouted to the kid, told her run. But the kid didn't get far enough. He shot her down like a dog. I couldn't stop him." Morgan's eyes were flat but Temeke knew he was scared.

"Let's talk about Kizzy. Is that OK with you?"

Morgan looked straight at Temeke and merely nodded.

"Did she die then?"

"No, I carried her back to the barn." Morgan took a deep breath and held it in for a moment. "I gave her some Nembutal to take away the pain."

"There's no heating in the barn, is there?"

"No."

"Did she have a blanket? Pillow? Anything?"

"She had me. She always had me."

"You stayed with her all night."

"Until dawn. She was a little scared, I think."

"So what did you and Kizzy talk about in the barn since you spent so much time together?"

"Her dad. How he was going to come and find her."

"There is something about her dad you might want to know, Morgan. He keeps a loaded gun under his pillow and he's not afraid to use it. Seems like he's training for something. I should have taken it from him when I had the chance. But I didn't."

Temeke watched the smile, the kind of smile that crept under the back of his shirt and made him sweat. Morgan wasn't buying any of it. "The pathology report said Kizzy Williams died at three o'clock in the afternoon. Did you know more people die at that time than any other time of day?" Temeke knew more people actually died at four o'clock in the morning but Morgan wasn't to know.

"Odin's hour."

"Who's Odin?"

"He's ruler of Asgard and the guider of souls."

Temeke couldn't help thinking he had overstepped something important. He remembered the god Odin in a school report he had done in tenth grade, a man with a long beard riding a horse with eight legs. According to the field investigator, a man with a long beard had been carved and painted on several tree trunks in the woods. A man with the word *Wodin* etched on his gnarly forehead.

"I want to be tried in Norway." Morgan rested his elbows on the table, fingers stretched briefly before forming a steeple in front of his mouth.

"Doesn't Norway have the largest plateau in Europe?" Temeke asked, wanting Eriksen to know he was on the ball, knew a thing or two. The accent didn't fool him either.

Morgan nodded, eyes glazing over as if haring off into the darkness for one last memory. "Hardangervidda. So many trees."

"We found a passport in the barn," Temeke said, flashing it under Morgan's nose. "In a black lockbox behind the fridge. Is this the man who shot Kizzy Williams?"

Morgan rolled his lips and gave a glossy stare.

"And this?" Temeke slid a photocopy of the passport across the table. It was a picture of a blond man alright, same smile, same slant of the head. Same last name. It could have been a relative at a squint. "A Mr. Ole Eriksen. Your best friend."

Silence.

"And where's your passport? Don't have one, do you? And as for your driving license, I hope it didn't get into the wrong hands."

More silence.

"You're no reindeer roast. Lived on the beach for most of your life, shacking up with women old enough to be your mother. Come to think of it, you were shacked up with Patti's mother when you moved to Albuquerque. That's how it all started, wasn't it? Only you fancied a bit of calf after you'd had the cow."

Morgan chewed his lower lip, as if a nagging doubt rose to the surface.

"It was all about money," Temeke continued. "Or was it the sex? Could have been both, I suppose." He watched the pursed lips, the slow skankish smile. The type of smile that stroked the pit of his stomach. "Before you answer that, Hardangervidda has no trees. It's about as sterile as your lunch pack."

Temeke saw Morgan's puzzled look and beamed at him, he also felt the earpiece vibrate with angry static. It wasn't quite true about the trees, but why was Morgan the only one allowed to lie?

"You liked Kizzy, didn't you, Morgan?"

"She was brave."

Kizzy was a great talker according to her dad. It had kept her alive longer than the others, two days longer if Temeke had calculated right. The others were all dead within nine hours of their kidnapping, although Morgan never admitted to killing them. He likely just stood there and watched.

There were body parts in that commercial fridge. Fingers, hair clippings, souvenirs of those he killed. The defense psychologist ruled that Morgan had acute distress disorder and PTSD, both of which would be thrown out by any jury since he'd never been in the military or suffered trauma of any kind. He was a liar. A very good one.

"She was worried her father would miss her," Morgan said, eyes burning with a rekindled fire.

Temeke studied Morgan a little more closely. He wasn't dirty-looking like a vagrant, not even when they picked him up. He had been freshly shaved with a pressed white shirt covered in Kizzy's blood. There was a smell of soap about him and if it wasn't for an armful of tattoos peeking beneath his sleeves, you would have thought he was a *resting* actor.

"She wanted me to believe she wasn't afraid."

"Wasn't afraid of what, Morgan?"

"Me."

The last word was chilling. Kizzy had to have been terrified of Morgan because he was her abductor. The one thing she'd been warned against. Talking to strangers.

"Did you believe her?" Temeke asked.

"Yes, until Wednesday morning."

Three days after the kidnap, Temeke thought.

"You think I killed her, don't you?"

"I'd like to rule you out."

Morgan nodded slowly. "Heads speak wisdom. That's what Odin says. So here I am accused of this crime."

"First degree murder and kidnap to mention a few."

"What if I didn't do it?"

"Then you'll stay here until we find out who did."

Morgan caught his breath and his eyes widened as if a thought had suddenly come to him. "You'll find your man of interest. Two priors for solicitation, breaking and entering, and a restraining order. Not much. But it's the restraining order you need to focus on."

"I'd like to point out there are a few class felonies in that list." Temeke grimaced.

"Yeah, *real* class."

Temeke wanted to reach over and grab Morgan by the collar. What was the point of having laws when they were blatantly ignored? "Well, that shouldn't be too hard to find amongst the several million we have on file. Better get to it."

Temeke scraped his chair back against the vinyl floor, snatched up the file and left the room. He almost hurled the earpiece into Stu's outstretched hand. "We're wasting our time. He's not our man."

NINE

Ole knew he was being followed, knew he was being watched. But just to be sure, a glass of wine yesterday had been a novel idea. He saw the cop in the lobby of The Press Club with a cell phone pressed against one ear. That's when he wiped the glass with his napkin and slipped out through the kitchens. In those few precious moments he'd lost the cop. But he never forgot a face.

Now he stood in an empty house on the south side of town, Smith Street, far away from the spotlessness of his Tuscan estate. This is where he disposed of the girls. There was only one thing he was truly sorry for. And that was shooting Patti in the leg. That soft sallow thigh was bruised and swollen and he'd done the best he could to clean it.

She wasn't perfect any more. She wasn't the happy dancing Patti, the light-as-a-cinder-on-the-wind Patti. A girl worth having. She stiffened when he held her in her sleep, murmuring for Morgan until the early hours. But snooping girls were stupid girls and he was tired of telling her what to do.

There was no way out of the bedroom. The door was bolted from the outside, windows locked. She could have screamed all day if she wanted to and nobody would have heard her. Now there was a four-day-old stench in his nostrils and a corpse on the kitchen floor.

He showered in the hottest water he could bear,

scrubbed his nails and then smeared his skin with a good dosing of hand sanitizer. It was the burn he was after. Made him feel refreshed and alert.

Time to call the detective.

"Who is this?" Ole heard him say.

"It doesn't really matter, does it? Not when you don't have any evidence."

"Well, that's where you're wrong. I just got lucky. Can't be too careful during these last days. You're leaving too many crumbs out for the birds."

Birds? Ole tapped the side of his head with the phone and then squeezed it against his ear. His mind was beginning to blur. "I'll give you Patti for Morgan," he offered.

"Put her on."

"I won't do that."

"How do I know she's still alive?"

"Ask me anything and I'll ask her."

The detective was quiet for a while and then, "What's her cat called."

Ole covered the mouthpiece and hesitated for a moment, enjoying a sense of the ridiculous. "She doesn't have a cat."

"A dog then?"

Ole hesitated again. "Yes."

"What's his name?"

"Buster."

The detective actually laughed. "She's dead, isn't she. You know how I know? Because Patti doesn't have a dog."

Ole shouted into a dead phone, heard the drone of the dialing tone. It was no use hurling curses at deaf ears. Patti had lied to him.

He saw faceless images of her. Smart, glittering Patti, nothing like the lone, staring thing slumped on the floor at his feet.

Then he shrugged and turned his attention to another girl he had followed two days ago. He thought of her now through the cloudy lens of his mind. A rare specimen with spotless, waxen skin and eyes sweeping with black eyeliner. Quite perfect.

Quite breathtaking.

And then came the provocative moment when he fell in behind her, so close he could smell the scent of her hair. His mind was a riot of madness and that's when he braced himself for that heart-grinding shiver before the downhill plunge.

This was a new girl whose infatuation was too good to pass up. He'd spoken to her a few times after that, asked her for directions from his nice black car, dropped his wallet in the mall right in front of her. She picked it up, of course, smiled shyly at him when he thanked her. He even sat right next to her in the dental office a few days later staring off in the distance and watching her out of the corner of his eye. You'd think she would have wondered if he was stalking her, wondered if he was just a little dangerous.

Asking her out was easy. Especially after he told her he was a cop.

She said yes a little too quickly, running her tongue along those generous red lips of hers. He took her to a Mexican restaurant for lunch, nothing pretentious. The white bustier she wore was laced low enough to reveal two mounds as sheer as a pair of stockings. He could hardly keep his eyes off them.

He promised to call her in a few days. It had been much more than that.

The stench from the cardboard box at his feet brought him back to the present. His most recent kill—one of Odin's darlings. This one would have to be disposed of on higher ground where bear and fox wouldn't make a meal of it.

He kept a container of her blood in the fridge, only he might need to take some of it where he was going. It would fool the police. It would fool everyone. That's why he kept Morgan's driving license and a few strands of his hair. That's why he used Morgan's identity now he was inside.

Morgan's face was on every newsstand in Albuquerque. The 9th Hour Killer. Ole loved the description, loved the attention. He was almost famous now.

He walked into the front room and saw the axe. It was dirty, so dirty. And so was the mattress. Fire was a cleansing thing and besides, he couldn't stay in the same place for too long.

With that nice black car in the garage he had already become an overnight sensation in the neighborhood. He only went out at night. So did the hoodlums in their low-riders desperate for weed, desperate to be noticed.

So incredibly ghetto.

He'd pay one to burn the house and then there would be nothing left. No evidence.

The rest of her was wrapped in a quilt, pink, flowery. Cold. Heaving the bundle over one shoulder, he took it out through the kitchen door into the garage where the sleek Camaro beckoned. The trunk was already open. He was practical like that. Once the car was packed with all his precious things he drove east along Central, following the silvery track of the moon, following it north on Tramway and then east again to where the road gave way to sand and green-gray sage.

He lugged the bundle as far as the foothills, propping her against a boulder so she could see what he saw— Albuquerque, the winking city with its legendary lights. Only she couldn't see anything now.

"Quite marvelous," he said, pulling out a packet of antiseptic wipes from his pocket. "So close to home.

You used to live up this way with your mom. In fact, I think I can see your house from here."

He'd never be able to sleep. Not after climbing a hill in a cold December wind. No, he'd need to drive around for a bit. Need to clear the fog from his mind.

Two minutes later, he found himself heading west on Alameda, listening to the fastest violin performance he had ever heard. It made his heart pump. It made the car go faster than a bullet all the way to the apartments at Puerta de Corrales. It was dawn when he got there, when he turned off the engine and watched the front entrance.

To the left, a cop car sat idle outside a ground floor apartment. He had a ripe young thing for a daughter who never drew her blinds. Like she knew someone was watching.

He thought about what he would do. How it would be. Sat there watching the vertical blinds behind the patio doors twitching in a warm draft of air. That's when a light flickered inside the bedroom and where a young girl swung olive legs from her bed, running fingers through a bob of black hair.

She was so beautiful.

The dark ones might be beautiful, he warned himself, but they were the tricksters, the seducers. He was used to them now, the black painted eyes, the moist lips, all there to invite a look. He had come to see it as part of the game.

It struck him suddenly that he ought to have left a single white rose on her door step, something to light up those smoky dark eyes, something to make that cop-of-a-pop all jittery and suspicious. There was something particularly enticing about tormenting those who hated him. Those who made him an outcast.

And so it was his commission to come back every night just to sit and wait. Until the natural rhythm of things told him when the time was right.

TEN

The sky was gray and heavy with snow. Malin squinted through the windshield trying to steer against a driving wind. She sensed Temeke's despair, his anger.

"She's dead, probably been dead for days," he said, finger soothing his upper lip. "I asked him the name of Patti's dog. You know what he said? Buster. Her mother said she didn't have a dog. They've never had a dog. He was lying. That disgusting cesspool of a man was lying!"

Malin couldn't stop wondering if Temeke was a liar. She'd seen him hugging Becky in the lobby, seen her tearstained face. Something about a man she liked, how he had stood her up after school yesterday. Even though Becky tried to hug him, Malin still wondered if he broke away because he thought he was being watched.

She watched him. All the time. Behind the bathroom door near the drinking fountain, through her make-up mirror when he sat at his desk. She tried not to look at him now out of the corner of her eye, tried to concentrate on the road. He was silent for a time before his hand flicked directions. On the left-hand side of the road she could see the serried ranks of Spanish style buildings, one of which was the Old Town post office.

"Want to know the real kicker?" he said as they parked. "Patti outwitted him even at the end. You wait until the results come back from Forensics. We've got a wine glass with his sodding spit all over it."

Malin couldn't scrape up even the tiniest whimper of a comment. She merely opened the door, glad to breathe in a blast of cold clean air.

Andrew Knife Wing was sitting on the bottom of the stairs leading to an upper terrace, thumbs dancing over a bright red phone. He looked normal to her and nothing like a psychic. But what did psychics look like anyway?

"Ma'iitsoh," Knife Wing said, waving one hand over his head as if wafting smoke from burning sage.

"What did he say," Malin whispered to Temeke as they approached.

"It means *big coyote* or *wolf*."

"Is that what he calls you?"

"No, it's what he calls the spirit he sees in his dreams." Temeke looked down at a fresh-faced man in his early thirties. "You said you wanted to see me."

Knife Wing gave a lazy smile, hesitating for a moment. "I had another dream. Well, it was a vision really. You got a light? Might need a cigarette for that light."

Malin studied the glossy-haired youth, five foot nine inches tall when he stood up, hair in a long ponytail, turquoise earrings. He was charismatic like the users she had interviewed in the county jail and she was aware of a small tremor of sadness in those laughing eyes. Temeke handed him a cigarette and pointed up the stairs.

The balcony looked out on a restaurant and a colonnade of art galleries. Navajo blankets were draped over the banisters and wind chimes clanging from the vigas.

"You said you had a dream," Temeke said. "You also said you had a name."

Knife Wing drew hard on his cigarette and blew out a thick cloud of smoke. "I said I had an *address*."

"But you did say a name."

Knife Wing slipped the phone in his shirt pocket and

took another drag of his cigarette. "Bought a truck from him a month ago."

"That's a stroke of luck. His name will be on the paperwork," Temeke said, peering over the bannister at a metallic gray truck with front fog lamps and alloy wheels.

"I don't keep paperwork."

"Clean title was it?"

Knife Wing shrugged. "Great price."

"I'm guessing that's a 2008 Chevy Colorado. Probably got the word *salvage* on that title. So what did this guy look like?"

"Thickset, braided hair, tattoos. Same man in my dream. Only that one had a bloody axe in one hand and a severed head in the other. Girl with pale blue eyes."

Temeke seemed to think about that for a moment, mouth twitching. "Any particular tattoos?"

"A snake round his arm, a sun and moon on his neck. He was saying stuff about the girl. Said a god had taken her. I just laughed. Thought he was crazy. But he grabbed me by the throat and said, 'She's a gift. A sacrifice for the father of victory.' I wasn't laughing much after that."

"When was this?"

"I said a month ago."

"And you didn't tell anyone?"

Knife Wing shook his head, treating Malin to a wink. "No one to tell."

"Have you seen him since?"

"Couldn't get hold of him after my truck died. But I remember where I bought it. Cream house on the corner of Smith and Walter, the only two story house in the street. There was a black Camaro parked behind the gate. Reckon it's his."

"Anything else you remember?"

Knife Wing shrugged and thought for a moment,

eyes grazing over Malin's face. "It had a crime-stoppers sticker in the window."

Temeke handed Knife Wing the pack of cigarettes and a yellow Bic lighter and started down the steps to the road. "You'll call me if you hear anything else?"

"Ma'iitsoh," Knife Wing said again. "Watch out for the spirit."

He saluted and grinned, eyes flicking toward Malin in that deliberate way of his. "Always best to watch your back. But then you cops know all about that, don't you?"

Malin couldn't help shivering all the way to the car. "Are the tattoos the same as Eriksen's?" she asked Temeke as she slammed the door and locked it.

"Not quite. And I doubt it was a snake round his arm. More like a Celtic knot. He did mention the man he saw had a shaved head and braids," Temeke said, sniffing. "Take Kathryn and I'll give you directions from there."

Malin pulled out sharply into oncoming traffic and skillfully steered into the right-hand lane. They were speeding along Kathryn Avenue, past Arno and Edith before Temeke told her to slow down.

"Didn't much like him, did you?" he said.

"I don't believe in psychics. They can see in the past. Not in the future."

"He's a shaman's son. Uses his eyes and sense of smell. He's an artist. Means he's got an eye for detail."

"Why do you think he wanted to talk to us?" Malin said, hearing the irritation in his voice.

"The visions won't go away unless he tells someone. He's got his ear to the ground. Watches people. Knows people. He might go off the grid for a while but he always calls me."

"And what does he get in return?"

"A few smokes."

Malin wondered what Temeke meant, what he alluded to with that tight little nod. They turned into

Walter and then Smith, and there was the house exactly as Knife Wing had described. It stood behind padlocked gates and a high stucco wall. There was no sign of a Camaro.

"What now?" she said, parking along the curb.

"What are walls for if we can't climb them," Temeke murmured.

Malin saw the tight-lipped smile and ground her teeth. Here they were trying to gain access to someone's house on the suggestion of a nutcase. "We don't have a warrant."

"Don't need a warrant for a break-in," Temeke muttered, slamming his door. He laced his hands and formed a stirrup.

Malin found herself sitting astride the wall, snow seeping through the seat of her pants. She briefly stared into an upper story window where curtains were frayed at the edges and the frame was peeling and rotten. Easing herself over the other side she narrowly missed a trash can, hearing the echo as it pinged off the opposite wall.

"Blimey girl, you'll wake the dead." Temeke was on the other side, quick as a cat. He held a finger to his lips, eyes wide, head nodding. "Take the north side. I'll take the south. If you find an open window—"

"We can't do this," Malin stammered, handing him a pair of latex gloves. "What if Hackett finds out."

But Temeke wasn't listening. He cocked his service pistol and edged around the south wall where he disappeared behind a rusted out Chevrolet Delray.

Malin sighed loudly and pulled on her gloves. Gun at low ready, she moved toward the north side of the house, seeing nothing but old car parts and an antique gas pump that stank of urine. It would just be her luck if there was an open window.

There was. With a gap wide enough to get her hand

under. *Walk away now...* It was the voice she always heard when her body moved stubbornly forward into a dangerous place. It was the same voice she heard when she first jumped out of an airplane, a charity jump. But it was the excitement of it all.

She hesitated for a moment, nose twitching at the bad breath of decay, and she tried to ignore the fluttering in her gut. What if there was a dog on the other side, all teeth and drool like a Rottweiler? A Rottweiler? Who was she kidding? There was nothing barking at her from behind the glass.

Lifting the window, she dropped inside. The heater hummed overhead blowing out hot air through the vents. The stench hit her as soon as she stood there, toxic, sharp. Not decay. Something else.

She covered her face with a hand and all she could see were five mattresses on the floor, laid out as if it were a temporary dormitory. There were no pillows or blankets to speak of and the one nearest the door was leaking wool from a slit and stained with food.

Or was it blood?

She had to take one hand away from her face and fumble for the small flashlight in her belt. Holding her breath, the beam prodded the darkness, light bouncing off the dark brown stain. An axe leaned against the wall with a dusting of tree bark on the blade, a pruning axe by the look of it. There was a bundle wrapped in a black trash bag and bound with duct tape.

A body?

No, not big enough for a body. She steadied her breathing, heart pounding louder now. Training the flashlight on the shiny black bag, she crouched, hearing a popping in her knees. She jabbed at the bag with the muzzle of her gun. It was soft like a pile of old rags.

There was a smell to those rags, oily, gassy, leaching out like the fumes of an antique car. It was everywhere, all over the carpet, the furniture, glistening on every surface. A garage smell, a man smell.

She stood up and swallowed the fear she felt inside, sobs racking her body. A place like this could go up in smoke.

She forced herself to stay calm, to give herself a mental shake. Biting her bottom lip always helped to center her focus, to keep her in touch with her surroundings. She had to get out and the longer she delayed the more likely something else would mess with her frazzled mind.

Movement. Something moved. Behind the chair.

"Hello," she whispered, throat quavering with dread. She trained the flashlight to one side of the chair, watching the wall for shadows.

ELEVEN

Whatever it was behind that chair was more afraid than she was. A small child perhaps, shivering with terror, or a war veteran suffering from some type of trauma.

"Sure I'm scared," Malin whispered out loud as if answering a question. "I'm scared of the dark. I'm scared of china dolls and their blinking eyes. I'm scared of going barefoot into the sea. But I'm more scared of what I can't see."

A sigh. Not a human sigh. The heater had stopped. And then her flashlight went out. She could smell sweat and fear, and she caught the glint of a knife just as something hit her, sending her head against the door frame.

The flashlight fell from her hand, a loud thud against the floor and then the gun. Fingers wrapped around her neck, pushing her back against the wall. There was hardly any room to move between his body and hers, but she strained and wriggled until she managed to reach up, clawing his face and jerking up a knee.

A scream of pain as her assailant broke free, trying to find the door knob, hands swishing along the wall. She crouched, fingers swinging out wildly across the floor until she grabbed the flashlight. Swinging it like a club, she heard the groan and a sharp crack of bone, only that didn't seem to stop him. He prized the door open and slipped out into the hall.

It wouldn't be the first time someone clipped the side of her head with a weapon, leaving her senseless on the floor. Only this man saw fit to fly up the stairs, taking three steps at a time.

Tall, she thought. And fit.

Light came from a crescent window in the hallway and she could see the gun on the floor now, only two feet from her right leg. She grabbed it and settled herself to channel her shame, angry he had got away so easily. If he went upstairs, chances were he would have to come down again, although she wondered why he hadn't just raced through the front door. And then she noticed it was armed with three tumbler locks and a solid chain.

That was why.

Malin peered up the stairs. Pitch black. No noise. She steered a tiptoeing course through a pile of boxes in the hallway, some leaning at an angle as if ready to topple. There was a kitchen on the south side and what appeared like a conservatory at the back of the living room. Dead plants, feathery plants. That's all she could see through the aisle of brown cardboard boxes.

She inched out a little further and stood at the foot of the stairs. There was a crack of light beneath the bedroom door. At least, she assumed it was a bedroom.

And then she heard it.

Light clumping footsteps as if someone was pacing back and forth, voice muffled. There was no variance in the noise. He wasn't coming downstairs and if he wasn't coming downstairs, she would have to go up.

She tried the first step, soft, carpeted. The second and the third made no noise and she was halfway up with her gun poised when she heard his voice.

"I've never seen it before."

Silence. Whispers.

"I don't know anything about that either. It's the first time I've seen it."

More whispers.

"It's cold, everywhere's cold. Don't you have your heater on?"

A muffled voice and then a grunt. Malin cocked an ear, wondering if the man was on the phone.

"I'm not going back inside—"

The door burst open before she had time to move and there was Temeke, pushing a gangly youth down the stairs and cuffing him with one hand.

"Meet Podger the lodger," Temeke said with a grin. "Found him skulking about in the cupboard with a cardboard box. Isn't that right, Podge?"

"It's Steve Pogar," the young man said.

"Oh, got a first name now. Always polite in front of the ladies, isn't that so Podge? Trouble is," Temeke said to Malin, "he wasn't lodging, he was trespassing, fiddling about with evidence."

"I didn't know it was evidence," the young man said.

"Well it was. And in case you were wondering, breaking and entering's a crime."

"Then how did *you* get in?" The young man asked, shoulder brushing past Malin.

"Same way you did, son. Listen, where's the rest of her?"

"Rest of who? I just came over the wall for a smoke. Where are you taking me?"

"You can ask the judge. Prison's not a nice place, son. Every hole's a goal. It might help to know a few throws and take downs. What's that smell?"

"What smell?" Podge said.

"Bleeding Nora, you trying to cover up a bit of weed with some spray-on gasoline?" Podge went quiet then, lips pressed into a thin line. Temeke tapped Malin on the shoulder. "By the way, there's a head in that box. Whatever you do don't touch it."

Malin nearly gagged, although not half as much as

she did when she saw it. A bloated face looked up at her, all teeth and blind staring eyes. A silver earring dangled in her left ear, a disk engraved with the number eight. She struggled to control her stomach and snapped the lid shut.

Slumping down on a small antique chair, she rocked gently to the rhythm of her breaths. There was a photograph on the dresser, a girl with long dark hair and pale, faraway eyes.

Patti Lucero. She wore no earrings then.

It was the writing on the back of the photograph that brought the bile to her throat. *Ole, you are the burning, glowing flame in my heart, Patti.* Tucking it in her pocket, Malin ran downstairs past the other boxes not wanting to look inside. She couldn't look inside. She'd really throw up if she did.

There was a gush of cool air coming from the back of the house and slipping through another tower of cardboard boxes, she found herself in the kitchen. On the countertop was a plump, wooden figurine, a Santa Claus with his mouth shaped in a small O. It was a handcrafted incense smoker. Probably helped to take away the stench.

The back door yawned open since the screws from a heavy duty padlock had been wrenched out of the jam. Temeke was in the front yard talking to the suspect and he eyed her with a cool nod.

"There's gasoline all over the front room," she said, panting out the words. "It's everywhere."

"Do me a favor," Temeke said, cocking his head at the sound of a radio. "Hop over the wall and answer that, will you? Sounds like Hackett's having a coronary."

Malin left Temeke to his relentless mocking and climbed over the wall. The car radio had been begging for attention to an empty car and she snatched up the handset. "Santiago."

"Finally! Where's Temeke?" It was Sergeant Moran with a bleat in his voice.

She gave Sarge the exact location and filled him in with what had happened. There was an edge to her voice she couldn't define and her hands were shaking.

You've done more murder cases than Perry Mason, she kept telling herself. Only she hadn't, not one like this. Not one where human heads had been packed in cardboard boxes and some pimply youth was trying to burn the evidence.

It was twenty-five minutes before the field investigators were inside taking samples and dusting for prints. Cameras whirred and flashed, and there was an eerie silence as the axe was wrapped in an evidence bag.

Temeke wandered off outside for a smoke. She saw him through the window, sitting on a tree stump, eyes turned up to the sky. He took one drag before grinding the cigarette under his shoe. Probably thought better of it with all that gasoline inside.

The field deputy medical investigator tapped her on the shoulder and smiled. He was a tall man with short gray hair, eyes a watery blue. "Name's Joe Vasillion and this is Jennifer Danes with the Journal." He nodded at a brunette, hair in a bun, large green eyes.

"Detective Santiago. *Malin,*" she said as an afterthought. She shook Jennifer's hand, saw a strange sparkle in her eye. She was pretty, probably sleeping with the doctor.

Vasillion's voice was clipped, a walking, talking academic. She hadn't seen many of those since leaving New Jersey. And he was handsome, too.

"Well, Malin, it looks like the head's been in the house for about three days. Probably around the time she was killed."

"And our suspect's been inside longer than that," she said more to herself than to them. "What's in the black bag, the one in the front room?"

"Clothes."

"Her clothes?"

"Hard to say. Come over to the car, will you?"

Malin complied, sensing he was unwilling to talk in front of Jennifer. The doctor laid the box in the back of his car and opened the flaps. He prodded the flesh with a latex covered finger.

"She's young," he said, studying the mouth. "Could be anywhere between fourteen and eighteen. My guess is she was decapitated with that axe. Blade's been cleaned, of course, but there're traces of wood chips around her neck. Might be a wooden block around here somewhere."

Malin's head was beginning to swim and she steadied herself against the car. "That's barbaric."

"Take a walk and some deep breaths," Vasillion said, closing up the box.

"Is this her?" Malin said, showing him the photograph.

"Can't say," he said. "Tell Temeke I'll call him later."

Malin clutched her stomach as the car pulled out, wondering what it was that made Vasillion such a genius. From what she'd read, he was certified in anatomic, clinical and forensic pathology, a fellow of the Board of Medicolegal Death Investigators. Quite breathtaking, she thought, hardly feeling Temeke's hand on her shoulder.

"I think someone asked Podge to get rid of the evidence." Temeke held up a finger as Jennifer tried to snap a photo of them. He took Malin around the side of the car and away from the path of the camera lens.

"Attempted arson?" she said.

Temeke nodded. "A regrettable coincidence we dropped round when we did. Looks like he took quite a beating. There's a nasty lump on his head and a scratch on his cheek. You wouldn't know anything about that, would you?"

"He tried to attack me, sir. What was I supposed to do?" Malin tried to swallow but there was no spit in her mouth. "Are there any other remains?"

"Nothing. They found a metal hook, tablespoons, bongs, roach clips. I just wish I knew what happened to the rest of her." He turned at the sound of the doctor's car horn and waved. "I see you met Vasillion, our resident CMI."

Malin nodded. She tried to ignore the sting of wind in her eyes as she waved, tried to ignore the fact that the Chief Medical Investigator would make a poor second best to the man beside her. Detective Temeke was all brawn *and* brains, and fine eloquent lines on a beautifully sculpted face.

"I found this gas bill in the kitchen made out to Morgan Eriksen," Temeke said, flapping two envelopes in his hand and thrusting them at her. "The other's a rental agreement from a Kelly Coldwell. Find out what you can."

Malin handed him the photograph and watched him turn it over. "She was in love with him."

"That was quick, Marl. Congratulations."

"She didn't know what he was, sir."

"Killers can be devils. But so can the police."

Malin walked back to the car and pulled the keys out of her trouser pocket. She glanced back one last time toward the house, nose twitching with the faint scent of gasoline.

The vision that popped into her head then was worse than morning breath on a pillow and she stumbled as she reached for the door frame.

"Sir, when you went out for a smoke, what were you sitting on?"

TWELVE

Darryl sat in a pew at Clemency Baptist Church, watching his girls in the front row of the choir. His sister, Maisie, stood in the back row, warbling like a canary and waving her arms about.

"Detective said he wasn't the right man," he said, fighting back a yawn. "Said he couldn't have done it."

"Then he knows the man who did," Pastor Razz said. "Remember what I said about forgiveness?"

Darryl nodded. "I finally forgave my dad for dying."

"Well good for you. 'Cos he couldn't exactly help it with cancer and all."

"Someone's been following me, stalking me. I can feel it."

"Nobody's following you, son."

"I've seen footprints in my back yard. Killer's footprints."

"How do you know they're not yours?"

Darryl shook his head. A wave of sadness bubbled up from the pit of his mind, blotting out any joy he could possibly have. "I'll kill him when I see him."

"No you won't." Razz leaned back, head tilted up at the vaulted ceiling. "They all say that at the beginning. They're all full of hate and bravado, jumping around and pumping the air. But they never do it. It's not worth spending the rest of your life in the same prison as the man that took her. That would be a hell on earth."

"It's hell now."

"What happens if that man asked God to forgive him one day? How would you feel if he sat next to you at the wedding feast?"

"He won't sit next to me at the wedding feast."

"What if there was a seating plan? God's got a sense of humor, you know."

Darryl thought about it for a moment and stretched out his legs. It wasn't funny. None of it was funny. But it would just be his luck if God decided to write out a pair of place names in big flowery letters. Darryl and…

What was the man's name?

"What if they never find him?" he said. "What if the case goes cold?"

"Pray about it."

Darryl didn't know how to pray. And he wasn't about to start. Prayer had been the one thing Maisie begged him to do, to pray every day no matter the circumstances.

Maisie. Big-hearted Maisie.

She looked after his girls when his wife died. Stepped right in and took over. And when he was too depressed to make them their lunch, too depressed to kiss them goodnight and too depressed to watch a cartoon now and then, she was there to stand in the gap.

"Say your wife's name," Razz said.

"Why?"

"Just say it."

Darryl rarely said her name unless he was half-asleep. "Carmel," he murmured. It felt strange after so many years.

"That's a beautiful name. We nearly called our youngest *Carmel*, only we didn't think you could handle it."

Darryl almost choked. His wife would have loved it. If only he had been less selfish. Less stubborn.

"Maisie's a good woman," Razz continued. "She's a marvel. I don't think she's missed one practice in twenty-five years. Not *one*. If it hadn't been for my beautiful Gloria, I might have married her."

Darryl tried to swallow that down with a shudder. He couldn't imagine Razz and Maisie. You know. Under a quilt. It just didn't seem right to him.

"And I know what you're thinking," Razz said, patting his belly. "You're thinking I'm a good looking guy. That Maisie would have jumped at the chance. Thing is though, she wanted to be a nun in Junior High."

"A nun?"

"Yeah, a nun. She said she didn't want to play the *game*. You know, the one where the woman pretends to be all mysterious and the man can't help himself because all that secret stuff's driving him crazy."

Darryl had no idea what Razz meant. He couldn't remember a day when his late wife had ever played games, except chess perhaps. She was good at chess.

"You're lucky to have her, Darryl. It could have been worse."

What was worse than this? Darryl smothered a yawn and glanced at his watch. "Feel like going for a drive in my Comet next week?" he asked, studying Razz's wide smiling face. It was the color of well-done steak and there were more jowls on him than a bulldog.

"If they'll let me out of the booth at Lightwalk. I'm beginning to wonder if anyone ever listens."

Darryl enjoyed the show, a combination of bible study and light comedy kicking out at the televangelists of the seventies. Razz had excellent delivery, especially in church. "Of course they listen. Got higher ratings than that weather man and his dogs on Channel 4. You could slice a demon in half with your wit."

They shook hands and Razz made his way to the front of the church to congratulate the music leader on another hour of trilling and jumping about. Darryl felt like he'd spent the greater part of his weekend in church.

As he drove home, he barely listened to the girls in the back seat, voices raised to a joke or two. Maisie was quiet beside him, fingers pinching her nose. The Comet was stinking of oil again, stronger this time than before.

He turned off McMahon and swung into San Timoteo, pulling into the first house after a vacant lot. It was made of brick and stucco, evoking the desert southwest. He had grown to love the arches, the exposed beams and the floodlit courtyards. There were two blood-red ristras under the porch and a twist of Christmas lights around the vigas. Bought with his late wife's life insurance money so there would always be a part of her there.

Maisie took the girls upstairs and he could hear them thumping along the corridors still singing How Great Thou Art. He poured himself a glass of milk and that's when the phone gave a shrill ring.

"Darryl, this is Detective Temeke. Sorry to call you so late."

The milk almost curdled in Darryl's stomach. What could he possibly want at this time of night?

"I just wanted you to know there might be a newsflash tomorrow morning. We found another victim today. Partial remains."

Darryl barely stuttered into the phone and he quickly found a chair at the kitchen table. "Where ... where did you find her?"

"Over on the south side of town in a private house. The doctor said it was the same cause of death. Only it looks like our man left a bit of himself behind so to speak."

Darryl had the beginnings of a nasty headache and began to massage one temple. "When you say a bit of himself—"

"A few strands of hair and some blood. But let's not get ahead of ourselves. We need to find a match first. In any case, it was the newsflash I was worried about." Darryl heard the long drag of a cigarette on the other end of the phone and then, "But we think it's the same guy."

"How did she die?"

"Manual strangulation. And then she was decapitated."

Darryl felt a bubble in his throat like a large bloat of gas and he thought he was going to throw up. "If Morgan Eriksen's inside, he couldn't have—"

"The remains could be older."

"So he could have done it."

"He could, yes. I'll be seeing him again tomorrow."

"I'd like to see him." The words were out of Darryl's mouth before he could stop them. "Face to face."

"You and I both know that wouldn't be a good idea, sir. You have a good evening now."

Darryl heard the soft click as the phone went dead and he let out a long sigh. Somebody would be told soon their daughter had been found and that same somebody would be crying bitter tears just like he had. It was probably the same girl that was on the news a month ago, missing, lost.

He walked over to the kitchen window and saw the fir tree covered in a fresh fleece of snow. The lower branches bowed under the weight, some flicking upwards at the sudden release of their burden. The solar lights gleamed across the yard and bounced off a black shape that seemed to glide along the wall. It tumbled over the other side and down the embankment, perhaps to the arroyo.

A coyote? No, it didn't move like a coyote. It was more rigid, like a man vaulting sideways, legs outstretched. Darryl leaned over the sink almost pressing his nose to the glass. He had to be seeing things again.

Although, it wouldn't hurt to look.

He opened the sliding glass doors on the back porch and in six long strides he was standing by the back wall, peering down into the arroyo. There was a path directly below and beyond that, sand mixed with snow and sagebrush.

Nothing moved. And then about a hundred yards to the left of Tuscany Park something did move in the shadows. Something lurching up a gravel incline toward Bandelier Drive.

Darryl saw the car lights red and small, and a steam of exhaust as the car spun into gear and headed south to who knows where. He couldn't see the model but he heard the low rumble from a loud exhaust.

A performance muffler.

Darryl wondered if it was the same car he'd seen outside work, black, aggressive front-end. Camaro SS Coupe. It wasn't like he would forget a car like that, the type that was on every teenage bedroom wall. If you made a thumbs up sign at the driver you were already part of an exclusive club and it was mutually understood you'd left yours at home.

Three nights ago the car was in the bank parking lot at closing time, all fired up and glowing. It was the same halo headlamps that followed him all the way to McMahon, the same glass-shattering roar, the same black tinted windows.

He'd never get to bed now, not with that Camaro in his head. Not when he knew someone was out there watching him.

THIRTEEN

Ole drove around for a few hours, enjoying the afterglow of his latest stakeout. He was wearing a horizontal carry over a crisp white shirt and weapon tucked neatly at his side. He must have looked like Special Ops.

What was it that haunted a man's soul? He didn't claim to know the answer. He only knew that men like Darryl Williams needed to be haunted in order to be broken.

Broken and haunted. Haunted and broken.

The car window was open to a gush of icy wind. The cold never bothered him, nor did he need a coat in thirty degree weather. He felt like the wolf in the darkness, his Loki. Sometimes he pretended he had thick skin and fur you could sink your hand in, sometimes he was just flesh like a man.

It was dusk when he'd made up his mind. Time for something different, he'd earned it after all. He liked to make sure the subject was in his sights long enough to create an impression and not enough to know he was there.

And this one was worth something.

The girl had an evening job at the Corrales Café and he waited outside until closing. Twirling a short flouncy skirt, she walked outside, painted nails dancing through black hair. She put her hand up over her eyes to shelter from the headlights of an oncoming car, then looked up at the trees as if searching for something. The moon, a constellation of stars. He had seen it often enough.

This was his fourth time of watching her. Unique, unforgettable. As always the loneliness of his situation pressed in, a strange blackening moment, and then a souring excitement fell deliciously over his soul.

Acting like a shadow was getting boring, especially as he was stoned most of the time. *Fun* in his mind meant a frenzy of blackouts and the whir of faces, and he never remembered much after the fact. Reliving his cruelties was no longer exciting. He needed so much more.

He knew how to stalk anybody, any*thing*, and he parked deep in the shadows under the trees and watched the girl. She unlocked the chain around the back tire and looked up a couple of times. She was probably uneasy, knew she was being watched. That was the part he liked the most, the part that ratcheted up the pace and made his heart pound.

There were eight other cars in the parking lot, his was the ninth, and she wouldn't have a clue where that feeling came from. Even as she brushed a hand through those blunt bangs of hers, she had no clue what was nagging at her senses, telling her to hurry up.

She flicked a glance in his direction because the Camaro, a dark stud of a machine, had a place in every girl's dreams. It had a place in her heart. She could only see her own reflection in the windshield, but she must have recognized it.

Even the cops gave him no mind at this strange hour as he waited outside the café watching the girl and the bright red bike. Part of being Ole was not looking at all like what he did.

By now she was unsettled enough to make a mistake, wobbling slightly as she pedaled away from the curb and out into the parking lot. That's when she noticed the tire. The one he'd slashed with his knife.

Ole was invisible inside that dark shiny shell, wheels hardly turning as the car coasted after the bike. She would be drawn to it like kids to an ice cream truck, only this one was offering more than a snow cone. Just as he was thinking that, her head snapped around and she came to a grinding halt in the middle of the parking lot.

He wouldn't jump out though. That was the oldest of all tricks. She might run for the trees if he did.

Forehead a frown and mouth working up a shout or two, her skin seemed whiter than he remembered. She was petite and slender, and that's what mattered. He powered down the window and stuck his head out.

"Becky. It's me."

She pressed one hand flat against her collarbone. The tiny smile, the nervous twitch. It was all fake. She knew his car well enough.

"Looks like the back tire," he said. "Leave it behind the dumpster."

She gave a tentative wave and walked beside the bike, looking back twice to see if he was still there. Then she hesitated at the crossing, even though no cars were coming.

"I've got a bicycle pump in the trunk," he shouted. The slash was too far gone for one of those but she wasn't to know.

She leaned the bike against the dumpster, fumbled with the chain and crouched down to wrap it around the back wheel.

Ole backed the car into an available space and slipped out of the driver's door. He leaned against the passenger side fender and watched her in the shadows.

She seemed to be taking her time.

Something throbbed inside him, a lingering burn of ancient lust. She turned then, eyes skimming down his body, visualizing things a young girl should never know. After the age of fourteen girls were no longer pure. They knew what they wanted. And this girl wanted him.

"It's slashed," she said, tucking her lower lip behind her top teeth. "I can't believe someone would do that."

Ole shook his head and shrugged. He was fascinated and thoroughly turned off at the same time. It was incredibly stupid to talk to a complete stranger, especially near a densely wooded path that led down into an arroyo. Only he wasn't a complete stranger. Not to her.

"Do you live around here?" she asked.

"Corrales," he lied.

She lowered her head, eyes flicking up to his. "I didn't know you lived so close."

"There's a lot of things about me you don't know." He couldn't keep the laughter from his voice and she half smiled in response. "Suppose I take you home and you tell me more about yourself on the way."

She didn't read the insult, the fact that her life would hardly fill the three long minutes to her front door. He wasn't sure he wanted to kiss those lips or touch any part of her. And he wasn't sure he wanted to slash her throat from ear to ear.

Not yet.

She eyed the gun in his belt and the car, and then nodded. He opened the passenger door, seeing the curve of her buttocks through that flimsy skirt. He wanted to look away, unable to form the simplest words.

He drove slowly, watching her out of the corner of his eye. She seemed to study the tuxedo shirt he wore, eyes fixed on the flesh at his collarbone. So strangely relaxed for one about to die, unless she was trying not to show any ounce of fear.

"Home," he murmured, parking in front of her ground floor apartment. He flexed his left hand, the hand that would snake around that tiny little neck in a moment.

She slipped off her seat belt and turned to face him. In utter silence she studied him, lifting her chin to expose her neck. "You remind me of someone. I can't think who."

Ole bobbed his head. He could see she was fortified by his smile. It was Morgan's face on every newspaper, long braid and tattoos etched into his temples. He doubted she would see the similarity. "Perhaps I have an ordinary face."

"No," she said, shaking her head. "You look like an actor."

That made all the difference to him. She would trust him if she thought he looked like someone else. He knuckled his forehead in mock concentration then snapped his fingers, rattling off a famous name. Her red painted lips parted, just wide enough to laugh.

"Trust," he whispered, "means walking down a dark, empty street without a gun."

"I've never held a gun, never touched one."

"You can touch mine," he whispered, knowing she hadn't missed the innuendo.

She lowered her eyes, shook her head. "They scare me."

"There's nothing to be afraid of," he murmured, trying to decide when to do it, when to lean over and kiss her, when to slide his hands around her neck and hear the frantic gurgle. "I won't tell your dad."

She looked at him then, eyes moist, like she suddenly knew what he was thinking. Only she was oblivious to what was going on his mind, even his hesitation. "How well do you know him?"

"Let's just say… better than he knows me."

He was getting closer to the edge, as if he would tumble into that ravine at any moment. How could it be so hot sitting next to her? Yet his mind was so cold.

Then he heard her say his name as if he'd been thinking for too long, grounding him, bring him back. She even smiled, brightened, like she was enjoying his company. He wasn't listening to her voice. Not really. It was just a blur of words, the type you hear in a bar, the type that bores the pants off any regular guy.

But he wasn't any regular guy. He was as welcome as a foreboding dream, as eloquent as grim poetry on a prison wall. Even when he took a single strand of her hair and wound it round his finger, he was still a killer.

She had got him at his name. *Ole*. It sounded odd and nice at the same time. He didn't feel vile, not anymore, not by a longshot. "Have you ever kissed a man?" he said.

There was nothing more exciting than a kiss. Doing it well was another matter.

"Yes," she said, cheeks flushing, hands flat on her thighs.

Ole threw up his head. "Show me."

When she hung back, he took the lead, kissing her lightly on the lips. And then on the cheeks and neck. She seemed to like it.

He liked it far more than he thought he would, and he stopped for a moment to look at her eyes. It was too dark to see details but there was a light across her face from the apartment office and for the first time in his life, he wasn't afraid of what he saw.

He'd been expecting the rise of bile in his throat, the screaming ravens in his head, the thick black smoke that threatened to suffocate him; but he felt none of those. It was like a cup of old whiskey in oak, streaming through his veins, fresh and delicate. The opiate of the rich.

He traced the line of her lips with a finger. "Do you know how hard it is for me to look at you?"

"No," she whispered.

He couldn't bear to look at those moist lips and not kiss them, and her tender, exquisite features only filled him with an ominous sadness. She wasn't vulnerable to the same things that he was, the insatiable desires, the raging anger, the repulsive smells each time he killed. It was his secret, a dangerous secret. It would compromise her to share in his world. But then again, she wasn't exactly Snow White.

Mustn't forget he was a cop, playing a cleaner role than the monster he was. He held on to that hand for a moment, sensing she wanted things to gallop ahead before he had a chance to show her how it was done.

"I should leave," he said, watching her face crumple like that of a child about to bawl.

"Don't," she murmured.

When he dropped her hand and said nothing she looked puzzled. "Don't you want my number?"

"I don't need it," he murmured in that fluid resonant voice she was clearly falling for. "I already know where you live." He leaned over and kissed her again. She wasn't going anywhere.

She had an inkling of what he was, monstrous and magnificent, a chimera. She didn't care. But it was hardly polite to kill a girl outside her own house.

"Let's go for a drive," he said, seeing the inflated cheeks and the smile beneath them.

He threw the car into reverse, felt the shudder of the powerful engine. He also felt an eagerness to get on the road, invigorated by the sudden change as if an invisible wall of darkness had somehow been breached. Instinctively, he tapped the stereo to life, listening for the pounding of the base.

Instead, a preacher's voice blared out over the sound of the engine.

… And no wonder, for Satan himself masquerades as an angel of light. It is not surprising, then, if his servants also masquerade as servants of righteousness. Their end will be what their actions deserve.

Ole balled his right hand into a fist and mashed the button.

FOURTEEN

Malin rubbed her eyes and yawned. It was nine o'clock in the evening now and Corrales Café had been closed for nearly an hour. No good wanting a decent meal at this time of night when all the best places were closed.

She glanced at the buff file on the coffee table. Morgan Eriksen. She had read it from cover to cover and she needed fresh air to clear her head.

Heads. Eriksen wanted heads. To tell the future, so he said. She remembered the Norse legend of Mimir, a wise man decapitated in a war between two groups of gods. Odin was said to have found the head and kept it so he could listen to its prophecy.

But the ninth hour? None of the girls had been killed within nine hours. According to the pathology report, time of death ranged between twenty-four and seventy-eight hours, all in the early part of the afternoon.

She cracked the sliding doors to her second floor apartment. It was too cold to sit on the balcony but she liked to listen to the water tumbling over a palisade of rocks at the front entrance. From her bedroom the soft susurration was a comfort at night, far better than one of those sound machines that mimicked waves on a sea shore.

Only tonight there was nothing but silence. The fountain was likely turned off due to the freezing temperatures and there was a fresh coating of snow on the floodlit monument sign which read Puerta de Corrales. Wind sighed through the branches of a cottonwood tree and there was the distinct smell of burning cedar wood in the air.

A young boy in a bright red sweater ran out into the parking lot. He pressed a ball of snow in his gloved hands and began to roll it along the ground. It was sticking. He'd have a snowman shaped in less than twenty minutes if he was lucky.

She wished she knew the Morans better, just enough to snatch a cup of coffee and a chat. Becky was a nice kid, smiley, friendly. It was the clothes that bothered Malin. She had seen how men looked at her, protective at first and then hungry. Old men, young men, men with needs.

Malin swallowed back a lump of shame. She'd messed up her life alright, working in back alley nudie bars and escorting the paunchy elite. How Hollister found out, she would never know. But there he was one night, leering up at her from a table in the front row. Just as she lifted her right leg against the pole, a black diamante stiletto flew from her foot and out into a cheering crowd. It gored Hollister in the groin, a bull's-eye she could never have managed no matter how hard she aimed. It had been funny then. But it wasn't funny now.

Minerva – she hadn't looked at the website for months. Opening the laptop on the coffee table, she keyed in her password and checked the email. A familiar feeling came crashing back and so did the same old men, wondering what had happened to her. And then she saw the email from Hollister. Just one sentence.

Where are you?

She was suddenly immobilized by a feeling of self-loathing. She'd been a stripper for crying out loud, shaking everything she'd got to a crowd of weirdos whose eyes were a ghostly shade of white, some larger than cups. It was as if they had never seen a naked woman before. What was that? Those rheumy eyes. Like dead men's eyes.

She deleted the message, deleted him. He was gone now at the tap of a button.

In spite of the chill on that dark night, she felt a trickle of perspiration at the small of her back and her hands were damp, too. Moonlight slithered through the blinds tussled by a night breeze and somewhere a coyote howled. She walked toward the patio doors and stared at the street below. The boy had gone, but there was a lump of snow in front of the office about five feet high.

It was then she saw the car, sleek and dark, purring along the road like a contented cat. It pulled in opposite the front office, headlights flaring through a haze of fresh sleet. It lingered under the amber glow of the streetlamps like a precious masterpiece in a museum, an artwork so dark it was beautiful.

She couldn't see the driver through the tinted window but she knew he was watching. Something.

Corvette? Camaro? One of those.

A plume of steam oozed from her mouth and curled in the breeze. Crouching, she peered through the balusters as the front tire slowly stuttered along the verge, gravel rattling against the exhaust. It was only a few seconds before the engine shuddered into life and the car arced back into the road, brakes squealing and taillights dwindling into the shadows.

Had he seen her crouching there with the light of the living room behind her? Had he even seen her face?

Malin blinked the sweat out of her eyes and retreated to the living room, locking the sliding doors. Her heart was pounding as she entertained the possibility that the car was Hollister's, that he had come to torment her.

It was impossible, of course. He was in New Jersey

and she was in New Mexico. But he could still get her number, her address, anything he wanted. He was a cop after all.

The thought gave her a headache and there was a buzzing in her right ear. Fear began to ebb but in its place was a surge of guilt.

Be careful, poppet. There's bad men out there.

It was her mother's voice, strained, sad. Malin had been close to her mom, iron-willed and always armed with a look of disapproval. There was something vulnerable about her at the end, something Malin had never seen before. It made her want to cry, knowing her mother had never told a soul.

"I wish I could just pick up the phone and call you, mom," she said out loud with a sob in her voice. "I wish there were phones that could reach to heaven. I just wish I could see you one more time."

She sighed and brushed away a tear. She wasn't going to cry. No use in crying. Not when it made your nose red and blotchy.

That was before the doorbell rang, heavy and menacing like a ship's muster. Her mouth went dry and her throat tightened. She wasn't expecting anyone and the thought of going out there in the freezing cold was anything but tempting.

There were only shadows through the spy hole and, grabbing her gun from a holster hung over the kitchen chair, she opened the door.

Crisp brown leaves whispered along the galleria, whirling through the bannisters and along the corridor like wood fragments from a carpenter's bench. Even though she moved out of the open doorway looking left and right along the dimly lit walls, the icy wind took her breath away. No one would be out in weather like this. No one sane, that is.

Hollister would no more follow her here than a call-girl to a brothel. He was too pleased with himself for that.

"Malin, it's me. Alex."

Malin heard the thudding of footfalls coming back up the stairs and she saw the boy with the bright red sweater. Alex Moran.

"I thought there was no one home," he said, lips curling. "Mom wants to know if you'd like to come over for dinner. It's not much, just spaghetti."

The sound of another human voice was such a relief, Malin almost hugged him. "I'd like that," she said, nodding.

"Were you crying?"

Malin was surprised at the observation. Her eyes were probably redder than a lobster's claw and there was no use saying no. "I miss my mom. She died this year."

"I'm sorry," Alex stammered. "That must be awful. To lose your mom, I mean."

"Here," Malin said, backing into the apartment. She handed Alex a fur coat that was hanging on a hook behind the door. "It was hers. It'll keep you warm."

"Cool!" Alex ran a hand up and down the collar, hem dragging on the floor. "Dad's home and he's made some apple cobbler. Do you like apple cobbler?"

Malin almost laughed. She enjoyed the refreshing chatter as they walked under a full moon where trees and shrubbery rustled and shadows curled across the front lawn. She pointed at the snowman, gave him a few tips on how to shape the head. Wasn't going to think of any more headless corpses tonight. She wasn't afraid any more.

Think of yourself like this, her mother used to say. *Pretend you're a master of self-defense. Not the black-belt type, the street type. The type that puts on an imaginary armor. Someone that knows the streets are not filled with human beings, but with demons. You'll be stronger then. Unbeatable.*

Malin had inherited some of those knife-edge debating skills – and tenacity – from her mother. She could pretend armor behind a Kevlar vest but she certainly couldn't pretend she was better than her opponent.

You better just hope you are, she thought.

It surprised her to see that the Moran's door faced the front drive just as hers did. Only theirs was a first floor apartment close to the main office, the second block near the cottonwood and the road.

Sarge stood in the kitchen wearing a butcher's apron directing operations with a wooden spoon.

"This is Rae," Sarge said, hugging his wife.

Malin liked Rae instantly. There was a sparkle in those small green eyes and warmth in two pudgy hands. Her eyes rolled over a steaming apple cobbler on the counter, edges bubbling with brown sugar. "Like cobbler?"

"Love it," Malin said.

Sarge pulled out a chair and ushered Malin over with a wave. "Anyone heard from Becky?"

"She's working late," Rae said. "Her boss called. Sounded foreign."

They all sat down to eat and Malin was surprised to hear a Christian blessing. She hadn't heard anything quite like it since leaving New Jersey.

"So Malin, any more news on the case?" Rae asked through a mouthful of noodles.

Malin shot a look at Sarge and he just nodded. "We found a… you know."

"Found what?" Alex said.

"A head," Malin said, wincing.

"Whose head?"

"We don't know yet." Malin cut into a blood red tomato, oozing with sauce. She knew the head belonged to Patti, and her stomach began to tighten.

"The man in prison couldn't have done it then," Alex said, spooning a few asparagus spears onto his plate. "If he didn't do it, then who did?"

"We'll find him," Sarge murmured, smoothing his moustache with two forefingers, eyes flicking to Malin.

"But we're not safe until he's inside," Alex said. "Not really. What if he's a cop hater? What if he knows where we live?"

"He doesn't know where we live." Sarge leaned across the table and gave Alex the eye. "We're not in the phone book."

"But dad—"

Sarge held up a finger. "Who's the best cop in the world?"

"You are."

"Then stop worrying. We'll find him in no time."

Malin's pulse began to speed. With forensics picking away at every last piece of evidence and Detective Temeke calling all units to pick up a nonexistent Camaro, she was almost angry with Sarge for giving his son a promise he couldn't possibly keep.

And there had been a dark car outside the apartment complex less than an hour ago. A Camaro, come to think of it. Just a coincidence. Lots of them about.

"I heard your mom passed recently," Rae said, steering the conversation to even less cheery news. "I'm so sorry for your loss."

I'm so sorry for your loss... Malin hated those words. They were unimaginative, stale. Everyone said it at funerals. There must be something better to say, something more uplifting. "It's not a loss you see. It's just a parting. I'll see her again someday."

"Yes, you will," Rae whispered. "And so will I."

Malin could feel a few pairs of eyes staring at her but she kept her head down, kept chewing on that blood red tomato. Conversation turned to school grades and Malin almost forgot she was a stranger in someone's house.

"Becky's got a boyfriend," Alex blurted. "And he speaks funny."

Sarge frowned. "Course Becky doesn't have a boyfriend."

"She does," Alex said, nodding. "She met him in the mall. He's old. Like dad."

Rae began to laugh. "Anyone's old when you're fourteen."

Malin conjured an image of an older man playing *father* to Becky's *child*. She knew how that felt. Strange. Exciting.

"How well do you know Temeke?" Sarge said.

The question took Malin by surprise and she felt the ache in the back of her throat. "Not well."

"Nobody likes him. Doesn't mince his words. Hurts everyone's little feelers. Thing is though, there's not much tweaking to his game. He knows exactly where to look."

"How do you mean?"

"They call him *the sniper*. It's like he can dial in his inner rifle and scope, and there's his quarry right in the crosshairs. Dead nuts on."

Malin grinned when she heard Alex laugh. "Now you're making him sound superhuman."

"That's the problem. He's got more up his sleeve than a gun. He's BAU. That's why we've got him."

Malin knew how hard the FBI trained its team of professionals in the Behavioral Analysis Unit in Quantico. How they focused on criminal behavior to better understand the criminal. Not only did they study all aspects of violent crime, they also studied the people they worked with. And half of them were nuttier than the nuts.

"He sees you," Sarge said, peering through a circle he

had made with his thumb and forefinger. "Any twitches, any false moves and its curtains."

Malin felt her stomach crunch with laughter, only she caught herself just in time. Detective Temeke wasn't a laughing matter. He was clearly the burr under everyone's saddle.

"And steer clear of Hackett. We call him *Lucifer* behind his back. Got a telescope in that corner office trained on rare birds. He might look like he needs a personal dresser but he drives like a supercar."

Malin began to grit her teeth. That was two dangerous bears she wouldn't be poking any time soon. "Lucifer?"

Sarge nodded and tapped his nose. "He roams the earth, the corridors and the toilets. Best keep your phone out of reach unless you want it tapped. Best keep your private life *private*."

Malin walked home in her mother's coat, Sarge on one side and Alex on the other. Their banter reminded her of home and how much she longed for one of her own. Not just any home. A home with a fire in the hearth and a husband of her own.

That night she lay in bed, fur coat bundled beside her like a curled black dog. She listened to the wind soughing in the roof and the creak of branches outside. It sounded like the scrape of dry bones against next door's window and, from time to time, she imagined a corpse in a wood, arms reaching out from under a pile of broken branches as if pleading to be found.

FIFTEEN

Temeke squinted at the digital clock on the nightstand. The display read four forty-seven in the morning and, as far as he knew, he'd slept in three-hour increments since the night before.

He was sweating again. It was that darn Albuquerque heat and then he remembered it was December and snowing.

Serena. Her body was on fire.

He remembered the day when she couldn't lift her arms to use the hairdryer, the day she called in sick. Serena had never been sick in her life, not that he remembered. She soldiered on through colds and flu, mostly coasting in overdrive even in the heat of the summer. She thrived on stress until the depression kicked in, until her hands started to shake.

Four years ago this month, that's when she left her job, left the rat-race behind. They said it was Graves Disease. Temeke said it was stress. And now a few pills managed the shakes, the sensitivity to heat, allowing her to live a near normal life.

Normal? There was nothing normal about a woman who stared into space, cried when the weather changed, called him incessantly until he got home. She was worried he'd been kidnapped or shot in the line of duty. He suddenly wished he had.

She was worried about his smoking. And as for any

intimacy, that had been given life without any chance of parole.

The phone shuddered on the nightstand, a reminder of what had woken him up in the first place. He snatched it before limbering beneath Serena's leg and rushing into the bathroom.

He muttered his name in the mouthpiece and studied two half-closed eyes in the bathroom mirror. It was Hackett.

"Bad news. Forensics said there was nothing on that wine glass. Nada. And second, I need you down at PNM this morning. Nine o'clock sharp. Warden says Eriksen keeps banging his head against the wall. Says his bed's not been slept in."

"My bed's not been slept in."

"Becky Moran didn't come home last night. Probably nothing to worry about. Got a boyfriend apparently. You wouldn't happen to know his name?"

Temeke felt the tightness in his gut and drew a deep breath. "Why would I know his name?"

"Rumor has it, she's into older men. Black men. I heard you messed up some evidence yesterday. Sat on a block of wood. Got those pants you were wearing?"

Temeke rubbed his rear end. He'd never get over that one, especially with half of the department listening into this call. "They're in a plastic bag, sir."

"Another monumental balls-up! Did it not occur to you…"

Temeke put the phone down on the vanity and began to ferret under the sink for a packet of smokes. But with Hackett cussing like a docker, he reluctantly put the phone back against his ear.

"Just when I thought we'd tied things up with Eriksen," Hackett shouted. "Better hope Judge Matthews doesn't get hold of it."

"Better hope the news doesn't get hold of it."

"I want this farce over with, do you hear? It's a copycat killer. Has to be."

"Very good, sir. I'll take a little drive to PNM and tell Erikson the good news."

"You'll do no such thing. It was his blood on the Williams girl's teeth after all. You'll get down there as soon as possible and you'll squeeze the bastard until he gives you a name."

"Talking of names, do we have one for the dead girl?"

"Not yet. And by the way, I'm fed up with you using that elevator. It's going up and down like a schoolgirl's skirt."

Temeke heard the click and shook his head. A diamond-bright moon shone down through a black sky peering through the window with a big round face. He could have watched it for hours, only the doorbell rang and gave him a start. It was too early to be Malin.

Creeping back into the bedroom, he watched the rise and fall of Serena's chest, the soft purring through an open mouth. Hauling on a pair of pants and grabbing his harness from an ottoman, he sprinted barefoot downstairs. There was a grill in the half-lite door and squinting through the glass, he saw a frosty beam. He pressed one hand against the frame and slowly turned the knob.

An icy wind tore into his chest like a thousand tiny knives. He had to shield his eyes against the glare of headlights from a departing car as it reversed up the driveway and swung out into the road. It was silent for a few seconds before the engine began revving behind a stand of sycamores before the driver hit the gas. Probably two teenagers parked in the front yard having a good snog and a grope.

Bloody kids, Temeke thought. He'd string them up next time.

It wasn't the first time they'd parked under those tall bushy trees, misting up the windows and bouncing the front bumper off the tarmac. But it would be the last.

Silence.

Only the leaves shuddered in the night breeze and moonlight blinked between the upper branches. He could still see exhaust vapors hanging two feet off the ground like a curl of angry ghosts, and there was another scent, familiar, sickly, like the inside of an old church.

He turned to go, foot brushing against a rolled up copy of the journal. Blimey, he thought. Newspapers were getting earlier every week. Just as he picked it up something slipped out and rattled onto the doorstep.

A charred bone. On his doormat.

Not a dog bone. Much longer than that. The shaft was slender and slightly arched, knuckled on one end and rounded on the other. A thigh bone.

A human bone.

Temeke shuddered as he crouched, heart hammering so hard his vision began to blur. He tried to work up some saliva by sucking on the roof of his mouth, fingers twitching, almost touching. And then he snatched his hand back. Why would kids leave a bone on his front doorstep?

Idiots, that's what.

He was hoping for a magic flash of inspiration and when none came, he picked the thing up in his fist, stashing the newspaper under one arm, and brought it inside. A macabre image of a corpse popped into his mind, one that was missing a leg, and he nearly dropped the damn thing on the threshold.

I need a smoke, he thought, slamming the door. What he actually needed was a drink. Reaching behind the antique coffee grinder on the top shelf of the kitchen cabinet, he retrieved a packet of Marlboros and a box of matches. He was startled by the sudden click of a timer at the base of the Christmas tree, lights suddenly winking through the darkness.

The blue numbers on the microwave said it was now four minutes before five, and trudging through the hallway to the kitchen he punched the start button on the coffee-maker, looking forward to that first cup of piñon roast.

First things first.

He placed the newspaper and then the bone on the breakfast table under a pendant cut-glass lamp. Gorge rising and bitter in the back of his throat, he saw no evidence of blood or tissue. The thing was smooth except for what appeared to be a piece missing near the top of the shaft. He couldn't be sure, but it looked like a gunshot wound.

Wrapping it up in the newspaper, he left it on the chair by the front door. It was a prank. That was all there was to it. But he'd have it examined by forensics just in case.

Sliding one of Serena's coats from a hanger in the hall closet and slipping on an old pair of gardening shoes, he took his coffee outside to a wrought iron table. The snow was just a light dusting of powder now and there was little of it on the patio.

What's with a bone? he thought, wondering if the teenagers hadn't left it after all. Wondering if it belonged to an Alpaca, those hairy goat things that grazed in a nearby meadow.

What if it had been left by next door's dog? An ornery brown poodle, unclipped and rugged and nothing like his frou-frou cousins. No, Harry didn't have the clipped yew-hedge look. He even had a full tail.

But would he have left a bone as big as that on Temeke's front door mat? He'd left other things. A squeaky toy, a rubber ball, three feet of water hose and, come to think of it, a half-eaten bone from the butcher.

It's just a bone, for goodness sake.

Temeke shook his head and took a sip of coffee. Dark roast, just how he liked it. And then he saw them. A set of footprints neatly carved in the snow and stalking toward the sitting room window. His breath was ragged now, heart-attack breath, and his hand slithered beneath that coat for his sidearm, a 9 mm German semi-automatic.

No one knew about the secret stash of weed in the downspout. No one knew it was wrapped in a Ziploc bag and covered with duct tape. No one knew he hadn't the guts to smoke the damn stuff anymore, not after Malin had mentioned it. The footprints had to be his. No point in squeezing off a few shots at nothing. He blew out a loud sigh as he replaced the gun in his holster.

Pulling out a cigarette, he let it sag between his lips, mind wandering to the night before. Serena was mad because she'd found another packet of cigarettes in the toilet cistern.

Scratching a match along the arm of his chair, he cupped one hand around the flame and watched it glow for a moment. The smell of fresh tobacco filled his nostrils and he blew the match out with a lungful of smoke.

The back yard was nothing much, just like the house. There was a block wall and plenty of trees to stop an intruder. The front was a different matter. It was open to everything, even horse manure.

That's how it was living in the nine hundred block of Guadalupe Trail. Maybe he needed a gate and a big fat padlock. Maybe he needed to get going. He took a few more drags and then ground the remains of the cigarette under his shoe, kicking it into a pile of leaves. Snatching a clean pair of socks and a polo shirt from the laundry basket, he shoved the cigarette packet down a side pocket.

A phone call brought him to the front door. Malin was outside in the Explorer, nodding through a tinted windshield. He waved and flicked up five fingers before grabbing a can of Hawaiian Aloha from the guest bathroom and giving the hallway a vigorous spray.

"Bye, love," he shouted, pressing his feet into a pair of dark brown combat assault boots.

He could see Serena's face over the bannisters and that narrow-eyed smile. Silken olive skin behind a satin baby-doll, she'd win Miss America hands down.

"Always in such a hurry to leave," she said, padding down the stairs. "Pity you can't stay and enjoy the Christmas tree."

"Christmas tree?"

"We could snuggle together on the couch and watch the lights."

What the heck was she on about? Temeke hoped she hadn't found the contraband on the lower tier. The fairy on top had a packet of Marlboros stuffed up its tutu.

"Truth or dare?" she said, head wobbling from side to side.

"If only I had the time, love," he said, stuffing the pants Hackett wanted in an evidence bag and grabbing the bone in the rolled up newspaper. "I'd be right there like a terrier down a rabbit hole."

"Happen to know about these?" she said, holding out a box of cards. "Went to play Bridge with the girls and guess what fell out? Not cards. Oh, no!"

Temeke suddenly found the front door of consuming interest. That was a third stash of cigarettes he'd forgotten about. "You don't have to tell me. I'm getting my sorry ass out of here before I get a walloping."

"What's that?"

"This?" he said, clamping the bone under one arm. "Evidence."

"Give it here."

"No, love. Trust me. You don't want to see this." He began to back out of the hallway, one hand raised. "Just going to see a dog about a bone. I'll be back at nine."

"What's that smell?"

"What smell?"

"Have you been smoking?" That's how it was with Serena. A quick sniff, an accusing word.

"No, my love. Must be next door, burning leaves again." Temeke bolted for the door.

SIXTEEN

Temeke put the evidence on the backseat of the Explorer and nodded at Malin. "Morning drill," he said, slipping a cigarette between his lips. "Need a smoke and a think. Meet me at the end of the drive."

He had a few long puffs as he listened to the rain pattering on the roof of his house, driven by a sudden gust of wind. Albuquerque, the city of roadrunners, of chile, of lobos, where one heard the dialects of Spain and Mexico. Where a menace lurked beneath the enormous sky – one who spoke none of those languages and who wiped away all evidence of his very existence.

He stood in the beam of Malin's headlights, flicked the lighted cigarette in next door's dumpster, half hoping it would go up in smoke and take away the stench of old socks. It wouldn't be the first time the thing caught fire. He'd thrown a lighted smoke in there a couple of weeks ago not knowing the neighbor had discarded an oily rag from his garage only moments before. The blaze was spectacular. And so was the heat.

He jumped into the car, noting Eriksen's files still sitting between the handbrake and the console. "Find anything?"

"I've been thinking, sir. The ninth hour doesn't mean the number of hours the victims were missing before they were killed. It means the hour of day. *Any* day."

Temeke stared ahead through the windshield,

watching the flash of traffic lights as they sped past. "Nine o'clock in the morning or nine o'clock at night?"

"That depends."

"On what?"

"On whether you're talking about Jewish or Gentile time."

"What's the difference?"

"From a Jewish perspective, the day begins at six o'clock in the evening and ends twenty-four hours later. So that means the ninth hour of the day would be three o'clock in the afternoon. Jesus of Nazareth is said to have breathed his last breath at the ninth hour – three hours before the day ended."

"Well, that's excellent news, Malin. Hackett will be pleased."

"Can't you see? It gives us more time."

"It's a gamble," he said, arranging his cigarettes within easy reach and flicking a match into life. He felt the heat of Malin's eyes as they searched his face, his mouth, his body. He began to wonder if she had come at Hollister with those large staring eyes all excited and dribbling.

Once a stripper, always a stripper, he thought, hoping she wouldn't push him in a tight corner and take off her top. She'd be disappointed if she did. Boobs did nothing for him. Never had. It was the ass he liked. And hers was as flat as a park bench.

"Let's get one thing straight," he said. "No lies, all right?"

"I don't lie, sir."

"Hollister was your boyfriend, wasn't he? Only he got mad when you signed up to be an escort on the Internet. Can't stand a woman getting the better of him. Sounds a bit like the nutcase we've got inside. Gawd!" he shouted, feeling the heat on his finger before shaking out the flame.

The car came to a screeching halt at the side of the road, rocks splattering against the side fenders. The seatbelt dug into his belly, squeezing out an almost audible belch.

"Cussing I can take," hissed Malin between clenched teeth. "Blaspheme and you'll be walking home."

Temeke shrank back from the onslaught but Malin was still on the attack, eyes black and glittering. He gave a half-hearted flutter of his hand. "I'm very sorry. I'm not at my best when I'm hungry."

"You're not at your best at any time."

As usual Malin was driving too fast, and Temeke was seriously beginning to like her. Her mood showed in her driving, swerving out onto Highway 550, twisting the wheel as they took the onramp to I-25.

He didn't mind seeing as ten minutes later they were sitting in a rest stop eating hot burritos and drinking coffee. She knew how to keep a man's stomach in order, knew when his needle was past hungry. His last partner ate refried beans and hot Doritos, and the air was ranker than dog breath.

"Looks like that shirt's been at the bottom of your laundry basket," she said, talking at last.

"It beats a deerstalker and cape." Temeke lit another cigarette. "This car is going to be our home for the next few days. We'll be tired and covered in sand. You'll spray whatever feminine stink you've got secreted in that duffle of yours and I'll smell like a pair of old socks."

He heard the ring of laughter over the scrunching of paper, and he watched her ball the bags and toss them into a nearby trash can.

"Catching this guy is our number one priority," he said, sighing a cloud of smoke. "Time you talked to Morgan. Time you gave him a real taste of Norway. Time he told us who he really is."

117

"You got a little sassy since you got the night off, sir," she said.

Temeke never felt his smile waver. "Got a little *sleep* since I got the night off."

"There's something about him," she said, face thin and nervous. "Creepy. You know."

"They're all creepy, *you know*." Temeke almost railed at her stupidity and then decided to stay calm. "He likes the dark ones."

"He hates the dark ones. He probably hates women. He's a monster."

"Like it or not, that monster's the difference between finding a body and solving the case. Every day's the same. You have to sniff the dirt like a dog each time you find a fresh kill. That's the way we find the deeper mysteries. But if you're scared, that fresh kill might just be you."

Temeke caught the forced smile, the hand that strayed to anchor a strand of loose hair. He continued to watch her with an uneasy silence, *uneasy* for her. "This isn't a bullet you can dodge, Marl, not with all the competition out there for a job like yours. No criminal has a face. This one's no different."

At least that's how he dealt with it. No face, no personality. Just a layer of membrane that barely puckered each time it spoke. It was the eyes that gave it all away, eyes that never lit up even when the mouth dared to smile.

"I found a few strange things in Eriksen's file," she murmured.

"You've gone and done your homework." He was glad she had.

"He says the dark ones are the dwarves, the swindlers of the blood of Kvasir. Norse mythology, sir."

"It's all superstitious drivel. What's all this swindling of blood?"

"Kvasir was killed by two dwarves. They drained him of his blood and mixed it with honey to make the mead of wisdom. Maybe that's what Eriksen did to these victims. Drained them of blood to make wine. And the heads? The only thing I can find about a severed head giving wisdom is the head of Mimir."

Temeke didn't know what to make of it. He didn't know what to make of Malin. A few minutes ago, she was spitting red sparks and now she was wistful, pleasant. He was glad though. He could have landed one of those beefy blond partners with a chest like a tugboat bumper.

"He'll keep killing unless we find him," he said, trying to keep his mind on the matter. "One a month, just like he promised."

"Got any leads?"

"Not unless the doctor comes back with a match. Incidentally, I found a nice little gift on my doorstep this morning. A thigh bone. Human. It's on the backseat if you want to take a look at it."

Malin curled her lip. "Is it all—"

"Clean as a whistle."

"Who would do a thing like that?"

"Saw a car pulling away. Thought it was kids at first."

Temeke took another sip of coffee, watching a blur of mesa to the west and a wilderness of browns and sage greens. He'd been wondering who the driver of the car was all morning, wondering why he hesitated in the road. For a moment he couldn't shake the feeling that he was being hunted by a wax doll infused with supernatural rage.

He saw a whole realm of possibilities he had never thought of before. If the killer was following him it wouldn't be a bad thing. Nothing wrong with lying in wait. It was knowing just where to lie. And let's face it,

119

with all this driving around the killer would never find him.

Temeke began to wonder if his suspect was like a wolf in a forest. Someone who could pick up the scent of a deer, knowing how many there were before he saw them. A man who killed without regret or compassion. A man who was unafraid, invincible.

Temeke would learn to be the same. To believe he had limitless stamina, to not feel the cold, to not feel anything. Rarely had he ever witnessed a killer's face without that faraway stare as if they had been pulled back to the past and into the worst possible pain.

This killer hadn't accounted for Temeke's skill at tracking. After all, he was a hunter too.

SEVENTEEN

Ole yawned and lifted his head. Sunlight crept through a gap in the blinds and he realized he had overslept.

He remembered the call he made to the police department yesterday, when he put on his best American accent and asked for Luis Alvarez. Captain Fowler wouldn't tell him much except that he was on leave for ten days. Depending on when he left, Ole calculated Alvarez could be back in a week. It wasn't long to wait.

He thought about the bone. He couldn't for the life of him remember who it belonged to, nor did he care. It was torn off a victim as easy as a drumstick and then he washed it, scrubbed it, and wrapped it in newspaper. Who more deserving than Detective Temeke to receive such a gift?

Probably be on the news.

He stretched his legs and sat up against a nest of pillows, grabbed the remote and turned on the TV. A power outage in Belen, a new currency law, and the divorce of a famous boxer.

Ole's mind drifted to the detective's house. He remembered the road all the way to Fourth and half a mile in, a narrow farm track to 9723 Guadalupe Trail. He parked outside a small white house with a sparkling green lawn so neatly clipped it would put any golf course to shame. A fake lawn so the man of the house wouldn't need to mow it.

It wasn't hard to vault over the back wall, keep his footprints to the perimeter and ply the stash of weed from the backyard downspout. Sitting in his car, he tore into the duct tape, crushed the leaves between his fingers and took a long lasting sniff.

He rolled a joint right there and then. No one could see him in the Camaro, dark tinted windows and shiny black paint. It was like a stealth bomber hovering amongst the trees, headlights at full beam. What a night of surprises. He'd just have to do it again sometime.

The vision faded as he stared at the TV. There was no news. Not even a postmortem report. He was a celebrity who had struck nine times and not even a ticker-tape announcement at the bottom of the screen.

Cursing loudly, he swung his legs out the bed, looked at the white phone on the bedside table and smiled. The girl stirred beside him, red lipstick smeared across her face. In the back of his mind there was a twisted morsel of hatred, the surging delight in finishing it just before she woke up. Even his hands itched, those strong hands that could easily twist off the stubborn lid of a pickle jar.

Killing her wouldn't be gentlemanly. Not before breakfast. Not before seeing how she looked at him, smiled at him, longed for him. And when she knew what he was, she would lie to him. Offer to call that cop-of-a-pop, reassure him she was OK, tell him she was in love. That she had run away.

That was the best of plans. The police would never find her, never suspect. And he could enjoy her all the more until he got tired of her. It was a simple noose for easy game. Hell, rabbits were smarter than this.

Leaving the phone by the bed and just within reach was half the fun. So he showered and went downstairs. Naked. He never felt hot or cold like most people did. Standing in front of a long mirror in the hallway, he studied his thighs, his belly, his chest. Blond hair settled around the nape of his neck, flipped out in a razor cut. Sunlight caught in his dark blue eyes and settled on the cusp of his cheekbones. He almost sobbed when he saw it. The pale skin, the ginger eyebrows, the sideways smile.

Morgan.

He found the cell phone in the bread bin and dialed the Penitentiary of New Mexico. The phone would be long gone by the time they traced it, washed down a storm drain like all the others.

The blood flooded to his brain when he heard Morgan's voice, felt the tingling in the veins of his face. His conscience should have been killing him.

"Where's Patti? What have you done with her?"

"Done with her?" Ole almost laughed. "Having a picnic, I should say, under the first tower."

"What do you mean?"

"Where a car can soar over the crest line, spanning wider than a man's hand." Ole stopped to listen to Morgan's brain as it rattled to understand. "They'll be letting you out soon."

"When?"

"Trust me. They'll be letting you out. I have something they want. Something very special."

"You don't know the detective. He's a tracker. He'll take you down slowly. Those are the rules of his game."

Ole felt a nudge of jealousy. "He doesn't hunt, not like I do."

"You're a fool if you think you can win this."

Ole could hear panic and a trace of hatred. It wouldn't be long before the detective picked away at Morgan's flesh until there was nothing left. "Killers belong together," he crooned. "Like brothers."

"We're not brothers. They know we're not brothers."

"They don't know anything."

"They know I didn't do it."

The tiny red numerals of the digital clock told Ole to ring off. He knew they were listening to him. He knew they were tracing him.

He snapped the phone back in the bread bin, craned his head round at a sound. A creak on the staircase and the subtle pop of a joint.

The girl was awake. In a way it excited him.

He let his head drop to one side, listening for the familiar whisper of carpet underfoot, the unmistakable catch of her breath. The soft rustle of clothes, the rasp of a zipper, all these things he heard as he took an anchor chain and two screw shackles from the hall closet. When he reached the top of the stairs there she was, standing in the shadows.

"Becky," he whispered. "Were you listening?"

She shook her head, eyes glistening, mouth slack.

He lunged for her then, clasping her around the waist with monstrous arms strong enough to rip her apart. Felt her lean toward him, heard her whisper.

"Please let me go."

He didn't answer. Didn't need to. He wanted to delay the killing this time, delighting in the texture of her skin, the beat of her heart. It would soon be the last vibration of consciousness.

"They know I'm missing," she said, wrestling with the shackles. There was a frown on her forehead when she said it, pupils large and black. "My dad knows where I am."

"No," he said, brushing a stray strand of hair out of her face, the tear under one eye. "He doesn't know where you are."

It hadn't occurred to him to dress. After all, killing was always best done naked. No evidence. There was a radiant glow about her face he hadn't noticed before and a distant stare.

She was a fragile flame in his cold world and the

more he thought about it, the more he longed for that first spurt of blood, sometimes on his cheeks, sometimes on his lips.

"Please!" she almost yelled.

He tied her to the bedhead, wrists pinned neatly in the shackles with a screwdriver. It was a good job, he thought as he took one last look.

"I promise I won't tell anyone," she said, tugging at the chain. "I won't. I hate the police, always have. They've never been good to me. I've wanted to run away since I was eight."

"So you have."

"No, you don't understand. Let me call my dad. I can tell him I ran away with you. That I'm in love."

There it was. The unimaginative things they always said. Same old, same old.

"You be a good girl, now," he said, holding up a finger. "Not a sound."

He knew how she must have felt. A tingling in her chest, a clenching of the stomach. Lightheadedness perhaps.

All in a good day's work.

"Ole, I can help you," she said. "I can…"

The girl's voice was soothing and strange. Sometimes it reminded him of the legends his mother told when he was a child. She had a voice he would never forget. A light that would never go out.

He dressed slowly in Morgan's clothes, held them up to his nose sometimes to inhale the scent. His mind began to scan over words, columns, photographs, as if turning the pages of his own headlines. Episodes returned in no particular order, screaming mouths, rasping breaths, clammy skin. He couldn't recall them all, except one.

Kizzy… Kizzy Williams. Daughter of Darryl Williams of 5024 Timoteo Avenue on the west side of town. A place of curiosity. Nice house. Shame about the bell tower.

It was more than a bell tower. There was a motion detector that set off a floodlight, illuminating the courtyard and the sweeping drive. He knew because he had been watching the house for weeks. Watching Kizzy's older sister, the girl Morgan was supposed to have taken in the first place.

The arroyo was just sand and scrub, and unless the Williams man had the audacity to raise his block wall, there was virtually nothing to stop anyone climbing in.

He pulled on a pair of shoes under faded jeans and slipped his gun in his belt. Grabbing a set of keys, he took one last look at the girl on the bed. She was quite beautiful in the early morning sun, hair burnished copper... just like Patti's.

He said nothing as he locked the bedroom door, engaging two deadbolts before hurrying downstairs. The living room was still dark behind closed blinds, kitchen darker still.

He could see in the dark, prided himself on the fact. Settling at the kitchen table, he watched the wall above the countertop where a sleek white phone hung by the door. Chin resting in one hand, he counted to five. And then came the moment he was hoping for. The blinking light, the static when he lifted the receiver.

She was on the other line.

A girl's voice, shrill and distant as if she kept turning her head to see if someone was coming. "Temeke, it's me."

"Becky... Where are you?"

"I don't know." Sobbing. "I don't know where I am."

"Who are you with?"

"He's gone. I don't know why I did this. I don't know why—"

"Give me his name. Becky. His name."

"Ole…"

"Describe where you are? When you look out of the window, what do you see?"

"A sloping roof, a pool… pine trees."

"Houses?"

"Yes, between the trees."

"What type of houses?"

"Adobe… brick… iron gates."

"Can you hear anything?"

"No." More sobbing and then, "He's going to kill me."

"Becky, describe the house, describe where you are."

"In the bedroom."

"Can you get out?"

"No. I'm chained to the bed."

"Stay with me. Stay on the line. How are you tied?"

"Shackles… on my hands."

"The pin in the shackle, can you twist it or does it need a screwdriver?"

"Screwdriver."

"Describe the bedroom."

"White walls, blue carpet, blue bedspread, cupboard by the door, bathroom …"

She was really sobbing now. Ole liked the sound. And then it struck him. Why did she call Temeke first? Why not her father?

He drew a deep sigh from the pit of his stomach and put down the phone. He made sure they heard the click, made sure the detective knew he was there.

He walked up the stairs, sensing the thumping of her heart almost as loud as the clock ticking on the landing. It was aching to be set free.

He unlocked the door, ripped the phone out of the wall and sat down on the bed.

"You know he'll never find you," he said at last.

She stiffened. She nodded. She knew.

EIGHTEEN

Malin looked up through the windshield at a vast gray sky. Clouds hung low and rain rattled on the roof of the car. Highway 14 was a cracked slip of a road that took them to the Penitentiary of New Mexico.

She listened to Temeke on the phone, listened to the disappointment in his voice. "So they got a trace, sir... northeast heights... can't be more specific?... No, we're not at the Pen yet. A curry?... I can't, sir. If I have another of those I'll blow."

Temeke ended the call, drew a large breath and released it before speaking. "The northeast heights are crawling with cops. They still haven't found her."

"They will, sir." Malin saw the pinched lips and the tapping fingers. "They always do."

"What do you mean they always do? How many murder books do we have in the archives where cases have gone cold? I've got several under my desk from the seventies."

He went quiet for a few moments, then muttered something about a tour to Old Main, the abandoned Cell Block 4. But a depressing tour in a ghost town was not what Malin had in mind, nor did she want to clutter her head with old scenes of prison riots. There was something in the air that bothered her, a sense of menace from Becky's kidnapping. Temeke had definitely picked up on it. He was milder to her now.

"Hackett said we're to be here by nine-thirty." she said, glimpsing at her watch. "It's already ten-fifteen."

"Hackett says a lot of foolish things. The kindest thing is to ignore him."

She caught sight of herself in the wing mirror, hair neatly tied back, no makeup. Her eyes were wide and the steering wheel felt oddly thin. Maybe she was squeezing it too hard. She began to pray.

"Are you nervous?" she asked Temeke. "You know, talking to Eriksen."

"Oh, I've already had the pleasure." He looked up from the file on his lap and gave her a peevish frown. "He should be scared of *me*."

"But he's not is he?"

"No," Temeke said, staring off into the distance. "He's not scared of anyone. And you shouldn't be either."

And yet she was scared, almost shivering with terror. Temeke was typical of the detective race, having a fascination for human beings and their behavior. The only difference was he had retained his Englishness even down to the ill-concealed sneer.

"Remember," he almost whispered, "most of these men were offered their first hit of dope by a family member and a snort of the hard stuff. They had the choice—"

"No they didn't. Not the ones that were offered a can of beer at the age of eight and told to nut up and be a man. Not the ones that were sodomized, bullied and lied to. Where's the nearest safe house for them?"

"Right now?" Temeke said, taking a deep breath. "Inside."

"It's already too late then."

"It's never too late. Whether you choose to admit it or not, each one of those correctional officers is a better leader to the inmates than whoever they looked up to on the outside. *We* are leaders to someone. The question is, who is that someone? Because that *someone* is counting on you."

He was right. She couldn't help feeling a terrible burden of guilt, as if this was all of her own making and just what she deserved.

Something caught her attention in the rearview mirror, a car so close it almost nudged her rear bumper. She sped up a little and Temeke intuitively turned his face to look at the wing mirror.

"Police cruiser," he said. "It'll overtake in a few."

And it did.

"Getting really sporty with their undercover cruisers now," she said, marveling at the shine on that black paint. "I've seen over fifteen of those since last week."

"Probably saw the same one fifteen times," Temeke muttered, eyes fixed on the car in that typical way men do. Probably wishing he had something as nice as that at home.

She turned off the east frontage road onto Veterans Memorial and then left onto the Turquoise Trail. When the highway merged into one lane, her stomach began another rumble, guts twisting and turning in their stressed out juices. It was then she wished she had taken an extra dose of vitamins and antioxidants.

You'll get cancer with all that worrying, her mother once said.

The desert was barren and so was the road. Lucky she wasn't doing this on her own. The penitentiary was a cold gray place, colder still than the December winds. It housed well over seven hundred inmates and consisted of three facilities. They rolled past a large wooden sign that read Penitentiary of New Mexico Complex where ranks of chain-link fences came into view, almost blurred out of focus by a curtain of sleet.

She turned off the engine and snatched the keys out

of the ignition. They jangled in her hand all the way to the entrance, jarring, condemning.

Temeke carried a wrapped up newspaper under one arm and an evidence bag in the other. He handed both to a corrections officer. "Have these taken back to forensics on the next shuttle. Got a little warm in the car and I don't want one of them going walkies."

A second correctional officer showed them to Level VI, Supermax they called it, white corridors and gray doors, and rectangular windows that framed a face or two.

She saw Morgan Eriksen through a sheet of glass, elbows on the table, chin resting on his knuckles. He leaned back when they entered, legs straight, chain clinking between his ankles. Malin noticed the two chairs opposite and a mirror behind, and she was glad to note the table was at least five foot wide.

"Oh, I see they've dressed you in yellow scrubs," Temeke said with a snap in his voice. "Pity they're not green. You'd be leaving then, wouldn't you?"

"Always the joker," Morgan said, jabbing a finger at Malin. "Who's she?"

"She's my partner. Malin's the name," Temeke said, sitting. "And yes, she's dark but a little taller I think you'll find than the regular dwarf. Looks like you don't like the short ones."

"You know *nothing*, detective."

"Well, you know what they say. Danger and pleasure go together."

Morgan's eyes suddenly snapped to the window, set high up and covered with bars. He had a bruise on his temple and another on his lip.

"How many times have you picked a fight in the yard?" Temeke asked. "Because quite frankly I've lost count."

"I do everything I can to block this out. That's why I

fight. So one day someone's going to crack my skull open and I'll end up in hospital. On the outside."

"Surely there's better ways to keep busy, son. What about counting how many sheets there are on a toilet roll? While we're on the subject of fights, I looked up your arrest record. It was Patti who sold you out. She was the one that made the phone call, not Mr. Levinson. You know, the caretaker. We found his body dumped in a ravine. I wonder who could have done such a terrible thing."

"You said you'd never spoken to Patti."

"So I lied. It's like a virus in here."

Morgan stared out of the window, eyes roaming the sky as if he could see something. "They've all flown away."

"We found a head in a house on Smith Street. Still waiting for the doctor's report. But it looked like her. Blue eyes, long brown hair. Bloated. Are you alright, Morgan? Look a little green around the gills." Temeke gave Morgan a hard smile. "There's nothing wrong with your feelers, son. Normal people can't hide stuff like that."

Morgan looked up at the window and squinted. "There's a storm coming."

"Is that what's been bothering you? I heard you had a sleepless night on account of the wall being too close to your bed. Probably got a headache and all."

"You're wrong, I don't feel anything."

"Anger is an emotion, Morgan, and you have plenty of that." Temeke flicked through his notes, mirroring the lack of empathy in any way he could. "I've seen dead men look more cheerful."

"Ah, so that's what you want to talk about. The dead."

"Since you brought it up—"

"I don't believe in death. I believe in reincarnation. I

believe in the mead of vision, of insight. Kvasir had so much of it, yet the dwarves squeezed every last ounce from his body."

"Bastards," whispered Temeke. "All those Norse legends have gone to your head."

"Only wine and pride goes to a man's head, detective."

Malin shifted in her seat. "He's quite the debater," she murmured.

"He's just warming up," Temeke whispered and then in a louder voice, "He's taken another girl, Morgan. You wouldn't know where we could find her?"

"You're not looking hard enough are you?"

"Couldn't give us a few hints?"

"Do you like to play golf, detective?"

"I've been known to putt a few balls now and then."

Morgan looked at the mirror behind them, cocking his head to one side as if studying the length of his hair. "You like coming here to see me, don't you? It's like a day out. Like going to the zoo."

"I can think of better things to do."

"Nah, you're smarter than that. There's only one of you. There's two of me."

"Psychotically speaking I would agree," Temeke said. "Physically speaking, either your eyes need testing or math isn't your strongest subject. There's two of us and one of you."

Malin saw the flicker of a smile behind drawn lips and wondered if Temeke saw it too. But there was more. It was like staring at two serpent eyes with slits for pupils. She felt as if she was being sucked inside, groping around in the deep blue. In that far place, she could pretend she was something special, an ambassador's wife, a famous singer. Only she wasn't and she felt it more now than ever before. The chill that plagued her wasn't from the December air or the lack of heating in the interview room. It came from within.

"Can you tell us where Patti is?" Temeke asked. "The rest of her that is. 'Cos we're dying to know."

"Where a car can soar over the crest line, spanning wider than a man's hand. Under the first tower, so I'm told." Morgan shut his eyes for a few seconds and then stared right at Malin. "They do a twelve-step program for problems like yours."

"Problems?" she stammered.

"You know what I mean," he said, leaning forward as far as he could. "*Sunbeam.*"

Malin swallowed back a ball of bile. He might have found her picture on the internet because inmates used computers like everyone else. Lucky they didn't have access to semi-nude pictures, pictures of her in feathers and the essential lace. She was classier than that. And class meant staying silent.

Temeke hardly flinched. "How often do you use a computer, Morgan?"

"Every Tuesday and Friday."

"Under supervision?"

"Not always."

Malin hoped Temeke would have a word with the officers about that. Inmates shouldn't be looking at porn. *Porn?* No, her stuff wasn't porn. Just the soft stuff, the stuff that made a man look. The stuff that made rich men pay through the nose.

"Then you know there are undercover officers posing as escorts," Temeke said, packing a bigger punch. "Keeps the pervs at bay."

"Are you saying I'm a pervert?"

"You were looking, weren't you? Isn't that how you met Patti? Looking."

Morgan stared past Temeke's right ear, a bleak stare that wavered now and then. "Her mother drank too much. Couldn't keep it together, couldn't pay the rent, couldn't keep a job. She slapped Patti a lot. Made her cry."

"Lucky you were there."

Morgan blew out a series of breaths. "After her mother went to bed one night, Patti begged me to take her away. She had nowhere else to go. She clung to me, tried to kiss me."

"Must have been hard for a red-blooded male like you to keep your paws in your pockets. She was underage."

"I didn't touch her, not then. I went straight to bed. In the sitting room that is."

"So in that highly charged and unfulfilled state, you wrapped yourself up in a blanket and had a nap on the couch?"

Morgan nodded.

"Blimey, you've got some serious self-control there, son."

Temeke saw Morgan's chin shoot up, saw the eyes widen. The boy was beginning to cave. "So when Patti and the little kid got shot, how did that make you feel?"

"Sad."

"I thought you said you never felt anything. You're in serious trouble and you're only making it worse with all these lies. Fat lot of good it's done you. That's why you're inside and the real killer's drinking Remy Martin on his patio," Temeke pointed out. "He used you, made you look like a fool. Just another victory notched on his cupboard door."

Morgan's eyes shot to a clerestory window again as if he was searching for a certain drop of rain. "The ravens know everything."

"Ravens?" Temeke turned slightly to look at a silvery veil of rain against the window pane. "If you're referring to the FBI that's one of the hazards of crime."

Malin resisted the temptation to keep following their

gaze. She studied Morgan's face, pinched with disapproval, lips drawn in a snarl.

"*Thought* and *Memory*," he murmured. "They fly around the earth and bring back news. Only I have no news. I haven't seen *Memory* in weeks."

"You'll tell us when you do see him," Temeke said, restraining what sounded like a stallion's snort.

Morgan turned his ear to the plummeting wind. "Do you hear that?"

"Hear what?"

"You know what they say. If a man has ears let him hear."

"You know as well as I do it wasn't just anyone who said that."

"It was Christ," Malin interrupted.

Morgan flinched and sat back in his chair. There was a tremor in his throat, greater than a swallow. "Endless war," he whispered, leaning forward again and placing his hands on the table. "With a single stroke the succession could be snatched away. Make no mistake. No one knows how it will end. *No one*."

"You're wrong," Malin said, lifting her chin a little higher. "The devil will drown in the lake of fire. Even he knows. That's why he fights a little harder. That's why he's running out of time."

"Odin casts the biggest shadows. He knows who lives and who dies. What's your next deception, Malin? Watch out for mine."

Malin sensed a gnawing in her mind and a surge of daring in her veins. "Who's the raven called *Thought*?"

Morgan gave her a cursory glance and then looked down at his hands. They were resting on the table again, picking, cleaning, fingernails torn right down to the quick.

"If you know about them," he said, "why do you ask?"

"Yes, I know about the ravens," she said in Norwegian. "But which one are you?"

Morgan pounced. It was so quick, Malin felt Temeke's body covering hers before she heard the growl and the scraping of a chair. Two officers burst into the room, restraining Morgan against the wall before taking him outside.

"Nice one, Marl," Temeke said, wiping a glob of spit from his cheek. "I think we're getting somewhere."

NINETEEN

The clouds were low and weepy when they left the Penitentiary and that was after a plate of chicken and mushroom pie in the warden's office.

Temeke curled his toes to get some life into them and rubbed his hands. They would need to drive a few more miles before the heater came on.

"Still nervous?" he asked, wondering why her lips were constantly working as if she was reciting another of those infernal prayers.

"Yes," she said. "What do you say to a family that have just lost their daughter to a psychopath?"

"Not lost. Not yet. Let's concentrate on Ole, on how his mind works. What's the betting he reacts to murder the same way he does about a cup of coffee. He feels nothing toward his victim. So what's his next move?"

"An exchange," Malin said.

Temeke shot her a look, saw the twitch of a smile. She was touching her hair again, twirling a strand around her finger. If she wasn't driving she probably would have leaned in for a smooch. "What are you thinking?" he said, trying to interrupt the momentum.

"I'm thinking your wife's a lucky woman. I'm thinking you're a nice guy."

"Nice guys never get the girl."

She smiled at that.

"You're not so nice yourself. Excellent job of riling

up the deviant. Keep the car on the road, Marl. You're swerving about like a jack rabbit."

He thought of Luis, called dispatch and asked them to raise K33 on the radio. No answer. Temeke shrugged it off with a yawn.

"Nothing grows out here," he said, staring out of the car window. "Mark Twain once described the territory around the sea of Galilee as *a blistering, naked, treeless land.* He should have come here."

"Wild that," Malin murmured. "Israel blossoms like a rose in the desert."

"Must be good irrigation."

"Must be a great King."

Temeke wasn't aware Israel had a king, unless she was referring to the current Prime Minister. It was Eriksen's words that kept drumming around in his head.

Where a car can soar over the crest line, spanning wider than a man's hand...

He glanced toward the west where the sky met the mesa and where rugged piñon trees ornamented the slopes. To the east lay the foothills of the San Pedro mountains and he could imagine the rutted trails that wound through spruce and pine all the way to the top. It would make a good hike if he ever had the time. He was longing to see the dark sprawl of the Sandia Crest, like a sleeping dragon in a bed of sand. Forty more minutes.

Be quicker to fly, he thought.

He couldn't stop his teeth chattering, nor could he get rid of the icy chill down his back. All he could think of was a man rushing at him with bared teeth, screeching louder than a trucker's brakes.

"Ravens... he's sicker than a bloody parrot," he said.

"*Memory* and *Thought*," she reminded.

"Yeah, Hocus and Pocus."

She was quiet for a few miles and then, "Thanks, by the way."

"Thanks for what?"

"For covering up the escort thing."

"Eriksen needs to know we're watching. Needs to know there's a camera in every room."

Malin pressed one hand against the vent, fingers flayed against the heat. "When he said there were two ravens, I wondered if he meant two people or one person with a split personality. You've known a few *splits*. What makes them do the things they do?"

Temeke's thinking was never cloudy, but today it was like hacking through a shroud of fog. And Malin squinting at the rearview mirror made matters worse. He declined to look back along that desolate stretch of highway for whatever it was she saw and, in spite of the warm air flowing through the heater vents, he was still cold.

"I interviewed a man thirteen years ago," he said, "a man so burdened by his other psyche, he wouldn't eat in order to starve the other out. And when that didn't work he was found hanging in his cell with a note pinned to the end of his bed. *He won't go away.* It said. *Not unless I die first.*

"A psychopath in my opinion is not as unique as a fingerprint. It could happen to any of us. Something snaps in the brain and then it grows inside like a worm. They see life as a killing-track, a blur of blood and faces that never go away. For a time they're untouchable, immortal, in a world of twilight and shadows. But they know something will destroy them and in a strange way they long for it. Eriksen's different though. I should have had the sod in an arm-lock against the wall. I don't believe a word."

"He doesn't expect you to. He's talking in riddles."

"He's talking himself to death row." Temeke turned briefly to look at Malin, to study her furrowed brow. "He's a bloody liar is what he is."

"He's waiting for something," she said, eyes following the windshield wipers. "Why do you think he kept looking out of the window? He's half scared to death."

"I think I would be if I saw two killer ravens with chainsaws for beaks. Calling all units! We have two suspects on the loose, black hair, feathers, last seen perched on a power line, should be easy to spot."

Malin was having a fit of giggles, chin almost bouncing off the steering wheel. "You're determined not to take this seriously."

"I'm determined not to let him get to me."

"Hackett's not going to be happy we didn't get a name."

"Hackett's happiness is not very high on my priority list at the moment. Eriksen was spoiling for a fight and we were told to leave for our own safety." Temeke turned the heater up.

"Sir, what was he talking about when he said a car clearing the crest line? NASCAR?"

Temeke thought of those mountainous trails, some black as night and silent as a spirit. Only this time he saw them from the air.

"The Peak Tram," he said. "It has the world's third longest single span."

He could sense her looking at him. No, not looking, it was more than that. She was reading him. *Not too close now*, he thought as a faint alarm began to tingle in the back of his brain. "So how did you get into the escort business?"

Malin's head moved slowly from side to side as if ignoring a bite of irritation. "Who wants to know?"

"*I* want to know. There's nothing to be ashamed of. You say I smoke a little weed now and then. Well, maybe I do. Maybe I do it to take away the filthy images we see now and then. But we're not talking about me, we're talking about you."

Malin squinted at the rearview mirror before answering. "John Frederick. He was thirty-five. I was barely sixteen."

Temeke had already scoured her files, the photos, the dirty old pervert of a high school teacher. He never thought much of men with long straggly hair and goatees. And this one looked like a porn star.

"He made me dance for money so he could buy drugs. And then he shot himself when I tried to leave him."

Temeke felt his mouth go dry. He had seen the pictures, blood spatters on the wall, a crumpled body on the floor. Photographs never lie.

"Thank you for giving me a chance," she said, cuffing away a tear.

"I didn't."

The phone rattled on the console and he frowned at the caller ID. *Private* it said. He snarled a greeting and listened to a heavy accented voice.

"I have number nine."

TWENTY

Ole stared at the security monitor. The street was clear and so was the back yard, no black and white cars patrolling the neighborhood. They were likely parked outside Northeast Area Command, only a few yards up the street.

He sat in the kitchen, glancing occasionally at the girl in the living room. She was curled in a ball on the couch, eyes flickering in sleep. It was the noise of the chain he couldn't stand each time she woke up and tried to yank it from the grate in the fireplace. He wasn't going to leave her behind and he wasn't going to kill her either. She was worth her weight, worth watching the detective squirm over.

"Can I ask you something?" he said, seeing her stirring on that couch, hair cascading down her face. "Are you ashamed of me?"

She gave him a one-eyed stare, brow wrinkled for a moment. "What do you mean?"

"What do you think I mean? You don't touch me, don't kiss me. Don't even want to sit with me."

She couldn't sit next to him. The chain wasn't long enough.

"You disappoint me," he continued in a whisper.

He waited for those lips to move, those dark eyes to brighten. But they didn't. He rubbed a silver earring in his hand, brushed it against his lips.

"I've got something for you."

It would make her happy, like it had the others.

He poured two ounces of whisky in his coffee and sat down beside her. Blowing into the cup, he drank it down in three short swallows.

"I'm in no hurry. Are you?"

"Let me go home." A pause, then a sob. "Please…"

"What good would that do? You're worth too much." He took the earring and passed it through a hole in her left ear, watched the dog disk shimmer in the evening sun. "It'll only be one more day, I promise. So, what shall we do… you and me? Shall we go out?"

She shook her head, scooting away from him and closer to the arm of the couch.

"Did you know I was following you? Well, I was. Every day. I followed you to school, to the mall. I followed you home. Watched you when you woke up, when you got dressed, when you brushed your hair. I must have sat next to you twenty times. You should have known."

Her lips were no longer glossy like they had been that first night. Come to think of it, she wasn't as loving as she had been on that first night.

"I'm sure what you think of me is wrong. But big risks come with big rewards. How long will it take you to get ready?"

He was mesmerized by her dark lustrous hair, her olive skin. Nothing was sweeter than flesh tanned by the sun, and hers sparkled behind a silver earring, set with a number 9 charm.

"Don't you want me?" The silence was almost unbearable under the soft murmur of his voice. It was going to be the longest twelve hours of his life. "Spit it out!"

She shuddered at that, chains rattling with each tremor. It reminded him of his father all those years ago, twitching in the chair by the fire. One hand anchoring the other, eyes darting around the room in the hope that no one was watching. He had Parkinson's.

"Why are you doing this?" she said.

"They've got my brother. I'm sure you understand. All going well, this could be a game-changer for you. We're so near the finishing line. Here's some good news. We're going out to see your *Temeke* today. Won't he be pleased to see you."

He took the cellphone from his pocket and dialed the penitentiary pay phone in the men's block. Ole told a rough voice to find Morgan. He heard back-noise, the clatter of doors, the buzz of an alarm. The raven had returned.

"How did you get this number?" Morgan asked.

"The same way I get every number."

"They found her head," Morgan sobbed. "You killed her, didn't you?"

"If they found her head—"

"It's just games and words with you," Morgan shouted.

"I better not step on my tongue." Ole chuckled. "Be patient. You'll be outside soon smelling the good fresh air. So you saw the detective?"

"Yesterday. He's too fond of his own ass to do all the dirty work. Brought someone else with him. Norwegian. Made me look like a fool."

Ole hadn't accounted for that. "Partner? What was he like?"

"Malin. Her name's *Malin*."

Ole sounded the name in his mind, keeping it locked tight in his memory. He knew a Malin once at school. Pulled her long hair so tightly around his fist in the bathrooms, she screamed bloody murder. That was when he was eleven. "Was she trying to identify with you?"

"No."

"What does she look like?"

"Small, dark."

Ole gave a chuckle. "Just how we like them."

"This one's different. She's like a rat with a nasty bite."

"Rats can be exterminated."

"She knows the Norse legends, knows a lot of things."

"Got an accent?"

"No."

"See, they're lying. So when's the Brit and his fancy woman coming back?"

"Today. This afternoon."

Ole couldn't believe his luck. Highway 14 was a racetrack of possibilities. "What excellent timing."

"How did she die?"

Ole thought of Patti, eyes bulging, body twitching. "Rather well." He tapped the screen and ended the call. He didn't want to talk any more.

They would trace the number all the way to the arroyo on the west side. To the Williams' house. That's where he found his new cell phone. Maisie Williams. Her purse had been right inside the sliding patio doors.

He could almost hear the whisper of a sharpie across a white board at the police station, officers writing lists, spinning out his profile. It would lean more toward an organized offender, good social skills, educated, unusual intelligence, probably into pornography. Attacks planned... a regular night owl. Ole burned everything in the woods. Except Patti. Unlike all the others, he wasn't able to burn her at all.

The new girl moaned and lifted her head. She looked around, shackles rattling against the chains.

"I scared you, I'm sorry," he murmured. "Do you remember where you are?"

She began to moan. It was the drugs. They always

gave a victim a nasty headache on the first day.

"I can make you a cup of tea. All you have to do is ask. You can ask, can't you?"

She didn't answer. Just let her head drop on the couch, face turned away from him.

"No point in being scared. You have me."

He watched her flinch when she touched him, felt the shudder of flesh under his fingers. Wanted to squeeze the breath out of those lungs because it wasn't him she wanted. She recoiled at the sound of his voice, began sobbing into the cushion.

"What if you have a baby in that belly?" he whispered. "What would you do then?"

She stopped crying and looked at him sideways, watching his hands, his eyes, his mouth. Tears fell from two beautiful eyes and he wanted her then because she was so vulnerable. "What would you do?" he said again.

"I would love it," she murmured.

Would she? He doubted it. The child would be torn from that belly and discarded. "Get up," he said. "It's time for a shower."

It was also time for some fun, time to find that dope-smoking detective and his Norwegian partner. Becky would enjoy the ride, the chase, the kill. And she would see her *Temeke* crushed under a mound of twisted metal.

Time to get Morgan out of jail.

TWENTY-ONE

Malin savagely slammed the car onto the frontage road until they reached the racetrack which most Albuquerque residents sensibly referred to as I-25.

"Clocking seventy-five, Marl," Temeke warned. "State cops get a little snarky around seventy-four."

She barely reduced her speed, probably desperate to get to PNM and home again. Working double shifts like the rest of them and who were the rest of them? Half the squad were down with the flu and the other half pretended a glut of illnesses Temeke had never even heard of.

Sarge was on family leave. It wouldn't take his mind off Becky, but it would certainly get his mind off Temeke. The car was quiet without the constant drone of Sarge's voice over the radio. Until the silence was broken with another voice.

"Got a description on the partial remains." Captain Fowler crackled over the radio. "Patti Lucero of 5341 Live Oak Lane. Last seen on Thursday, November 27th outside Cibola High in the parking lot. Aged seventeen, dark hair, 127 pounds, five feet five inches tall."

"Any surveillance videos?"

"Too grainy."

So there were videos. It had been three weeks since Patti was last seen. "Any chance we can get NASA to clear up the video."

"I'm working on it. Two things, her mother didn't know Patti had a boyfriend. Didn't even know where she was living. The doctor found no fingerprints on the remains in the box. No other blood samples besides hers. Oh, and guess who's fingerprints were on the bone you sent over on Tuesday?" Fowler paused for extra clout. "Yours."

Temeke shook his head at the sound of laughter coming through the radio. "You've got eyes sharper than a spectroscope, Captain. Course they're mine."

"The doctor confirmed ballistic trauma to the femur. Same as those found on the body of Bonner Levinson. He also found the leftovers of meat and fries in her teeth. Since there wasn't a stomach to do a contents check, he was quite pleased to know that was her last meal. It gave me the creeps. I had a burger for lunch yesterday."

"If you get kidnapped and decapitated, we'll know there's a connection. What else?"

"Nothing much on your pants. But DNA came back on that strand of blond hair found on the victim. It belongs to Morgan Eriksen."

Temeke turned off the radio, sick to the stomach. "That's not possible," he murmured, turning to Malin. "Not unless our killer was wearing Morgan's clothes. Let's say Patti had a burger and chips, that says this girl had a good appetite for someone that's been kidnapped."

"She was in love with him. Didn't think he was going to kill her."

"After a gunshot wound?"

"I'd still be hungry in that many hours. Probably want to build myself up so I could put up a good fight."

"Maybe. But burger and fries is fast food. Food on the go. Food in the car. It's not like a home cooked meal of steak and baked potato."

"So you're saying they were driving around."

"I think that's exactly what I'm saying." Temeke

pulled out a cigarette and sucked on it for a while. "We know Eriksen's inside so he can't have done it. Even if the fridge in the barn kept those heads nice and fresh. No maggots, no real time of death. Patti's head was left in a nice warm house, getting moldier by the minute. A little easier to read wouldn't you say? Not like he can run back to the Shelby Ranch and burn them. He'd only get himself wrapped up in crime scene tape."

"Who's *he*?"

Temeke was lulled briefly by the metrical beat of the windshield wipers. "The man in the passport. The man that calls Morgan from time to time on stolen phones. The man they call Ole Eriksen."

"But we know Morgan doesn't have any brothers."

"Morgan doesn't. Ole does."

Malin's head twisted around and Temeke could feel those steely eyes trained on him as if she had no idea what he was talking about.

"According to his files, Ole never committed any crimes in Norway. That's why he wasn't showing up in the database. Morgan Eriksen wasn't there in Patti's case. But he saw what happened to the others. He knows the drill."

"And Becky's number nine." Malin glanced up at the rearview mirror.

The wind whistled, driving sand and snow across the road. Temeke's nose began to twitch, testing the air. He heard the loud boom and felt the car lurch forward, rushing along the highway at a speed way beyond the Explorer's capacity.

"It's the cop car," Malin shouted over grinding metal, trying to straighten the steering wheel.

Like a bullet rushing past a man's ear, the car overtook and roared into first place. It hung there for a while and then accelerated over the brow of a hill, leaving a cloud of dust behind.

"You OK?" Temeke said. He saw Malin nod before picking up the handset and calling it in.

It was a Camaro SS Coupe with at least four hundred horsepower and window tints darker than state requirements. There was no license plate. No car number. Nada.

"I've heard of undercover. But this is underhand," he said over a ghastly rattling in the rear. He looked through the wing mirror and saw the bumper dangling by a thread and scraping along the tarmac. "No need to rush. He'll be waiting over the next hill."

And he was, hanging by a hard shoulder some seventy feet ahead and revving up a fog.

"Go slow. We don't want three large hacks to jump out of that tiny trunk with an armful of semi-automatics."

Temeke's cell phone rattled on the console beside him. The caller ID flashed with the name Maisie Williams. He tapped the speakerphone icon and an unfamiliar voice claimed the air. "Speak two names, Detective. A raven needs a name."

"Who is this?" Temeke snapped a look at Malin.

"You tell me." There was a hint of amusement in that gravelly voice, a hint of an accent.

Temeke took his time to answer. *I mean, why not?* He was still half-dazed from that big old thud and his neck had almost snapped off its stem. "How about *Memory* and *Thought*?"

"Very good," the voice replied. "The last detective I spoke to was too ignorant to know it. But then you know what I do with ignorant people."

Temeke remembered what had happened to his predecessor, tried not to think of that dead cat either. They were fifty feet from the Camaro now. Near enough.

"I pulled him from his car, Detective. You should have seen his eyes."

"Nobody called it in for three days."

"Nobody knew where he was."

Temeke pressed the phone to his chest and whispered, "It's the daft bugger in that Camaro. How'd he get hold of Maisie William's phone?"

"Are you smart, Detective?" the voice said.

"Smart as any man." Temeke flapped a hand at Malin and indicated for her to pull over.

"Of course you're wondering how I got hold of Maisie William's cell phone. Better take it up with your surveillance team. Looks like they're not doing their job."

Temeke had visions of a well-dressed man, late thirties, nicely gelled hair and smelling of aftershave. He let him rant on while he lit a cigarette and then realized Malin was giving him a wide-eyed glare. He opened the window and flicked it at a large clump of melting snow.

"Smart men don't find themselves in places like this. Smart men aren't lead investigators of cases they can't solve. And you won't solve this case, detective. It's out of your reach. So call off your dogs, there's a sport."

"I'd like to stare you in the eye and ask you why."

"Maybe you will. Maybe you won't. And yes, I am the daft old bugger in the Camaro."

Temeke took a measured breath. He was suddenly sick of all these foreigners. They should all go home, he thought, and then realized that was a bit ripe coming from him.

"What's your price?" he said, knowing there was one.

"Morgan Eriksen for Becky Moran."

Temeke listened to the engine humming over the radio, wishing he could haul-ass up the hard shoulder and stuff the muzzle of his gun through the Camaro window.

"You mean her remains," he said, taking a deep

breath. "Her body."

"I never leave bodies. Just the head. Living heads. Dark heads. In her case, she has both."

Temeke had a feeling in his gut, a sense Becky was in the car with him. "Put her on."

He heard the sluggish voice. "Temeke... Temeke..."

"Becky—"

"If you follow me," the man grunted, "I'll kill her. And that's a fact. You've got nothing. No evidence. No chance. Winner takes all."

"If I could tell you how many criminals I've met in the last twenty-four years claiming I had no chance, your claws would curl."

"Sarcasm cuts both ways. And you have so much of it. The blood samples aren't mine. The DNA doesn't match any crime stain profile."

"So we found out. Cleaner ways don't win wars, Mr.... . you never did give me your name."

"That's why I asked you if you were smart. You're a legendary lawman. I'd like to meet you in the flesh."

"I'm right behind you," Temeke said with a smile. He could hear a girl whimpering in the background, making his heart race faster than it was meant to.

"Another time perhaps. I'm guessing you'll go back to the drawing board. You never know. You might have missed something."

The death rattle of the dial tone was drowned by the surge of tires over gravel. The Camaro surged off like a missile and was lost behind the next rise.

Temeke called it in, shouted at Fowler to alert all units. He put a restraining hand on Malin's arm, told her to slow down. "He was using Maisie William's cell phone. If he didn't take it from her purse, he must have taken it from the house. Either way, he's getting too close."

"You mean he broke in?"

Temeke felt himself nod, felt himself shiver. Darryl was in danger and so were his girls.

"He said there were other heads out there, sir. Living heads. Dark heads. He told us to call off the dogs. There's something out there in the woods. Something we missed."

"He doesn't mean a row of severed heads singing nursery rhymes in a freezer. He means young girls he's been stalking."

"*Dark*, sir. A girl he should have taken in the first place."

Temeke watched her, read the expression in her eyes, heard the tremor in her voice. He knew what she was thinking.

TWENTY-TWO

It was a gray day. One of those days when the clouds were pale overhead and the streets were slick with rain. Ole felt wired. He had been feeling it for days. When there was a change in the weather, a change in the light, it was like a stirring in the blood that wouldn't go away.

Sometimes he sensed Odin in the wind. But for the last five days, he hadn't sensed him at all. Something was different. He needed to go back to the woods. He needed to see Loki.

He had to get out. Couldn't stand the smell of the house, the darkness behind the blinds where only one light burned in the kitchen. He felt like he was floating under the surface of water, hands pushing up against a thick wall of ice.

Swiping the screen of his new cellphone, he hit the contacts button. There was a number for *Temeke*. Just as he expected.

"Remember me? We spoke yesterday," Ole said with a smile in his voice. "I hadn't heard from you. Thought I should follow up."

"I'm glad you did," detective Temeke said, "because I was beginning to wonder if you'd acquired another phone. It's a bugger trying to trace someone without a phone. Or a valid number."

Ole wondered at the sarcasm, wondered if it should cost Becky a finger. He'd already tightened those shackles with a screwdriver, only the right one was full of dried blood and needed to be scraped clean. They were different to the ones Patti had. These were screw shackles instead of a twist pin. There was no way Becky could get out of these. "There are three cabins near the Shelby ranch. One is still standing. Make sure you leave Morgan by the fire."

"Does he want a cup of tea? Or shall I make it a beer?"

Ole felt a wave of heat, mind racing to understand the response. "Just you and Morgan, Detective. Or Becky dies. Capitch?"

"No, it's *capiche*, son. That's how they pronounce it over here. Italian, you know. Anyway, nip along to the cabin and bring Morgan alone. I got it."

"Tomorrow."

"Well, that's the thing, see. Tomorrow's Sunday. The Sabbath. Nobody works on Sunday."

"Are you Jewish, Detective?"

"No, but quite suddenly I wish I was."

"Then you know the Sabbath begins on Friday and ends on Saturday night."

"Since you put a dent in the Explorer," the detective said, "the car's in the shop. Like I say, mechanics don't work on Sunday. I could go on foot, only it might take a week or two."

Ole wondered if the detective was hard of hearing or just plain stupid. The warning buzzer was going off in his brain and it was beginning to give him a headache. He'd been on the phone for a minute and a half. Time to ring off.

He put the screwdriver on the window sill and stretched his aching fingers. The girl lay on the bed, cheek swollen and bruised. It happened when she cracked her head against the window yesterday. When he rammed the Camaro into the Explorer. Should have seen her face when she heard the detective's voice. Should have heard her scream when he pulled away.

That was over seventeen hours ago. She was sleeping now. And he was hungry.

"Becky," he murmured, sitting on the bed. He touched her arm, felt no response. "Looks like your *Temeke* wants to wait. He doesn't love you. He doesn't even care."

He leaned down to kiss her cheek, flicked a wisp of hair from her mouth. She was chained to the bedhead, wrists clamped tightly together and resting on the pillow. He couldn't remember the dosage this time, probably no more than two hundred milligrams.

He looked about for a needle, something to poke that skinny arm with just to see if she was faking. He picked up the flat-blade screwdriver and he let it hover over her skin. She'd feel the change in air current just like a common house fly if she knew how close he was. He pressed it against her shoulder, saw the flesh crater under the pressure. Not a shiver. Not a sound.

She was out cold.

"I'm not your enemy," he whispered. "Never was. I would have loved you if you had loved me. But you didn't. I am good, you know. Much better than you think. I was perfect once. When mamma loved me. I don't know why she left papa, my kind, smart, goodhearted, papa. I don't know why things have to change. But they do. When did you change, Becky? When did you really know?"

He liked the feel of her skin, the smell of it. And he liked those dark eyelashes that would have been stained with five-day old make-up if he hadn't taken a glob of Vaseline and wiped the residue away.

"You will be going home, babe. I'll make sure of that." He lowered his lips to her ear and whispered, "In tiny little pieces."

Two minutes later he was driving north on Osuna to the Gridiron Café. He parked in his usual spot, almost directly across from the front door. There were cops sipping shots of dark espresso in one corner and a group of businessmen in the other. If he was lucky, he might see Alvarez and follow him home.

He liked being out in the open where everyone could see him. Only no one even gave him the time of day. That was the best part. He was anonymous in a town where all the worst nightmares were all his fault.

By ten o'clock he was having a light breakfast and scanning the crime pages of the Journal. He couldn't help feeling the flutter in his belly as he read the headlines, a warning sign. It wasn't a feeling he could interpret right away and he put it down to the dark clouds and the sweep of rain against the window he sat next to.

Albuquerque's Murder Count Reaches Eight. Morgan Eriksen, charged with seven counts of murder and kidnapping, and two counts of first-degree assault against a law enforcement officer, has pleaded guilty to kidnapping, but not to murder. Are Police hiding the identity of a second killer?

Ole pulled the phone out of his pocket and tried Jennifer Danes at the Journal. Her line was busy. He left her a message, only this time in his best British accent.

Jen, it's me. And don't go telling anyone I called. But we've been looking in all the wrong places.

Sounded likely enough.

Looks like Morgan Eriksen had nothing to do with it.

Well, that wasn't quite true. Morgan stalked the girls, quite enjoyed the money until he found out Ole wasn't about date rape.

Just doesn't fit the profile.

Too damned stupid to fit the profile.

Off the record, Jen, we're looking at one of the

victims' fathers, Darryl Williams. Seems he may have had something to do with his wife's death.

There. Seed sown. Ole didn't leave a name. Didn't have to. He'd be visiting the Williams man as soon as he'd had his breakfast.

He hung up and sipped a frothy cup of coffee, eyeing a couple of girls behind the counter. One was fat and blond, thighs begging to be set free from a pair of tight black pants. The other was a redhead with a face full of freckles. She reminded him of someone. He stared at her a little too long, caught her attention, made her smile.

It didn't come as a surprise.

He cut the burger in half and took a bite, savoring the sharp taste of cheese, paying no attention to the waitress at his elbow offering him a refill.

A refill?

They don't do refills on cappuccinos. It was the redhead beaming down at him, bill in one hand and pot poised over his cup. "I thought you'd like it. On the house."

He wondered what else was on the house and spread the newspaper out on the table as if both pages were a pair of white thighs.

"What's your name?" he asked.

"Fawn," she said, screwing up her nose as if she hated the name.

"Bringing a bill this early makes a guest feel unwelcome. Like you want me to leave."

"Oh no, sir. I'm sorry. I can bring it back later if you want."

"Olafr," he said, tapping his chest. "It means *ancestor's descendent.*"

"Are you German?"

"Norwegian."

"I love your accent."

Of course she did. They all did. He stared her down,

flicking a hand in front of his nose as if to get rid of a bad smell. Her eyes widened, hip no longer hiking up and down as she backed away.

There was no sign of the cop and that bothered him. The music bothered him too. A Germanic hum that reminded him of the secret tongue he once shared with his mamma.

A hymn.

Something about taking the veil from our faces, the vile from our heart.

His heart wasn't vile, was it?

He mouthed the words as he remembered them, words that ran too fast for others to understand. They were kind words, special words. But sometimes they were words that hurt papa and made the whole world tremble, words that drove poor little Morgan to the pantry cupboard because they were quarrelling again.

It was an hour later when Fawn left the bill on the table. He saw her phone number written on the corner and he wrote *no thanks* underneath. He paid in cash and studied the pen. At least it wasn't one of those pink furry things or worse – a huge sunflower with a smiley face. This one had a silver shaft with a blunt end as if it would fit into a countersunk hole. A screwdriver.

Becky…

He couldn't remember leaving the restaurant. All he did remember was the sound of tires screeching through a red light on Wyoming and speeding down Osuna to the house.

He went in through the kitchen, saw the sliding doors to the patio smeared with blood and rain.

On the outside.

He opened the door and stepped down onto the flagstones, shoes crunching on broken glass. Craning his neck up to the shattered bedroom window, he saw shards trickling down from the angled roof and trapped in a clump of cattails below. A six foot chain and shackles lay abandoned by the pool where lights once shimmered blue beneath the surface of the water. He followed the footprints through the back gate toward the road and there, by a storm drain was the screwdriver.

That's when he howled.

TWENTY-THREE

Darryl pulled the blanket up over his youngest daughter, Sharek. *Youngest* now that Kizzy was gone. Another bad dream, another bad night. Beads of sweat had collected on her forehead and he touched her with the back of his hand.

Flu. He'd keep her home tomorrow.

He listened to every breath, wondering how often she woke in the night and used her inhaler. Asthma wasn't the only thing she had inherited from her mother. Looks, temperament and the kindest heart. How he loved that heart.

There was a small nightlight beside her bed in the shape of a hollowed-out tree. Inside it were three brown bears sitting at a table drinking tea. The glow from a single watt bulb was no brighter than a candle, shedding a rosy glow across the room.

Outside the window was a young pine tree, spiky leaves hanging limp and drizzled with snow. Thousands upon thousands of flakes were illuminated by the headlights of a passing car, incrusted like jewels on a wedding veil.

He recalled a fragment of their conversation earlier at dinner.

If you think someone's watching, daddy, they usually are. Like ghosts in the shadows. Like a really bad dream.

When he asked her what she meant she merely shrugged and stared at her elder sister, Tess. Sharek talked about a man outside the school, a man who had called her by name. And when Darryl asked her what the man looked like she just turned her face toward her older sister, eyes vacant as if she saw right through her. Tess just looked like she'd swallowed a piece of meat without chewing, forehead creased with a line or two.

He knew there was an elusive truth to that look. It was all there if only he cared to notice. He wondered how he managed to keep living day after day, feeling the way he did.

Sharek's grades were dropping at school and her teachers put it all down to emotional stress. It had been nearly two months since Kizzy disappeared, two nightmarish months. No closure, no funeral. It was hard for an eleven year old.

Her conversation was often peppered with cryptic nonsense and he wondered if she would ever be the same. He sensed that not every strange statement she made was half as eerie as it seemed. Morbid visions of a man behind a tree, a man sitting on Kizzy's swing, a man with a crooked smile. He wondered if the child needed a dog, something to take her mind off it all. She had been closest to Kizzy after all.

Tess was asleep in the next room, probably in those hiking boots if she had her way. Clemency Christian School's best sprinter, 400 meters in fifty seconds. He peered into her room, eyes glancing from her bed to the window and the courtyard beyond. The fountain was still floodlit and the pavers glimmered like diamond chips under a full moon.

It was the sound of a car reversing from the west side of the house that got his attention. The tail lights cast a rosy blush along the street and Darryl walked around the bed to take a closer look.

It was a Camaro lazing under a street lamp, dark gray or black, he couldn't work it out and the windows were gloomier than his cellphone screen. No one had called him in days.

He thought of calling the police. At least it would be someone to talk to. But you didn't just call 911 for a chat and besides, what if the guy was looking at the empty lot next door.

At eleven forty-five at night?

It was parked on the wrong side of the street in front of the vacant lot and about thirty feet from the courtyard wall. It seemed to shimmer like a black beetle in the sand, brake lights casting a blood-red beam along the ground.

Darryl sensed the driver was watching, sensed he was enjoying the moment as if he hoped Darryl was just a mouthful of jittering teeth.

"I won't be the rabbit to your hungry fox," he murmured, padding barefoot to his bedroom at the back of the house.

There was a short-barreled .44 magnum pistol in his bedside drawer, Israeli-made and fed with a detachable magazine. If two rounds could take down an elk, they would certainly poke a few holes in a gas tank.

"That'll frighten him off," said Darryl, seeing the sense in it. He'd also put a few holes in those wide tires while he was at it.

Creeping out of the front door into the courtyard, he was careful to dodge the floodlights, bare feet crunching through snow. He felt a spasm of cold shooting up through his calves and he berated himself for not wearing shoes. He could see the back of the car clearly now through a wooden grill in the adobe wall and he could see the Chevy emblem above the rear bumper.

The engine purred to life and the car slowly moved forward, turning sideways onto the dirt lot as if attempting a three point turn. Although Darryl didn't see anything threatening or out of the ordinary, the car stopped and sat there for a time, headlights shining over the arroyo. He couldn't make out a driver until he heard the humming of the window motor, revealing a pale face that seemed to be staring right at him.

Darryl ducked instinctively, wincing from the sting of ice beneath his feet. The saliva seemed to evaporate from his mouth and he wondered what the man was doing beneath the amber lightfall of the street lamp.

The only other sound he could hear was the drift of falling leaves and the hammering of his heart. At least the driver couldn't see him behind the five foot wall.

Something sped through the riven sky, a zip of light that illuminated the courtyard and filtered through the grill. It was a powerful flashlight, big and fat, and the silvery beam scurried along the top of the wall before going out altogether.

Darryl crouched in the darkness, listening for the car door to open, and when it didn't he inched back toward the wooden grill in the wall, chin resting on the ledge.

It was then he heard the voice, low and rasping. At first he thought it was the neighbor across the street until he heard the sound of his name.

"I can see you, Darryl Williams. I know you're there."

Darryl wanted to run. He didn't care about the madman with the whispering voice, the shallow puddles of melting snow or the pine needles underfoot. He just wanted to get back into the warmth and safety of his house, until he remembered the gun he was squeezing in his right hand.

"What are you afraid of, Darryl Williams? Are you afraid I'll cut off your head?"

Darryl knew the man out there wasn't a man any more. He had been taken over, slaughtered, conquered, devoured. By a demon.

"I take heads, Darryl Williams, because I need the wisdom. Young. Teenage. Girls. So you have nothing to fear."

God help me! Darryl's mind screamed. This man had all the supernatural power he needed to scale the wall and no locked door would keep him out.

"I need more heads, Darryl Williams. More, do you understand? You can spare me another of your little dark-eyed girls, surely."

Darryl was sickened by talk of death and dark-eyed girls, and here he was hunkered beneath a drain spout where the snow had melted to water, splattering against the pavers and down the small of his back.

He had to move.

He squeezed the rubberized grip of his gun, eyes scanning the ambidextrous safety. He'd stripped and cleaned it last week because a clean gun was a functioning gun. The magazine was nearly the size of an AR magazine, a beast of a gun with a little recoil.

"You have girls, Darryl Williams. Young, dark-eyed girls. Just like Kizzy."

That was enough for Darryl to remove the safety. He twisted around, wrists resting on the wall and aimed. Pulling the trigger was the most satisfying thing he'd done all week, squeezing off the first three rounds in frantic haste. He heard the thunderous boom and saw the car almost list to one side.

The driver merely turned to look at Darryl as if frozen in anger, eyes wide and luminous, eyes that wouldn't stop staring.

Was he dead? Surely not. Not one of those slugs was aimed at the driver's door.

No he wasn't dead, thought Darryl, not with all that laughing. It was a deep guttural laugh that made him madder by the second.

He squeezed off shot after shot, explosions cracking along the rear fender and the rear door panel until he had emptied the magazine. The car shot backwards then, tires spinning against sand, loose rock ricocheting off the sidewalk.

His stomach twisted with nausea and the muscles in his forearms began to ache as he lowered the gun. What was he doing on this cold December night, standing barefoot in the snow and shooting at strangers? It was then he heard the rain, felt it against his cheeks, pinging and snapping off the roof in a tuneless anthem.

Somehow he was pumped with his own bravado, smelling gasoline and grinning through gritted teeth. He wanted to shout. He wanted to cheer, only he'd wake half the neighborhood. As it was a few lights blinked on and off from nearby houses and then he streaked across the courtyard and out into the street.

He headed west after the car, leaping over a low stone wall and a box hedge that delineated the subdivision from the main road. It wasn't until he stubbed his foot against a rock that he came to stop, realizing his bare feet were likely torn to shreds. He was in agony and freezing, and he couldn't help seeing fingers, pale and cold, reaching out of the darkness. They were dead fingers only inches from the nape of his neck.

He turned suddenly. There was no one there.

Why should there be? The man was going ten times his speed in a car that clocked zero to sixty in just over five seconds. He was probably half way to Gallup by now.

Gasping for breath and nearly doubled-over in agony, Darryl hobbled back along the sidewalk toward his house, wincing from needle-sharp shards of rock. House after house, floodlights speared out of the darkness triggered by motion detectors and the deep throated growl of a German Shepherd almost made him jump.

"Quiet boy," he whispered.

The growl soon turned into a whimper and two ears pricked, snout reaching between the bars of a restraining gate. Darryl brushed his hand against a wet nose, letting the dog remap his scent. He was surprised at how dogs warmed to him, surprised he never had one of his own.

He heard no one, saw no one, and he realized a shot fired in the night might sound like a car backfiring heightened by the squeal of tires. This was several shots from a .44 magnum and he doubted any residents would be eager to scout the streets. The dog was frightened enough.

He still felt a rush of exhilaration as he pushed open the weathered gate and the hinges groaned as he latched it. There were no little faces pressed against the living room window, none peering around the frame of the open door.

His girls were sound sleepers. Even Maisie. But he checked their rooms all the same, pulled back each quilt to study the rise and fall of their precious chests, checked the closets and behind every door.

Then he set his gun on the hall table before squatting and collapsing on the floor. Lying on his back and staring up at the skylight, he could just make out a cluster of stars that seemed to rain down from the night sky. He wasn't shivering anymore and his fingers began to tingle from the radiant heat beneath the travertine floor.

As he listened to the lulling tick of the hall clock and police sirens in the distance, an idea hatched in his mind. The driver would be back to get revenge.

Only this time, Darryl would be waiting for him.

TWENTY-FOUR

Malin squinted through a downpour of rain that spattered against the windshield. Just as the call came in about a girl who had turned up in the women's hospital on Montgomery.

Becky.

Malin saw the look on Temeke's face. The relief, the misty-eyed stare. Saw him jot down the details of where she'd been held.

"Bastard had her for five days. Gave her one meal a day and shot her up with sedatives. God alone only knows what he did to her while she slept."

Malin looked at the clock on the console. They arrived at 5024 Timoteo Avenue around eleven forty-five in the evening. Dispatch had responded to a possible shooting near the Williams house sending a couple of units ahead. Temeke and Malin were the second of those units to pull up alongside the vacant lot. It was a busy night.

A few lights blinked on and off, residents awakened by the police activity. Temeke jumped out, opened the passenger door. He grabbed a bullet-proof vest and a flowery pink notepad. He saw the look on her face and nodded. "It's all they had at Walmart. If I don't write it down, it didn't happen." He zipped up his leather jacket, face puckered and grim. "You stay out here and wait for the field investigator."

He slammed the car door before Malin had time to argue. He probably wanted to have a smoke and think. He was probably mad at his brother-in-law for being on leave. He had to have lunch with her now.

She took her flashlight and walked to the vacant lot. The police unit was parked on the other side of the street, still idling by the sound of a worn out engine and the sagging front seat.

"There's a puddle of blood over there and gasoline," officer Jarvis said, pointing. "I took what I could." He held up a plastic sample container.

Malin gave a tolerant smile and turned her back. She couldn't stand the man, pink, pasty and full of—

"I'd be careful if I were you," he shouted.

Too late. She was facing the lot now, shoes sloshing around in a bloody puddle, watching a pounding rain that threatened to flatten the channels the tires had made. Wide tires, curling back about fifteen feet and then veering off toward Bandelier. The car had clearly idled on the lot for a time, reversing back into the road at high speed.

Jarvis had already marked off several shell casings and a slither of rubber, and there was a smear of blood seeping off the curb into the road. The driver had been hit all right.

Malin was still staring at the blood spatter when the field investigator arrived. That was her cue. Whether Temeke had told her to wait outside or not, she was going in.

She opened the front gate, a heavy cedar door with a speakeasy grill, and found herself in a courtyard scented with damp mud brick. Metal lanterns with frosted globes—some round, some cylindrical—threw an amber glow on the pavers and a fountain graced the center, three lug-handled urns feeding into a shallow basin filled with pebbles. It would have sounded glorious in the summer months, an endless calming trickle.

Temeke was standing in the foyer with the Williams man, head down, scratching a diagram in that little pink book. There was a pistol on the hall table, a car-buster by the look of it.

Darryl looked up at her and gave a long hard stare. It was difficult to break away from a look like that and she half wondered if he was still in shock. He nodded as she wiped her feet on the doormat and then gave a wistful smile.

"Thought I told you to wait in the car," Temeke said, head cocked to one side.

"It's cold out there," Malin said, rubbing her hands.

Temeke turned back to Darryl. "You said you got a good look at him through the driver's window. What did he look like?"

"White, very white actually," Darryl said.

"What were you aiming for?"

"The gas tank mostly."

"Any chance you hit the driver?" Temeke leaned toward Darryl even though his eyes were locked on some distant object across the hall.

"None."

Darryl hardly noticed as Temeke drifted into the living room to answer his phone. He sat on the arm of a leather chair and began flipping through a gun magazine. It was Luis he was talking to by the sounds of things.

"Features?" Malin prompted. She noticed Darryl seemed to relax a little more and his demeanor became warmer the closer he moved toward her.

"Blunt nose, you know, the type that looks like it's been under a knight's helmet for too long."

"Age?"

"Late thirties." Darryl shrugged.

"Hair?"

"Short, blond," he nodded.

"Anything else unusual?" Malin examined Darryl's eyes. They were normal now, not wide and lifeless as they had been a moment ago. Although she could smell something tart on his breath.

"He had an accent come to think of it. Foreign. Couldn't tell you where. I was mad, that's why I did it. I just couldn't help myself."

"Where did you get that gun?" Malin pointed at the hall table.

"The Eagle? I bought it at Conway's two months ago. Thought I should protect the girls."

Malin gave Temeke a cursory look. He was looking through a pair of binoculars he'd found on the coffee table.

"Anything missing?" she asked.

Darryl frowned and shook his head. "Maisie lost her cell phone a day or so ago. We think she dropped it in the street. So I got her another. Would you like some tea?"

Malin shook her head, wondering if she should have offered to make him one instead.

"Got anything stronger?" Temeke said as he walked back into the hall. "Just a sip—to keep out the chill."

They followed Darryl through a stone archway into a spacious kitchen. Malin knew Temeke had smelled the odor from Darryl's mouth, probably thought he'd had too much to drink.

The cabinets were a rustic style with pendant lights over an island and wooden beams on the ceiling. A large white mantel dominated the back wall and beneath it was an antique range. There was a bottle of red wine on the granite countertop with yellow flowers and blueberries on the label. Home-made it promised.

Malin watched Darryl pour two small glasses with a shaky hand. Either he was nervous or just dog tired. He must have been exhausted working up all that adrenaline to shoot a man.

"Are you sure I can't get you anything?" he said, looking at her with a wrinkled brow. There was a spark of mischief in his eyes as he stood there, hands clutching two full glasses.

"I'm fine thanks," Malin said, feeling the heat from those eyes. She instinctively turned toward Temeke, wondering what possessed him to sample the wine.

"You identified the car as a dark colored Camaro," Temeke said, saluting Darryl with his glass before taking a large gulp.

"Goes down like silk," Darryl said, holding up a warning hand, "and then comes the punch."

Malin saw Temeke's shoulders hunch as he began to sputter, and then the fit of coughing stopped. "Oh, man! That tastes like hot creosote."

Darryl laughed, showing a perfect set of white teeth. "Too much and it's a laxative."

"Now he tells me," Temeke said, handing the glass to Malin.

"The car," Darryl began. "I've seen it before. No license plate. Just sits outside the bank and watches. He followed me home last week and I could have sworn he was the same man in my back yard. He jumped over the wall and down into the arroyo. But tonight it was different. Like he wanted something."

"Anything else unusual about the car?"

Darryl shook his head.

"You said he spoke to you?"

"He knew I was hiding. Said he took heads, young girl's heads. Like Kizzy's. Said he wanted me to give him one of my daughters."

"So you shot him."

Darryl stared blankly as if mystified. "I shot at the car. What would you have done?"

Malin could hear the silence over the buzz in her

ears. The wine tiptoed down her throat, tasting of bitter fruit until the explosion hit her empty stomach. The room was starting to blur around the edges and it took a great deal of effort to focus on Darryl's face.

"I would have called the cops," Temeke said quietly, face puckered. "That's a high-powered set of binoculars you've got in there. Unusual birds in the neighborhood?"

Darryl licked his lips. "I usually use them for hunting. I've seen the car a few times, tried to read his license plate. I would have called it in if he had one. You'd have thought the cops would have pulled him over by now."

You would, thought Malin. She flicked a hand at Jarvis and asked him to check for footprints in the back yard.

"Seems like the Journal has their own slant on things, Darryl," Temeke said. "Don't be surprised if they start pointing fingers in your direction. Parents first. Our friendly journalist claims she's got a new source. With a British accent."

Darryl knotted his brows and shook his head. "You're kidding?"

"A pain in the—" Temeke shot Malin a look and seemed to change his mind. "And talking of cops, we've got both entrances of Clemency Christian School covered. My brother-in-law called. Just got back from a fishing trip. Said he'll be covering the afternoon shift. Lt. Luis Alvarez. I'll make sure he says hello to the girls."

"Thank you, Detective."

"We'll put some security cameras around your house, a telephone-tap, that kind of thing. I'll leave you my vest." Temeke pointed at the hall chair where it was draped over the seat. "Until then, if you hear any funny noises, practice barking. Most intruders are scared of dogs. Most detectives are scared of dogs." Temeke reached into a cargo pocket and pulled out a photograph. "Does this look like the man you saw?"

Darryl frowned and peered at the photograph through half closed eyes. "Yeah, that's him."

Malin looked down at the photo in Temeke's hand. It was Morgan Eriksen. The only photograph he had.

TWENTY-FIVE

Darryl stared at a plate of bacon and eggs, heartbeat racing. His stomach was rock hard and he had no idea why. Sharek's fever was down, but her cough was worse. It might have been that hacking cough and the crowds in the Village Inn that made him feel sick.

He had been mad about the newspaper article on Friday morning. It painted him out to be a suspect, a tragic loner whose wife died under suspicious circumstances. If you could call an asthma attack *suspicious* then so be it.

What had been more suspicious was his boss's reaction to it. Morty Coben, a man who groomed his moustache more than his staff, had called him into his office that same morning and thought it appropriate to let him go. After all, it was in his own interests.

Lucky he gave him a big fat pay check otherwise Darryl would have punched his teeth out.

He tried to smile at Sharek with her stack of pancakes, tried to smile at Tess as she stared around the restaurant. Maisie's eyes flicked here and there, fork picking at a sloppy pile of scrambled eggs. He wanted to say something to make them laugh, something clever like he used to in the old days.

The best he could do was stare at his iPad, at the real-time video of every room in his house. It was then he realized something serious and profound was happening.

The sliding door to the patio had been left open.

He couldn't remember excusing himself from the table, pushing past Maisie, telling her to look after the girls. He raced home, tires skidding in the driveway and leaped from the driver's seat without closing the door. To his surprise there were no signs of the police, no alarms, just the melodic splash of the fountain in the front yard.

Fountain, he mouthed. It wasn't possible.

The water had been drained out almost a month ago, every last drop sucked out with a power vacuum. Sure enough, water trickled over the lip of the first urn and dropped into the next. He was as clueless as he was baffled.

The motion detector in the bell tower should have sensed movement as he came through the front gate. He'd set it when he left and there was no beam winking between the columns, no alarm buzzing outside. His phone hadn't sent him a text. It hadn't even rung.

He walked toward the front door, saw the gap between the frame and the jam, and pushed it open with one hand.

He saw nothing unusual, only shadows in the hall and sunlight streaming in through the skylight. The smell of fresh air streaked through the house, and he could hear the pat-pat-pat of the window blinds.

At the end of the hall was the kitchen and he walked stiff-legged toward it. Sucking in a deep cool breath, he peered into the living room, no furniture overturned, no smashed glass underfoot.

The blinds began to snap back and forth as a stream of cold air shot through the house. He'd been holding his breath as he went through each room and he let it out in one big sigh.

Just as he was about to close the patio door, he saw footprints carved into muddy slush on the pavers, a crisscross pattern like those on the bottom of a moccasin. They seemed to be heading toward the back wall, stopping at the footing as if someone had jumped right over it.

They were inside the house too, etched in the light beige carpet all the way back to the front door. He hadn't noticed them when he came in. But there they were, just dark enough to make out on the travertine floor.

This way, he said to himself, walking toward the sitting room, eyeing the mantel, seven photographs in their neat silver frames.

Something was different.

Two were missing. The one of Kizzy on her swing and Tess proudly holding a medal. He saw the revolving pendulum on the clock, the glass screen, the reflection of a man's face. His face. He nearly gasped when he saw it. Pasty, like a ghost.

Then he heard a sound, like the clip and slide of a gun. It came from the other side of the house, the garage if he guessed right. Inhaling slowly, he was convinced the intruder would hear each drawn breath, that he would track the very warmth of it with those supernatural powers of his.

Not an intruder. A hunter.

That was the worst thing. When his intuition kicked in and told him the intruder was somehow supernatural. A predator with sharper senses than a dog. How did he get in without tripping the alarms?

Darryl sensed his time was running out, that the hunter would find him at any moment, that he was being tracked and scented. As he started forward, another fear replaced the first. What if the intruder had a gun?

He eased around the furniture, eyes flicking toward the hall. He had to get his gun. The one in the nightstand. It was only seven steps to his bedroom, only five if he ran for it. The corridor was deserted. The only thing that moved was an army of dust motes, twisting beneath the skylight.

Sprinting down the hall, he reached the bedroom in three ragged breaths. The nightstand drawer gaped open. The gun was gone.

"No," he murmured, fingers searching under the pillows on his bed, between the mattress and the box spring.

His first instinct was to call the police, but the noise would only carry around the house and attract the intruder's attention.

But he could text.

Snatching the phone from his pocket, he found Detective Temeke in his contacts and clicked off four words.

Intruder in the house.

He checked the volume. The sound was off.

Then he sat on the edge of his bed and took three small breaths, listening to a chiming clock in the living room. He looked from the dresser to the open door and then to the closet on the other side. It was all the same, just how he had left it.

The phone vibrated in his hand and a red light blinked in the top left corner.

"Thank God," he murmured.

He swiped the screen and stared at an unfamiliar number. There were four words in the message.

Can't find your gun?

In spite of the terror he felt, Darryl knew better than to answer it. The security features on the phone had somehow been compromised and Detective Temeke was no longer getting his messages. The deep gloom that surrounded him got thicker by the second and he wished he'd kept the landline, the old dial phone that once sat beside the bed.

He saw the next text surrounded by a speech balloon.

It looked so flippant in light of the message.

Should take care of your things Darryl. Should have taken care of your daughter.

What day was it? Sunday. Darryl had almost forgotten. His girls were eating breakfast with their aunt. They would be safe from this maniac.

Should always lock the door. Always check the alarms.

Darryl was already sick to the stomach. Texts flying out of nowhere. All he needed to do was get to the front door and out into the street. Anything to warn the girls just in case they came home.

A good father is a protective father. Remember that.

For some reason he couldn't grasp, Darryl was reminded of his car before he entered the house. Had he locked it? Abruptly he felt poised on the brink of panic. If everything he had was systematically being taken away from him, what then? What did he have left to escape with? What did he have left to fight with?

The baseball bat. Behind the door.

Rather than hole himself up in his bedroom, he stumbled for the door, staring at the blank space between the carpet and the wall. He was sure he had left it there, sure it was there two days ago. And then he felt the vibration of his phone again.

A baseball bat? You must be hard up.

Darryl heard the pounding of his heart, so loud he thought it would break through his rib cage. The hunter was in the kitchen, watching every room in the house from the security monitor.

It was then his mind went back to the mantel shelf, to the clock, to the pictures. Why had he taken those two pictures? And the sound of a clip and slide? It was next door's garage door. He could hear it closing as they drove away.

He wanted to shout out then, wanted to warn the

intruder that he would protect his youngest from a mind sicker than sick. He wanted to rush out and squeeze that neck with both hands.

Trouble was, he didn't have a weapon. But he did have a bullet-proof vest. In the closet.

I know what you're thinking, Darryl. You're thinking you'd like to run.

Darryl tried to stay calm. He tried to stop twitching. The hunter was already picking up every tiny nuance of fear, every rush of blood from vein to vein. He could probably hear it too, first like a waterfall and then a gushing stream from an underground pipe.

You're thinking I'm down the hall.

It suddenly occurred to Darryl that the texts included apostrophes—something the self-editing feature didn't always pick up.

You probably think I'm in the kitchen.

If this guy was taking his time to correct his texts, he certainly wasn't paying attention to the surveillance monitor. It also occurred to Darryl that he might have bought himself some time, especially now he was standing directly beneath the camera.

You'd be wrong of course. I'm everywhere.

He took a few steps back toward the closet, opened the sliding the door and grabbed the Kevlar vest.

That's when the phone vibrated again, ominously this time.

Now you're just hiding.

"My kind doesn't hide," he murmured through gritted teeth, realizing he was standing in a blind spot, realizing he felt oddly empowered by it.

Such a beautiful girl. Enchanting.

He could see the hallway between the jamb and the door frame, and the front door beyond it. He decided to make a run for it, only his legs felt like two steel girders until he started thinking of Sharek. The asthma, the inhaler. The Village Inn.

So beautiful, the text repeated. *You have nine hours.*

"You won't get her," he said, and then, "Please God don't let him get her."

He pitched forward and scrambled for the hallway, feet slipping on carpet and tile. Just as he bolted for the front door, he saw the shadow of a man before falling on his stomach, wind sucked from his lungs.

TWENTY-SIX

A rage kindled in Ole as he packed up the house. He could still smell her, a seductive smell, delicious like caramel or butterscotch. Fainter on the stairs, but it was there all right. He liked Becky the moment he saw her, longed to be alone with her to ask her things, to tell her things.

He was angry his car was peppered with holes. But he had other ideas. First the cop, then the Williams girl. All in good time. He liked order and he hadn't had much of that lately.

All of a sudden he began to laugh. The Williams man actually thought he was there yesterday. In the house. He had been a little earlier, of course, when the idiot was out at breakfast. He had crept over the back wall, keeping an eye on Alvarez and that nice black charger in the street. Alvarez was a fool. He'd lose more than his pips and ribbons now.

That's when Ole took the gun, the baseball bat and the photographs. He took some other things too, things the girl might need. He wanted her to feel comfortable, wanted her to feel secure. Then he came home, switched on his monitors and watched the Williams house. Wanted to get a good look at the girl, a good feel for what was to come. Wanted to send a few texts just to freak the old man out.

Today, the spare lot was still stained red with Patti's blood and not in a container where he kept it. Odin would have no mead to drink, no wisdom. There would be a price to pay for that.

And the car? What use was a car peppered with holes and leaking gasoline. It was at the bottom of the Rio Grande river now.

He hitched a ride to Haynes Park on the west side of town, sat on a swing watching the white house with the blue trim across the street. Regular as clockwork, Alvarez opened the garage door and started the car, letting it idle for a moment to warm up. He always left the driver's window open, always checked his computer and never noticed a man edging along the side of the car, with a gun in his hand.

It was quick and Ole had a few seconds to feed off a pair of bewildered eyes, especially at the end. Opening the passenger door, he pulled the cop across into the passenger seat, sprinted around to the driver's seat and drove the car to the northeast heights. Lucky Lt. Alvarez was far from home now, lying face down in an arroyo on Pennsylvania Avenue. And luckier still Ole had a car sleeker than a rocket powered aircraft.

Although nothing in his life was a coincidence. He was guided by a fierce and uncontrollable drive which directed him to leave the bone on the detective's front door step. He would have left a packet of weed there as well if he'd had a sense of humor.

Ole hadn't laughed much until he met Morgan, the reawakening of his brother. He'd changed since his death, aged almost beyond recognition. But a body couldn't be expected to stay the same, not after a gunshot wound to the head and time in lonely limbo.

Morgan. Sea warrior. Transformed.

He was stronger now, a lifeguard, coming out of the Californian sea four years ago, body a shine of oil. Ole found him on the Internet, same age, same build, same last name. He offered him a home when he had none, a family when they disowned him and three million dollars when he was no better than a pauper.

And Morgan took it all.

He became Ole's brother, shaved his head, braided his hair. Even tattooed one side of that shaved head with sun, moon and stars. He wanted to belong.

Only now the sucker was in jail. He wasn't allowed a razor unless he was locked in a shower stall and that was only to shave his face. Ole had grown his hair out too. They were twins, weren't they?

He felt weightless, airborne, driving down the street in his brand new car wishing he was flying like that bird up there. A hawk it was, almost the size of a cat.

He counted the windows on every building he passed. He counted the trees and, if he was close enough, he counted the remaining leaves, subtracting them by the days of the week and the ratio of daily molt. That's how he knew how long it would be before they were completely bare. He was dedicated to the finer things in life, the things that others couldn't see.

They wouldn't see him in the Dodge Charger, not one with a police badge on the side panel. He drove down El Pueblo Road that sunny Monday afternoon. He wasn't there because he wanted to be. Not really. He was there to do what Odin wanted, and what Odin wanted was a fresh cup of mead.

He hadn't been the same since that ill-fated afternoon when Becky disappeared. Slipping up, making mistakes, sleeping at night when he never used to. Becky wasn't a freshly laundered shirt, pressed and perfect, without stain. When he kissed her she wasn't as stiff as a statue, rather hungry and a little too eager.

When they arrived at his house, she'd sprung out of the car like a rabbit from a trap, kissing him, running her

185

hands through his hair, laughing. If it hadn't been for the voice on the radio he would have been just as hungry.

The more he thought of Becky, the more he wanted her. Something different. Something priceless. Striking like the last sparkle on the ocean before the sun went down. That's before she ran away.

Now it was afternoon and he backed his car in the school parking lot and to the right of the front entrance. He watched the children as they came out, evaluating each through a pair of dark glasses, wearing a badge and duty belt.

Badge and duty belt. He nearly laughed.

He looked down at the cell phone and flipped through Alvarez's messages, mapping his wording, his style. There was only one girl to pick up today. The other was home with flu.

"We're going to ace this, you and me," he whispered to himself, elbow resting on the door frame, arm half covering his face. He nodded at another police car in the driveway, fingers flexed to a wave.

Lt. Alvarez was due to take over the afternoon shift and he was Alvarez, wasn't he? The morning unit pulled out and hardly gave him a second look. It was that easy.

Ole wanted nothing more than to smash the accelerator to the floor, fly down Central, lights flashing, sirens screaming. The power, the energy, it was worth all the frenzied fuss, cars pulling over in front of him, drivers mesmerized as he cast as little as a glance in their direction. They would be watching those pulsing emergency lights, glaring like white fire. And they would be watching him.

Ole liked to watch too, and the girl he watched today stood on the front steps of the school, staring out into the road, elegant as a black swan. It wasn't the first time he'd watched her, talked to her, laughed with her. Taller, eyes furtive as if she had already sensed him. Swinging a backpack on a slender arm, legs like silk beneath a tiny tartan skirt, she waited for her ride.

She waited for Alvarez.

The sluggish breeze carried the scent of her hair, only soon it would carry an air of mold and decay. She would never have gray hair and squint through thick rimmed glasses, clothes stale with the fragrance of camphor. She would be forever young.

He slipped out of the car and gave her a smile. "Ms. Williams?" he said, without a trace of an accent.

She nodded, head inclined, brow puckered.

"Your dad called. Your uncle's sick so he asked me to pick you up instead."

She nodded at that and handed him her backpack. Hand instinctively pulled down the sleeves of a round-necked sweater, hands covered in its thick weave.

"You can go to the office and call him if you want."

He knew she wouldn't. She was far too fascinated with him to do that.

"No, that's OK," she said, avoiding his eyes, giving a small nod. "I have a cell phone. I can call him in the car."

He opened the back door of the car, watched her slip behind the driver's seat, hand smoothing down that tiny little skirt. She wore hiking boots with high traction soles, a strange outfit for a girl like that. He wanted to tell her he was sorry. That he would kill and mutilate her without hesitation.

"Thirsty?" he asked.

She took the bottle and thanked him. If he kept her talking she wouldn't have to use that cell phone.

He pulled out of the parking lot, automatic locks in place. That's when her told her his name. "Officer Eriksen," he said, glancing through his rearview mirror. "But you can call me Ole."

No recognition. No reaction. She was drinking the

water instead.

There was a misty, haunted air to the afternoon and Ole wondered when she would know, when she would start to cry. Did Alvarez offer her the front or the back seat? It must have felt different. Somehow.

He kept driving and studying her through the rearview mirror. It would be miles before she woke up in the forest, in an unfamiliar bed. No one would suspect a killer of going back to the scene of the crime, not with all that crime scene tape snaking around the barn.

Her eyes were fixed through the side window, shifting back and forth to catch the sights. Oval eyes with a mix of hazel and green. She was a thinker and thinkers were secretive, dangerous.

"You can turn left here," she said with a slur to her voice.

He drove right toward the interstate, glancing occasionally up at the rearview mirror. That's when her head fell back against the seat and her eyes snapped shut.

That's when he stopped and placed her in the trunk. His imagination was suddenly captured by this strange princess and he felt a stab of fear. It was Kizzy all over again, Kizzy come back to life.

He couldn't see her any more. She was silent in the trunk, gagged and bound and lying on a bed of spare clothes. She'd sleep if she had any sense, because tomorrow she would be lying on her back on the forest floor where sunlight came through the trees in thin, dusty shafts of light.

He loved the drowsy fragrance of wet leaves and where spiders wove their elaborate webs between the twigs, each dappled with drops of dew. It was a good place to sleep. A good place to die.

TWENTY-SEVEN

"Rise and shine," Temeke said, ambling toward the duty desk and slapping it with his hand. Sarge lifted his chin, suddenly jolted awake by the noise. "I don't know how you can sleep with Hackett going up and down in the lift."

"Elevator, sir. *Elevator*."

"How's Becky?"

"Taking visitors tomorrow. You can go and see her if you like. Go lightly though. I don't want her to relive the ordeal." Sarge cleared his throat and looked away. "Oh, and Hackett's looking for you. Looks mad if you ask me."

"He was cussing like a detective," Jarvis chimed in from his tiny little cubicle. "Had a pink slip in his hand."

"That's a layoff notice to you foreigners," Captain Fowler chimed in to a burst of raucous laughter. He was standing at the door of his plush, white office. "What's this I hear about Malin calling you *sir*?"

Temeke lifted his chin and grinned. He'd seen the way Fowler looked at Malin, seen the way a lumbering walk quickly turned into a swagger. "I prefer a little distance myself. Pretty, isn't she?"

"Is she? I hadn't noticed."

"She gets five hundred dollars extra for being my partner. That's a lot more than your bonus once a year, isn't it?"

Temeke was the only one who laughed as he sauntered up the stairs and he swore long and feebly into the empty corridor. Creeping past Hackett's closed door, he found Malin poking through the filing cabinet in his office. She turned when she saw him, hand cupping her mouth.

"Something's happened, sir. You better sit down."

"I've been sitting down all weekend."

"Mr. Williams called. Tess didn't come home from school this afternoon."

"Not another one." Temeke unzipped his coat and flung it over the back of his chair. His eye was drawn to the window where the trees shuddered in the wind. At night the temperatures plummeted to below ten degrees. "What was she wearing?"

"A black sweater, black jacket, yellow and red plaid skirt and hiking boots. Mr. Williams said there was an intruder in his house yesterday. He said he didn't see anyone. But there were muddy footprints leading as far as the back yard. Someone's been tampering with his phone, sending him weird text messages. Should be able to get a trace on it." Malin turned and pushed the drawer closed with her back. "Why didn't you tell him about Maisie's phone?"

"Didn't want to spook him any more than he already is. There should have been a unit outside his house."

"There was. Lt. Alvarez. He's back from vacation. He saw Darryl arrive home in a hurry. Saw his car idling in the driveway. Then he found him on the floor in the hallway. He was OK but he was terrified."

"Luis is on this afternoon's shift at Clemency Christian. He hasn't called, has he?"

Malin shook her head. "I tried calling him an hour ago. Wanted to ask him to get a photograph of Tess from the house when he dropped her off."

Temeke could hear Hackett honking into a

handkerchief next door and dabbing what must have been a bright red nose. "Hackett seem OK to you?" he said, feeling a little sick himself.

She gave him a hostile glare and brushed a wisp of dark hair from her eyes. "Been like a bear with a bee up his nose. Heard him shouting at Jennifer Danes on the phone. She accused him of keeping valuable information about the 9th Hour Killer from the public. Says she's writing an article for tomorrow's Journal."

Temeke unwound his scarf and left it hanging around his neck. He had a strange feeling he'd be going out again. "And what bit of news are we keeping?"

"The bit where there's two of them. Not just the one."

"Oh, that bit. Anything else?"

Malin lowered her voice. "The bit where the police are now interested in Darryl Williams. Apparently, you called the Journal and told them."

"Why would I do a thing like that? It's Eriksen. Obviously he's got a way with words and an armory of accents."

"Andrew Knife Wing called a few times. Something about a dream. He shouldn't be messing around with strange spirits, sir."

"Any spirits in his house are the liquid kind."

Temeke called Luis and listened to the dialing tone. Probably got his sirens on full blast and couldn't hear the phone. He listened to the message from Knife Wing instead. A vision. A dead body wrapped in a pink quilt lying behind a boulder, which basically narrowed it down to the whole of bleeding New Mexico.

"The land of enchantment they call it," he said out loud. "More like the land of bloody *entrapment*."

That's how he felt after living here for so many years. Trapped. Like he'd blown in from Europe on holiday and never quite made it back. Something about the scent of cedar and sage everywhere. And the skies... those big blue skies that stretched as far as the eye could see, a vivid vault over a thirsty land.

"Get me a coffee, will you?" Temeke sensed Malin's narrowed eyes, the shake of her head. He pretended to pat a few papers into a neat pile.

What was the password to his computer this week? *H8st8P0lice* or *Hackettsux*. Typing the latter sent him quickly to an email from Hackett demanding an update on the investigation and driveling on about how Temeke's phone was permanently on voicemail and how many times Captain Fowler had tried to get hold of him in the last twenty-four hours.

There was another email from the local TV station hankering to do an interview and one from Jennifer at the Journal threatening to write her own opinion if he didn't return her calls.

Temeke deleted them all and opened the database for homicides and kidnap. He found eighteen Eriksens listed, none with the initial *O*. There was a listing in the NPIS, the immigration service in Norway. An Ole Eriksen born October 3rd, 1977 in Tromsø.

Blond, blue eyed, square jaw, but that's where the similarity ended. Darryl could easily be forgiven for thinking Morgan Eriksen's picture belonged to the man he saw. Put them together in a line up and he wouldn't be so sure.

According to the file, Ole had a twin brother, Morgan. He had died at the age of nine in a hunting accident. A newspaper article showed pictures of a boy lying under a tree as if he was sleeping. There was nothing remarkable about it until closer examination revealed a hole in his head resulting from an old battle rifle. Temeke had seen something similar, an AG-3 fitted with a railed forend and an Aimpoint red dot sight.

"No BB gun," he muttered. Not even then.

The hunter, a Johannes Elgar, who lived three miles from the Eriksen house, claimed he mistook one of the boys for small game. He was given a life sentence due to a weapon that hardly fell into the collector category according to the Norwegian Firearm Weapons Act.

The Eriksen family owned the Bergenposten, a well-known newspaper on the west coast of Norway and, by all accounts, Eriksen's father had at one time written an article citing Elgar for buying and selling illegal weapons.

"Revenge," Temeke said, suddenly sensing Malin in the doorway with two cups of coffee.

"Revenge?" she echoed.

"Little Morgan Eriksen." Temeke grabbed the cup and read out the article. "He was in the wrong place at the wrong time. But there's more. There's always more."

"More, sir?"

"It's lonely out in those woods, lonely for a beautiful woman. Ole's mother was only seventeen. Marja her name was." He took a deep breath and blew over the rim of his cup. "Looks like he moved to California in 2001. Followed her here. Tried to find her, only she'd committed suicide a few years earlier. He has an aunt in San Francisco. Might want to talk to that aunt."

"Already tried that, sir. She passed away. Last June."

Temeke looked up at Malin and gave a curt nod. He didn't want her to think he was too grateful. Didn't want her to think he was disappointed either. "And Johannes Elgar had a heart attack in jail."

Malin sucked on the lip of her coffee cup. "Died with a photograph of Marja in his hand and the very first letter she ever wrote him."

Temeke had already read the transcript. It was the last sentence that seemed to spin, slowing down as he remembered it. *Hans, you are the burning, glowing flame in my heart, Marja.* The very same words Patti had written to Ole in a card. Words he had wanted her to write.

"His father's dead. Parkinson's," Temeke said, looking at the picture of a well-dressed man in his sixties. "Ole was put up for adoption."

"He went from foster home to foster home, sir."

Temeke sensed his vision blurring as he read that screen, but he wasn't going to let it overwhelm him. "Talking of hunting rifles, did you see the Bonner Levinson file, the caretaker at the Shelby ranch?"

Malin nodded and walked around to his side of the desk, eyes following the cursor on the computer as it flew across the screen. "His body was found at the bottom of a seventy foot ravine. He must have seen something."

"That's the trouble with our witnesses," Temeke muttered, leaning back in his chair. "They're all dead."

"Yet here's an elderly man shot four times at close range. There might be some muzzle staining on that gun if only we can find it, and as for the killer's clothes, a nice blood spatter to go with it."

"According to this," Temeke said, finger stabbing the screen, "the caretaker had other injuries consistent with a body being pulled down the ravine post mortem. Time of death, around midnight on the evening of Wednesday October 29th. Looks like they found a .22 caliber shell case at the top of the ravine and a walking stick. Levinson's prints were on the stick but look at this. There's part of a shoe imprint in the lining of the coat he wore. Forensics say it's a gripper outsole with the Sebago logo. A leather moccasin."

"Those are going to be hard to find," Malin muttered. "The print on the lining isn't enough to tell us the shoe size."

Temeke cast a glance at the ballistic evidence. The bullet was said to be grooved, found to have come from a Sears or a Revelation. So far the gun had never been found.

His raw instinct told him the ranch area wasn't saturated with offenders. It wasn't exactly saturated with neighbors. "Any guns in the house on Walter?"

Malin shook her head. "Podge said this man had a thing for teenage girls. School girls."

"Podge was a sucker for booze and the old green dragon. Probably too high to know anything about the girls. He was scared when we found him."

Malin crossed one arm over her stomach and drained her cup. "I took a look at the yearbooks at Cibola High. Jaelyn Gains, Lavonne Jackson, Mikaela May, Lyana Durgins, Elizabeth Moya and Mandy Guzman. 6 victims from the same school, all taken within a month of each other. The only difference was Kizzy Williams. She was at Clemency Christian School."

"Where were they taken?"

"From parks, malls, parking lots. Lyana was taken only five hundred yards from her home. She was walking the dog."

"And Becky?"

"Last seen at Corrales Café after she finished work. I remember her mother saying Becky's boss had called to say she would be late. Had an accent. When I spoke to him he had no recollection of such a phone call. Nor did he have an accent."

Temeke studied Malin's face. Her eyes for all their listless stare were moist. "Anything wrong?"

"I wanted to ask you something. I wanted to ask if you said anything to Hollister?"

Temeke felt the beginnings of a belly ache. The coffee wasn't going down well either. "What makes you say that?"

"Because he left me an email. Wanted to know where I was."

Temeke pursed his lips, gave her a sheepish smile. "I gave him a tinkle, man to man. And he knows if he sets one foot in my nice shiny police station and gives so much as a wink to my partner, he's toast." That made her smile. It even made her snigger. "So who does the house on Smith belong to?"

"Kelly Coldwell, realtor with Desert Sun Properties. They said she's on a cruise in the Caribbean. Left ten days ago."

Temeke sucked in a long breath. He was hoping for a concrete lead, not more checking up to do. "If the driver of that Camaro is Ole Eriksen, he ought to be in hospital."

"Dr. Vasillion called half an hour ago, sir. He said the blood in the street belonged to Patti Lucero."

Temeke thought he hadn't heard her correctly and shut his mouth before a string of cuss words crossed the gap between them. If it had any significance he couldn't see it.

"The bone was analyzed on Friday, sir. Funny the one thing he tried to hide about the victim ended up on your doorstep."

"He wants us to find him, that's why. Wants the publicity."

Malin swallowed like she had a sore throat. "They found traces of polyethylene in the sample. He was carrying Patti's blood around in a milk carton."

Temeke made a face, although he was forced to admit it was the only thing that made sense. "If we don't find him soon, I'll have to buy a wig and send myself in as decoy."

Malin grinned and then seemed to pause to consider her next words. "Dr. Vasillion said when he examined the girl's head it had no brain. Like it had been completely sucked out. I think he wants to see us down at the lab."

Temeke's eyes flicked toward Hackett's office, finger pressed to his lips. He wasn't about to pay him a visit, not after that sodding email. "We'll grab a sandwich on the way, Marl. Make sure you bring some cash."

TWENTY-EIGHT

The office of the medical investigator was located in a large blue and white glass building near the Big I. New, immaculate, state of the art, a facility after Temeke's own heart.

After being buzzed in by security personnel, he had a strange feeling they weren't expected.

"You didn't need to come down here, Detective. I could have sooner talked to you on the phone," Dr. Vasillion said, cinched tightly in a plastic apron and standing behind an autopsy table.

Temeke shot Malin a look and raised one eyebrow. "Always better to see you in person. Isn't that right Malin?"

Malin gave a tight nod, eyes falling on a human skull which had been placed upside down on a roll of duct tape.

"I usually prefer a lot more meat on them," the doctor said picking up the skull, "but we'll use Hector here as our model. We know the girls were drugged and decapitated with the hatchet we found. Are either of you familiar with Egyptian mummification?"

Temeke nodded, seeing Malin's cheeks graying out of the corner of his eye. What was the betting she threw up?

"The Egyptians used a metal hook which was inserted up through the nostril into the brain case." Dr.

Vasillion demonstrated with a finger. "I found a second incision where the spinal cord exits the skull which appears to have been smashed with a mallet."

"So he cracked her skull and scooped out the brain," Temeke said.

The doctor nodded, giving Malin a sideways glance. "Hence the metal hook, a mallet and a spoon. Basic, but very effective. The head was completely exsanguinated. I'm confident the cocktail of drugs didn't kill her. It was the axe that did."

"Didn't see a metal hook in the house," Temeke said, reading the message in the doctor's expression. "Did you see a hook, Marl?"

He looked down at his partner bent over a stainless steel sink. The sound of her breakfast gurgling down the drain reminded him he needed to see to his waste disposal when he got home. He ambled over and patted her between the shoulders. "Got room now for a sandwich."

The doctor escorted her to a chair and gave her a cup of water. Temeke saw him nod and grin, and walk back along the corridor swinging Hector like a bowling ball.

"I don't know what happened," Malin said ten minutes later as she sat in the passenger seat of the Explorer. "Couldn't feel my legs."

"I'll tell you what happened. You came over all queasy at the thought of blood and brains." Temeke started the car and turned the heater on high. "Not the first time a cop has made a complete prat of themselves in front of the doc. And it won't be the last."

When he'd finished telling about the other five, they were already on the west side of town and parked in the front parking lot of Northwest Area Command. Malin had been unusually quiet all the way.

"Take the car and go home," Temeke said, feeling a twinge of frustration. "I'll tell Hackett you've come down with flu."

"But I haven't got the flu," she said, rubbing one red eye.

Temeke opened the car door and lit a cigarette. He puffed out a smoke ring and watched it curl around the wing mirror before disappearing altogether. "Are you getting anything out of being a detective?" he asked. It was a pitiful stare she gave him, eyes watery. "I'm not sure you've got the stomach for it."

"I love my job," she snapped. "I wouldn't be here if I didn't."

"Got PMS?" he asked, knowing he wouldn't like the answer.

"Don't you dare. I've put up with your spite all the way from the northeast heights—"

"Can't be PMS then."

"No, it's not PMS. I don't get PMS," she said, snatching a pile of papers from the glove compartment.

"Can't come to work in a bad mood, Marl. Detective work is no joy. It's bloody miserable actually, especially out in the field. Know what I mean?"

"Yes, sir. I know what you mean."

"Throw up again on my watch and I'll have you suspended. I can't say fairer than that."

"You can't suspend someone for throwing up, *sir*!" Malin's smile flickered and then sputtered out.

"And where are my gas receipts?" he said to the empty passenger seat. She was already running up the steps to the front door.

"Women," he muttered and slammed the car door, grinding what was left of his cigarette underfoot.

He switched on his best smile for Sarge in the front lobby and nodded a greeting. "Any news on that surveillance video?"

"Still in Imaging, sir," Sarge said without looking up. He was looking at the Best of Swimsuit Models in the

Sports Illustrated.

"When you've quite finished poring over underage Busty Brenda there, I'd like a word."

"All I know," Sarge said, closing the magazine, "is that the wretched thing was too grainy to make a positive ID."

"Why aren't you at the hospital?"

"I've been there all day, sir. Watched her cry, watched her sleep. I'm glad she's alive, but I don't know what to say. Rae's with her now. She'll know what to do."

"Right," Temeke said, rubbing his forehead.

Sarge blew his nose and seemed to nod away the memory. "Oh, and I got a phone call this afternoon from an Edna Barnes. Said she saw a cop outside Cibola High about the time when Patti was taken. Said she used to be a police composite artist. Made her very own sketch and then went and gave it to Jennifer Danes."

"She did what?"

"Headline news now. Oh and Edna's a bit hard of hearing by the way."

Temeke made a note to see this Edna Barnes in the morning and reluctantly climbed the stairs to his office. Hackett's door opened and he poked his big fat head out. "Can I have a word?"

Brilliant, thought Temeke, pretending to dig deep into his pockets for those gas receipts. "I'm not playing pocket snooker, sir, if that's what you're thinking. I just can't seem to find—"

Hackett pulled him in and closed the door. "You can quit your bellyaching. Malin already gave them to me. First things first. The public got a taste of Eriksen in the morning news. A sketch drawn by a witness. Pity she didn't bring it to us first."

"The police don't pay for sketches, sir. I expect she got a tidy sum from the Journal."

"I take it you know what this means?"

"It's all over the canteen and our killer's gone to ground."

Hackett sat down on his chair and huffed out a loud breath. He stared at the ceiling, cheeks redder than a baboon's ass. "It's a shame my officers couldn't find poor little Becky Moran. She had to come home all by herself."

"Not home, sir. St Joseph's hospital. By all accounts she was helped in by one of their security guards. Similar uniform. Should pass as one of us."

"You know what I mean. It's embarrassing. Makes us look incompetent."

"You feeling alright, sir?" Temeke wondered why the poor old git reminded him of something out of a Bram Stoker novel.

"Sit down, David." Hackett blew out a large breath, rocking his chair on its two back legs. He suddenly found a rubber band on his desk that required his immediate attention.

Temeke noted the use of his first name, felt the blood pumping in his head.

"Luis Alvarez has gone missing. There was blood on the floor of his garage. *His* blood by the look of it. His wife wondered why the garage door was still open." Hackett looked over his half-moon spectacles at the rubber band so he didn't have to look at Temeke. "He's highest on our priority list right now. Especially since his nice new Charger's nowhere to be found."

"How much blood?"

"A lot."

"Are you telling me he's dead?"

"There's no murder case without a body. You know that."

"I'll get on to it right away, sir."

Hackett held up a hand. "Since he's family I think it

best if you didn't. Like I said before, I want you and Malin out in the field. And I mean *out*. Oh, and before I forget, your jeep."

"My jeep?"

"Slight accident. Someone backed into it. Took off the back fender."

Temeke felt the heat rise to his cheeks, felt his hands ball into two tight fists. "It's bloody Sarge. I've told him to check his wing mirrors every time he reverses. But, no! He has to put his bleeding foot down and bang goes my antique Hotchkiss. I bet it's got a dent and all."

Hackett leaned in a little closer. "It may have escaped your smug British ass that Sarge parks around the front. And your Hotchkiss is hardly an antique if it's a rebuild. I'm sick of you correcting my English, sick of you calling Americans *Yanks*, and sick of you coming to work with stains down your pants. Anyone would think you've been having a bit in the bathrooms."

Temeke looked down at his pants and sure enough, there was a nasty white stain on his fly. Probably mayonnaise from the sandwich he had at lunch.

"Were you sleeping with Becky Moran?"

There was an audible snap as Temeke's head jerked up. "Of course I wasn't sleeping with Becky Moran. She's a kid."

"I'm glad you noticed. Are you sleeping with Officer Lopez?"

"Who?"

"You heard."

"You mean Flossy from Fingerprinting? You've got a bloody nerve. How am I supposed to get my leg over with all this overtime?"

"Go home," Hackett said. "Malin will give you a ride."

No she bloody won't, Temeke thought. He'd already told her to get lost. And what was this sudden interest in his sex life?

He heaved a sigh and stalked back to his office, sinking his rear deep into a leather chair. He'd hardly be fit for anything if he didn't go home and get a nap. Sniffing the air he could smell traces of perfume and he lit up a cigarette just to get rid of it. Pushing out a series of smoke rings he let his mind wander to the last time he saw Luis flashing that big white smile of his.

He wasn't dead. He'd probably just gone down to the Fat Jacks for a pint or two. As for his Charger, it was probably parked around the back.

He stared at the victims' pictures on his wall, eyes darting from one girl to another. They were all alike in a way, same bright oval eyes, same smooth dark skin. Some darker than others. Patti's eyes were pale blue though. That was the only difference.

Glancing through the window at the rear parking lot, he saw the empty space where his jeep had once been. Might never be the same, he thought, hearing the toll of a funeral bell in his mind.

He didn't want to go home to a wife who froze him out because he was never there and kept her legs tightly closed when he was. A wife who was culinary-challenged and could only whip up a scrambled egg on good days. A wife who if she ever found his stash of weed in the backyard downspout wouldn't hesitate to blow the whistle and get him fired.

He deserved it. All of it.

He felt a soreness in his throat when he thought of Serena. Sometimes he wanted to run from her, sometimes he wanted to run to her. He took a few deep breaths, hand rubbing his chin. Surely, her pain was worse than his.

My Serena.

He was suddenly thirsty and he opened his desk drawer. There were a few quarters in his piggy bank, just enough to buy him a drink from the vending machine. He was a coffee man himself and it was the first time in years he felt like a good cup of tea.

A cold shiver trickled down his back and he felt uneasy. It was colder in his office than in the morgue, and all he could hear was Hackett's voice raining down on him like a meteor shower.

There's no murder case without a body.

TWENTY-NINE

Darryl began to shake. He couldn't remember the last time he had eaten. It was sometime yesterday, two hours before Tess disappeared. He was teetering on the edge of some dark crater and if he wasn't careful, he'd fall in for good.

It was no secret now that he wanted to end his life. He was tired of living the darkness, tired of the tears. Maisie had taken Sharek to stay with Pastor Razz. They were safer there. And here he was all by himself again, feeling uneasy, like he'd just woken up and found a hate-message written on his mirror in lipstick. There was something odd in the silence, something that gripped at his conscience.

Why him? Why his girls?

His stomach lurched into a state of panic. What if all this had somehow been his fault? The bad dreams had beaten him senseless and all he wanted now was peace. He caressed the phone with his fingers, willing the police to give him good news. Any news. And when it didn't ring he opened the front door, heard the gentle roar of wind over the mesa. It was cold and he shivered in a flimsy button-down shirt and bare feet.

The sun tried to break through a cloud over the Sandia mountains, peaks gray in the waning light. It was a sight he would never forget and the more he thought about it, the more he felt a sick sensation in the pit of his gut.

He knew today was his last.

He could hear voices beyond the courtyard, cars pulling up in the road, laughter. He looked through the speakeasy grill and he was almost blinded by a sudden flash.

"Mr. Williams!"

Voices shouted, cameras whirred.

"Where's your daughter?"

Rattling and hammering against the garden gate.

"Where's Tess, Mr. Williams?"

"Have you heard from her?"

"Do you know where she is?"

He ran back into the house and locked the door behind him, heart thumping like those fists at his gate. They couldn't access the courtyard but they could climb over the back wall. He closed the patio blinds. There was no sign of them yet, but he knew their accusing voices would find their way into his home somehow.

The phone buzzed on the kitchen table and he lurched toward it with a big gasp.

"Mr. Williams, this is Carey Johns from Eyewitness News. Both your daughters have gone missing within a month of each other. How do you feel about that?"

Darryl couldn't speak, couldn't breathe. He couldn't take the phone away from his ear either.

"You've read the article in the Journal... the one that cited you as the kidnapper? I would want to argue that if I were you. Would you like to comment?"

The silence was longer this time and Darryl was suddenly shrouded in an emotional fog. A comment? Yes, he had a comment.

"Do you know what it's like to lose your little girl to a serial killer? Have you any idea what he did to her? And now he's got my Tess. And you're accusing me of taking her?"

"I'm not accusing you, Mr. Williams, the people are saying—"

"What are they saying?"

"They're saying if you didn't do it, who did? And if you didn't do it, Mr. Williams, you should be out there looking for her. You're no longer working at the bank, right?"

How did she know he had been fired? All he wanted to do was grieve. He muttered something into the mouthpiece, gave her a piece of his mind.

"When you say *grieve*, Mr. Williams, are you saying she's dead? Are you saying Tess is dead?"

Darryl snapped the phone shut and threw it across the room. He walked into the living room and slumped onto the couch, listening to it ring again.

He didn't remember how long he sobbed, and then his whole world began to spin before it went black. He heard a faint buzzing like a dragonfly bouncing from stalk to stalk and the trees beyond the patio doors seemed to pulse with life as if something moved in the shadows.

Snow fell in clumps from dirty gray clouds that scudded in from the west and a far-away howl suggested a coyote nearby. Narrowing his eyes to the snow, he sensed in that moment that his body was not his own and his mind was the only part functioning.

A whimpering sound made him turn his head toward the chair by the fire. Huddled in her usual place was Kizzy, head thrown back in sleep. He hardly recognized her voice, faint, sweet over the crackling flames in the hearth. He was too afraid to move.

"Daddy." It was only a whisper but he heard it all right. His heart throbbed so hard it almost hurt. Same green blazer, same pleated skirt.

He took his time standing, managing little more than a hobble. He could just make out two braids and a wealth of black hair, and large brown eyes that suddenly blinked to life.

She was not a blackened corpse as he expected and he wanted to take her in his arms, to feel the grip of her fingers. He began coaxing her with a slight tug. That's when her head wobbled from her shoulders and fell with a thud to the floor.

He screamed himself awake, looked around the room to the same old dreary emptiness. It was love he needed, love he craved, but that love was long gone.

Funny how the dead don't linger, not even to say goodbye.

Words replayed in his mind, a mind full of verse and song. They were good words, too. Something about being convinced that neither death nor life, neither angels nor demons, nor the present, nor the future… What came next?

Think, Darryl, think! *Take a deep breath and recite that old verse, the first verse you ever recited at church.*

He had been nine then, the same age as Kizzy was when she died. A new beginning for him. A violent end for her. He had always believed he had a lion's heart. Always thought he was a good father.

Had he been a good father? Had he done enough?

"I'm sick of crying!" he yelled. "I'm so sick of it. Please God take it away. *Please.*"

When God didn't answer he sank to his knees, both hands gripping the coffee table. His favorite black and white tie slouched over a leather bound bible, a reminder of better days. Days when he had the money to provide. Days when people looked up to him, honked their horns in the parking lot. They even opened doors for him.

Days when his assistant told him how much she liked that tie. It looked good on him. Always turned a few heads.

Now they turned their backs, pretended not to hear.

Walked down the other side of the street, sidestepping him in the grocery store. He felt like a beggar, an outcast, a thief.

He prayed in the bad times, asked God to show him what he should do. The only words he heard were those of his pastor.

Open the book, son. Read. That's how you'll know His voice.

How could he open the book? He couldn't get past the first page. All that separating of light and darkness, and stuff about trees bearing fruit. Although God saw it was good, when he made man, he saw it was *very* good.

Darryl wondered how he was supposed to fit into that scenario. He wasn't *very* good. He wasn't even mediocre. He'd been fired, for crying out loud.

Although he had gone forth and multiplied.

And look what happened. His wife was dead. His youngest daughter mutilated. His eldest daughter missing, presumed mutilated, and last but not least, the middle one with a great future ahead of her if the police didn't find the killer.

He snatched up that tie and walked into the garage. He had a better use for it now. That's where the rafters were. Two sturdy beams across the roof, load bearing up to a thousand pounds. It would be brief. He wouldn't feel a thing. Would he?

Taking the stepladder from behind the kitchen door, he climbed as far as the top step, hand out against the rafter. It was good and firm, just like he imagined. He put on that tie, that beautiful black and white tie. Carmel's tie, the one she had given him as a gift. It takes class to know class.

He wanted those blood-sucking journalists to see what they had done, to realize they had pushed him to an act of such horrifying consequence.

His life began to replay itself in those final moments,

a blur of faces just beyond his reach, floating in the sky. He would be floating with them in less than a minute. At least he hoped it was less than a minute.

Wait a minute. How long did a good strangling take? He wished he'd looked it up on the Internet first. Only they probably didn't show purple faces dangling at the end of a rope. And there was probably no such thing as a *How To* website.

Unnerved to the point of shaking, he climbed back down.

THIRTY

Temeke wiped a trail of spittle from his mouth and stretched. It wasn't the first time he'd slept in his office, neck stiff and trousers wrinkled. Flakes of snow and sleet began to tap against the window and he wondered if the storm would ever stop.

It was seven forty-two in the morning according to the clock on the wall. He fired up his computer and found an email from Hackett. The poor old sod was at home with a bad case of the flu. With any luck he'd be off for a month.

No news on Luis.

Attached to the email was a video file confirmed to be the voice and face of Patti Lucero. It had been emailed by an anonymous subscriber yesterday whose IP address Stu Andersen described as anywhere between Roswell and outer space.

The video showed Patti sitting on a couch with a sandwich in her lap and leaning against a pink quilt. The background was different. Not the house on Smith and Walter. Somewhere else.

The other party's voice had been edited out so it could not be traced and she appeared to be giggling, as if the question she had been asked was uncomfortable and funny at the same time. Then she went quiet, eyes dazed, head slumping against her chest.

The picture faded after that.

Behind her was a small window, blackened by the darkness. There was something on the sill that caught his eye. A small wooden figure of a chubby Santa smoking a pipe like the one in the house on Smith and Walter. When incense was placed inside, the figure blew out smoke rings. It was German if he could bet on it.

To take away the stench.

His mind was trapped by the medical report which confirmed the wooden block had traces of Patti's blood and so did the axe. A luminol sweep had been done of the back yard at the house on Smith street and the concrete apron lit up like a beacon. Cause of death was manual strangulation which seemed almost redundant in Temeke's opinion. But what caught his eye was the pink quilt.

Just as Knife Wing had said.

Patti had been drugged and killed at the house and the rest of her might well be lying behind a boulder. A flicker of heat arced through his body as he expounded Knife Wing's theory in his head.

I saw a dead body wrapped in a pink quilt. Behind a boulder… beneath Turtle Rock.

Temeke looked at his watch to see he had just enough time to get a burrito before ferreting about in the foothills. Grabbing his leather jacket, he raced out into the corridor and ran down the stairs.

"Sir? Where you going?"

"Oh, there you are, Marl," he said. "I was just going out for a smoke."

"I'm coming," she shouted, sprinting down the stairs and dragging a padded ski jacket. Her woolen scarf was already wrapped around her neck, pockets spilling with latex gloves. She knew where he was going.

"You feeling better," he said as they headed for the door.

213

"Need some fresh air."

"Might not be that fresh where we're going."

"Anything's fresher than a can of coughing cops."

He was inclined to agree. The office was beginning to fill with crumpled tissues, all stinking of snot.

They reached the upper parking lot of the Peak Tram at eight-thirty in the morning and there was a tram waiting at the gate already filling with passengers.

Temeke stuffed a few evidence bags in his jacket pocket and grabbed two bottles of water.

"Vicks?" he said, throwing her a small container and smiling as he did it. "Wrap that scarf round your nose," he warned.

They walked beneath the tram cables, showing their badges to an official before striding off into the foothills. It was hard work steaming up a narrow path between boulders and sagebrush. Clumps of snow nested between grass stems and, occasionally, the wind blew a spray into the air.

"Ever been up in one of those?" Malin said, surveying the tram as it sailed over a ridge.

"Not bloody likely."

"Don't like heights, do you?"

"Don't like nosy parkers much either. Get a move on."

The first tower rose up out of the sand, a blue painted frame that held the cables between the terminals. There was no disturbed soil beneath it, except the unmistakable tracks of bear and fox pressed into the sand and snow. Mountain lion were scarce and were rarely seen so close to the city limits.

As Temeke stared at the scene, he saw something flapping in the wind like a tiny pennant. He took the pen out of his jacket pocket and stabbed at a soiled wipe that had hooked itself to a clump of grass. He lifted it up to the sun, hoping there were traces of the killer somewhere deep down in the weave of that fabric. A distant memory began to crank to life in his mind, playing out like a sequel to the Kizzy Williams murder.

The field investigators had combed a two mile stretch of the trails and forest, and found twenty-eight bloodstained wipes, evidence that someone had tried to remove all essence of Kizzy from his skin. They ran the DNA evidence against the CODIS database and found no match.

"I know you're here," Temeke whispered under his breath as he bagged the wipe. The killing field was now more widespread and frequent.

He kept seeing Kizzy's wholesome face staring back at him, in his dreams, in his thoughts. He never told anyone, never took her picture down from beside his desk. There was Patti with her long brown hair and pale blue eyes, and Mikaela May with her heart-shaped face and dimples. They were all there on his wall. All in his heart.

He no longer cared when Malin signaled for lunch. He shook his head and crouched amongst the boulders, searching, sniffing. For four more long hours.

A tram car trundled above him, inquisitive faces pressed against the glass. Temeke watched it disappear behind a steep knoll where a turtle-shaped boulder jutted out against a pale blue sky. He almost ran toward it, hearing the crunch of gravel under Malin's feet behind him. Crouching in the dirt, he felt a mix of sand and wet snow between his fingers. He must have searched for two more hours before he found a shard of denim stained with blood.

He snapped on a pair of latex gloves before bagging the item and waving it at Malin. The last flush of sunlight would soon give way to dusk, leaving behind a hazy moon to light up the deep tones of a New Mexico sky.

"Higher," he shouted, nodding at the path.

The chill was internal, a sense there was something out there, a dark shadow flitting about in the trees. If a bear was as inquisitive as the tourists, he'd have a problem.

He glanced at where the path curled upwards around a steep knoll, coming to a head at the foot of a boulder and a piñon sapling. Listening to a whisper of wind from the crevices above, his forehead began to prickle with sweat and his hands were damp. Surely, there were no bears up there. He would have seen one by now.

In spite of the feeling that continued to plague him, he tried to stop his ragged breathing and his pounding heart. There was a sour taste in his mouth. Something had spooked him.

"She was dragged up there," he heard Malin say, teeth chattering in the night air. "There's broken twigs and stuff. We're close. She's got to be here somewhere."

The higher they went, Temeke began to see more broken branches, as if something had been hauled at least fifteen feet to a natural gulley bristling with stickers.

"… Temeke…"

The whisper was irrefutably clear.

"… left a little…"

Something about the voice was otherworldly, familiar.

"… there now…"

He turned to the sound, aware of a sensation like a thousand insects trailing down his spine. He watched Malin poking around in the dirt, occasionally stopping to look up at the mountain and back at the horizon. Not like she had a masculine voice. Nor was she prone to whispering.

It was his voice and he knew it.

He turned his collar up against the damp chill and

picked his way through waist-high sage flowering on each side of the path. What he did find odd was a downy drift along the path, some of which stuck to his lips and tasted of cotton. The worst of it was the stench, strong now as they climbed around the knoll.

"Blimey, Malin, what's that stink," he said, sniffing what seemed like the sour breath of the city's worst dumpsters. "Not you, I hope."

"This way, sir." Malin led him off the path, trampling through a tangle of weeds that clung to his calves.

Winding his scarf around his face and nose, Temeke began to take shorter breaths. It was warmer that way, only he'd be hard pressed to fit a smoke through thick layers of wool. Night was creeping across the mesa now and above it was a sky stippled with stars. To the east a large orange moon lounged above the Sandias and to the west a single slash of sunlight, bloody like a hunter's blade cleaving the sky from the desert.

He turned on his flashlight, training the beam on the hard-packed earth, looking for anything that might be peaking between tufts of sagebrush. It amazed him how strong that smell was, even over the fresh air. From here it reminded him of a teenager's bedsit, sickly and stale.

Temeke snapped his fingers when he saw the bundle tied with rope and partially covered with a pink quilt. It was propped up against a boulder, a torso of a young girl, *young* he assumed by the angel charm bracelet wrapped around the wrist. He prodded it with a foot.

"Well past its best," he muttered, wishing he'd smeared a large dollop of Vicks on his upper lip a little sooner. Wishing Malin would open her eyes and stop talking to herself. "And she's past prayer and all."

"Animals have had a go at her," Malin whispered, hand pressed against her scarf. She appeared to be holding back a heave or two. Then she stared at where the head should have been, imagining the face perhaps, imagining the girl's last moments.

Temeke could see what she meant. Bloody paw marks pressed against one leg where chunks had been torn from the waist and thighs, and remnants of a denim shirt were strewn about her feet. Mountain lion, he thought, judging by the three lobes he could just make out on the back edge of the heel pad.

Where the other leg was he couldn't fathom until he suddenly remembered the bone on his front door mat. If it belonged to this body, the 9th Hour Killer had a titanic ego. He put his flashlight down and fumbled for a packet of cigarettes.

"Don't talk and you won't have to taste the smell of it. Here," he said, handing her a cigarette. He struck a match on the rugged face of a boulder and cupped a hand around the flame.

She took it even though she didn't smoke and the coughing wasn't as severe as he thought it would be. She'd smoked before.

"See the quilt," he said, picking up the flashlight and pointing it at shreds of pink flowery squares. "Looks like he had a little empathy for this one, but it's not the case. He's getting sloppy. Each victim is the chink in his armor because he's leaving clues. I should have taken Knife Wing more seriously. He was right about the quilt."

He took the cigarette Malin returned and unwound his scarf. It was worth getting cold over a much-needed drag.

"Doctor's report said something about a tranquilizer," she said. "Nembutal, I think he mentioned."

"Must have given her a bloody big dose."

Crouching closer, he pulled the quilt out from under the right side of the body and ran the beam of the flashlight up and down the exposed flesh from shoulder to buttocks. There were signs of insect activity even in the low temperatures and Temeke wondered if the forensic entomologist would concur she had been killed elsewhere.

"I reckon this one wasn't left in a house for several days while the killer decided what to do with it."

"What do you mean, sir?"

"See how she's wrapped up nice and warm. Propped up against the rock like she's looking out at something. If this is Patti Lucero, her mother lives down there."

Malin looked at the direction of his finger and flinched. "That's so sad. So sick. I can't imagine what dragons she saw."

Temeke looked up in time to see Malin cuff away a tear. "G. K. Chesterton once said, 'Fairy tales are more than true, not because they tell us dragons exist, but because they tell us dragons can be beaten.'"

She jutted her chin at the scrunch of material Temeke had in his hand. "What's that on the quilt?"

There was a brown stain on the topside, streaking outwards in two wide smears. At first glance, it looked like a rough sketch of a bird with outstretched wings.

Temeke took another lungful of smoke and exhaled loudly. "It's where the killer wiped the axe."

THIRTY-ONE

It was an icebox of an apartment, nothing more than a studio with a tiny trundle bed in one corner and a stove in the other. Malin tried to keep the disgust from her face, tried not to flinch at the stench of stale cigarette smoke, tried not to put herself above the old lady who squinted through a pair of blue-rimmed glasses.

Tess had been gone three days and not one phone call. Not one clue. Not one witness. Until now.

It was ten after nine in the morning according to a digital clock on the mantelshelf and there was a roaring wind outside. The front door faced a large parking lot and, by the look of the gap in the door, most of that wind streaked in beneath it.

Edna was a tiny woman, no more than five foot tall, no more than sixty, with swollen ankles stuffed into a pair of pink furry slippers. "Rank and name?" she insisted.

Malin watched Temeke fumble in his pocket for an ID and stick it under her nose. It wasn't long before a kettle was singing on the stove. Edna dropped one tea bag in a cup and drowned it with boiling water, dipping the same bag between three mugs before flinging it in the vague vicinity of the bin.

Temeke leaned closer to Malin and whispered, "Hello… either there's stale water in that pot or Edna's boiling her drawers."

Malin stifled a smile and refused to react to Temeke's raised eyebrow. That dry sense of humor was hardly appropriate in such spartan surroundings and she knew she'd start giggling if she let herself.

"You heard he died," Edna said, walking back with a tray. "Heart attack, they said. I didn't believe it for a minute. More like indigestion."

"Who died?" Temeke said.

"Alan Barnes. He was a good man." Edna brushed a small cactus plant out of the way with the edge of the tray before putting it down on the coffee table. She handed Temeke a mug. "Used to work for district nineteen."

Temeke knotted his brows. "Oh no, not Senator 'Lucky' Barnes. I heard he keeled over on the golf course in the summer. Can't have been indigestion."

"No, not him," she said, shuffling to her chair. "Alan. My husband. He used to clip their hedges. You know, those big ones outside the Round House. Course they're not like that now."

"Oh," Temeke said, winking at Malin and handing her a mug. "*That* Alan Barnes."

"Muffin?" Edna said, pointing at a plate on the tray.

Temeke shook his head and a raised hand. "You've been keeping up with the news, I take it?"

"That poor girl. Patti, they said her name was. She was headline news. More like *deadline* news."

"Tell me about the man you saw, the one at the school," he said.

"Big." Edna's hand hovered over the muffin plate. "Like you."

Not that tall then, thought Malin. But then anything must have been tall to her. Temeke was, what... five foot ten? Slim build though bulked out with muscle. The more she thought of that muscle the more she hated herself. Liking a married man wasn't right. But then

221

again, nothing in her life had been right. Until now.

"About what time was that?" Temeke said.

"Just before four o'clock. My granddaughter had detention after school. Often does."

Malin wrapped her hands around the mug hardly hearing the questions Temeke asked. At least the tea was hot, only she couldn't drink it. The rim smelled of moldy old rags and as for the muffins, at least one had grown a beard.

Edna merely peeled off the blue gingham liner of her second muffin, stuffing it between two cracked lips and chewed for a time. The glasses she wore were well past their prescription, judging by the look of that squint.

"So what was he doing?" Temeke took a sip of his tea, made a face and promptly replaced the mug on the tray.

"Waiting by the crossing like he was looking for someone. And then he spotted her."

"Who?"

"That Patti. She didn't hug him or say hello. But she smiled a lot, shy like, you know."

"And then what happened?"

Edna cupped a hand over her ear and leaned over the coffee table.

"And then what happened?" Temeke repeated, raising his voice a little. He took out a cigarette and waved it at her. She nodded and they both lit up.

"They got in his car," Edna said, blowing a spray of crumbs and smoke down a fair isle cardigan. "It was disgusting."

"What was?"

"Put his arm round the back of her seat and kissed her on the mouth. Made me feel sick. He was old enough to be her dad. I'm telling you, those cops have no business picking up girls."

"What made you think he was a cop?" Temeke said,

pulling his chair a little closer.

"It was the car."

"Could you tell me the model?"

"It was black, fast looking."

Temeke drew on his cigarette and blew smoke out of the corner of his mouth. "What happened after that?"

"They drove right past me," she said, eyes shifting about as if she followed her thoughts. "I didn't like to stare."

Temeke turned to Malin and gave her a wink and then used one of the abandoned muffin liners as an ashtray.

"What was he wearing?"

Edna shrugged and stared long and hard at her muffin.

"Jeans, shirt, hat?" Malin asked, trying to jog her memory.

Edna looked at her and shook her head. "Had one of them pictures on his head. Can't have had a hat on if I saw that."

Temeke flashed Malin a look, one that conveyed the old lady wasn't as blind as she was letting on. "A tattoo?" he said. "How big was it?"

"Big enough. Looked like a circle and something else. Had a chain one on his arm."

A Celtic knot, thought Malin, wondering why the man was out in the freezing cold in nothing but a flimsy t-shirt, showing off more than his livelihood. A man who looked nothing like a regular cop.

"Edna, did you notice anything else unusual?" Malin asked.

"A kid came out of the school wearing a ram's head and riding a toilet plunger. Creepy if you ask me."

"No, I mean about the man."

Edna wiped her mouth and took a sip of tea. "Did this man do something bad?"

Temeke dropped the remainder of his cigarette in his tea and went to stand against the mantle. He seemed to study an old antique jar. "We're just trying to find out who he is, Mrs. Barnes. Nothing to worry about. How long have you had this?"

Edna merely peered over the rim of her glasses and raised one eyebrow.

"Retirement gift from Governor Bendish," she said. "Worth a buck or two. There's some toffee inside if you want some."

Temeke took a couple and walked back to his chair. "You said you used to be a composite artist?"

Edna nodded and took a slip of paper from her cardigan pocket, unfolded it and slapped it on the table between them. "This is him," she said, jabbing a pudgy finger on the drawing. It revealed a faint smile in the finely chiseled mouth and eyes that seemed to contradict the expression.

Temeke popped the candy in his mouth. He stared and blinked. And stared again. He seemed to chew for a while and then eased the toffee from his back teeth with a finger. "Sitting there for a long time, were you?"

"I can do them in five minutes." Edna stuffed her cigarette in the cactus pot and stared into space.

"Are you sure that's him?"

"One hundred and fifty percent sure. Can't get any surer than that. There was something else…"

Temeke leaned forward in his chair, nostrils quivering like a pointer. And when that *something else* never came he said, "What else?"

"Darned if I can remember."

"So you'd recognize him again if you saw him."

"Oh, yes. Handsome. Nice eyes."

"Thank you for the tea, Mrs. Barnes," Temeke said, lifting himself out of the chair and grabbing the sketch. "We should be going."

Malin left her card on the table, feeling uneasy as she watched the old lady fumble for the door. She had good eyesight; that much was certain.

Temeke's cell phone made a loud clattering sound in its plastic holster and he was already frowning at the screen.

"It's cold outside," he said to Edna, not bothering to cover up a yawn. "Be sure to lock your door."

He rushed toward the car, phone pressed against his ear. Malin heard the loud expletive, saw the look on his face. She wanted to run after him but Edna was right behind her, fingers wrapped around her arm.

"You're a pretty one." Edna jerked a thumb at Malin's face. "You better lock your door and all."

"I'll be OK," Malin heard herself say as she patted her holster. "I can look after myself."

"That's what it was," Edna said, slapping her thigh. "He was packed too."

That's when Malin paused, felt the cold wind against her cheeks and heard a faint buzzing in her ears. "He had a gun?"

"In his waistband."

"Like a cop?"

Edna shook her head. "Slipped down the back of his pants like he was hiding it."

"Thank you," said Malin, trying to keep the tremor from her voice as she walked toward the car.

"Next time, I'll bake a cake," Edna shouted, before shuffling back inside her apartment.

Malin faked a smile as she hauled herself into the driver's seat and slammed the door. "Who was on the phone?"

She heard the hammering of her heart against her rib cage, heard the desperate hitch to her voice.

"They found Luis in the northeast heights." Temeke lowered his head and stared at his hands. "In a ditch.

Bullet grazed the side of his head and nearly took his ear off. No sign of his car. No sign of Tess Williams."

THIRTY-TWO

Ole looked at the girl on the bed, dark and delicious like the coffee he had in his hand. Sitting astride a wheel-back chair, he rested his cup on the top rail and listened to her breathing. It wasn't late. It was just dark.

The urge to be caught was becoming stronger every day and he left clues, like a trail of crumbs in the dirt. He listened to the snow dropping from the gutters and the intermittent drip of water. It reminded him of ringing bells. He wanted to sing then.

Untouchable. That's what he was. No one would find him in the hunter's cabin. No one knew it was there.

He'd dreamed last night of bright lights like dragon's eyes blinking in the darkness. It was all he could do to shield his face when the lights grew brighter, like the blaze of sun and moon. He saw trees burning and then guttering out, leaving a misty trail along the ground. And he knew what it meant.

It was Odin's calling.

With a deep voice, be began to sing.

The hardy Norseman's house of yore,
Was on the foaming wave!
And there he gathered bright renown,
The bravest of the brave.
Oh! ne'er should we forget our sires,
Wherever we may be;

They bravely won a gallant name,
And rul'd the stormy sea.

The girl's eyes blinked open, face inclined to his voice. Illuminated by a silvery moon through an open window, she reminded him of a Botticelli angel.

It must have taken her a while to focus, eyes flicking around the room, settling first on the door and then back to him. There was a deep-seated fear behind them as if she was scraping together every last scrap of courage.

What tho our pow'r be weaker now
Than it was wont to be,
When boldly forth our fathers sail'd,
And conquer'd Normandie!
We still may sing their deeds of fame,
In thrilling harmony;
For they did win a gallant name
And rul'd the stormy sea.

When he finished, her eyes narrowed and she tucked her knees up against her chest. A mild breeze came in through the open window and he watched her pull down the arms of that thick black sweater.

"Where are we?" she asked.

He thought it was a respectful question, the way she included him, and dipped his head. After all, most girls stared wildly around the room as if he would sooner hurt them than talk. That always made him angry. He wasn't frightening to look at. Quite the contrary.

"Cimarron," he said, realizing his voice was taut, words slow and sharp. He saw her look at the photographs on a chest of drawers, the ones he'd taken from her house. She would feel at home now. With her sister.

"You're not a police officer, are you?"

Ole smiled slightly. "It's a shameless disguise. Hardly original, is it?"

"No," she said, looking down at her boots. "Are you the man that took my sister?"

"I am." Ole found himself staring at her, drinking in those deep brown eyes. She was a very brave girl. "It was you I wanted. You probably want something to eat." Her eyes seemed to widen at that.

"May I have a sandwich, sir?" she said.

The voice struck him as reverent, humble. What was it about her that made him want to hesitate. To delay.

"Call me Ole."

"Well, Mr. Ole, I'm sure glad to meet you."

And she held out her hand. Just like that. A beautiful brown hand he really wanted to shake. He remembered what he was and ducked his head instead. Shouldn't touch the angels and dirty them. Odin wouldn't like that.

He studied the sparkle in those brown eyes where there was only a hint of white in each corner. Perhaps she would like to know about the ravens. Who wouldn't want to know about the ravens?

"Do you know about the ravens?" he said, feeling more content than he had been in days.

She didn't flinch. She merely cocked her head to one side as if she could hear better. "No," she said, trembling a little. It was the cold because he knew she wasn't afraid.

"Odin gave them names. *Thought* and *Memory*. They were his eyes, his mind, flying out at dawn and coming back at dusk. They knew every man's whisper, every man's dream. That's why Odin's so wise. But there's always a price to pay. Mimir knew what that price was. And so will you. That's why you're here."

"Who's Odin?"

A voice so perfect, something in the diction. Like the children in Scandinavia. Sophisticated. A cut above the rest.

"He's the god of creation." Even as he said it, he felt a flutter in his belly.

"No," she murmured. "That's not his name. It's Yahweh. You know, our Father, who art in heaven. Remember?"

She smiled when she said it. Like God was a movie star or something.

"He made us in his image. He made you," she said. "In fact you probably look just like Him. Same chin, same eyes, same nose. Only a little smaller."

Ole felt himself smile. It came from somewhere deep inside. A gushing, like the curtain of snow that had just begun to flicker outside in the darkness. It caught his attention for a brief moment and he turned to the window, setting the cup of coffee on the sill. He saw each flake bigger than he ever remembered them.

Whiter.

That's when he remembered the horse his father used to ride when he went hunting. Glidehoof... that was his name. There wasn't a drop of gray on him, not even on his muzzle. He was like a ghost in the snow.

He loved his old papa and the gentle shake in his hands. He wasn't perfect. Ole wasn't perfect. Not even close, not with a heart blacker than the coal mines of Svalbard. "Why is there so much hate in here?" he said, pumping his chest with a fist. "Why am I so different?"

"Adam messed up," Tess said. "That's when everyone's hearts turned black. Mine. Yours."

He found himself staring at the angel on his bed. His little Botticelli angel. She would have to fly away soon. He didn't believe in what she believed. All fairy tales. Lies. If he told her the words would only come out of his mouth in a foul drivel, a tiger's snarl, and he wished he could articulate his feelings in the same perfect way she did.

It made his intestines twist and boil. Like the snake in his mind, black and yellow with stripes around its head. And where was Odin? That unseen ghost of a god that promised Morgan his life.

He wanted to tell Tess all about Kizzy, how she used to sing. It was a hymn come to think of it. Something about walking by faith and not by sight.

All he remembered of that night was how he'd thrown up after he killed her. Couldn't stop. Why was it so harrowing to do what he was born to do? Kill.

"Please may I have something to eat, sir?" Tess said, cutting into his thoughts again. Smiling.

Ole smiled back. She said *please*, didn't she?

He knew once he'd left the room she would pace around like a lioness, looking through the window at a thick wall of trees and wondering if it was worth the jump. If he took his time, she'd be out faster than a cat from a burning house. The thought excited him.

He locked the door and rushed down the stairs to the kitchen. If she jumped, that tender young mind would be the most resourceful yet. Only she'd break a leg if she did.

That's why he had stuffed her in the trunk and would have forgotten about her if it wasn't for her moaning. She could barely walk when he took her out, had to lift her up the stairs into the bedroom. Pity he left that tight metal chain behind. It would have been handy if only he'd thought to bring it.

It reminded him of Patti just after she had tried to run away with the little one. He'd locked her in the downstairs bathroom and he could still hear her crying if he listened for long enough, like a distant scream of wind in a lonely tree. But she wasn't there. She wasn't sitting on the floor leaning against the sink, rope grinding around the pedestal each time she moved.

He stood in the kitchen remembering those pale eyes,

still beautiful behind a curtain of dark hair. She wanted him to stay with her, kiss her. He had said no to both. But when he saw those lips, sweet and honeyed with tears, he bent down and kissed them and he heard the tender voice against his ear.

"Untie me... please. I won't run away."

He wanted to hold her and feel her skin against his. He wanted to believe what she said. They had once had common thoughts, common dreams. She was the only palpable loving creature he knew.

"Later," he said, running a finger beneath her chin, sensing a breath of turmoil.

He left her in the dark, left her to a welter of tears.

No point dreaming of the dead, he thought. No point feeling... what was he feeling? Couldn't put it into words even if he tried.

Standing in front of the kitchen counter, he pasted a ball of peanut butter on a single slice of bread. Reaching for the bottle in the cupboard above, he prized apart the two yellow capsules, sprinkling the powder liberally before folding the bread in two. The hatchet leaned against the wall, head and shaft drop-forged from one piece of steel. Brand new.

He had to do it. And quickly.

He lifted his head at a grating sound, heard his car keys rattle on a nearby hook, intermittent, like the chattering of teeth. Footfalls, slipping, sliding and then something smashed on the pavers below. A tile.

Tess was on the roof.

Ole grabbed a gut-hook hunting knife – it was all he could find – and rushed up the stairs to the bedroom. It was bathed in an iron-gray pall from the moon, bedspread rumpled where she had once been. There was no sign of her. He didn't expect there to be. When he leaned out of the window he saw a limping shadow rushing for the trees, heading west toward a stand of maple before barreling through a thicket.

He followed her as far as the thicket, hunching low as he slipped through it, sniffing the air and listening. She was about thirty yards to the north of him, he could hear the snapping twigs, the screech of a bird that lifted into the sky. She was unstoppable, immortal, tearing off like a great black dog with wild eyes and gritted teeth.

She was fast, although there was no reason to assume she was as fast as he was. Large hamstrings, thighs like a tree branch, he was designed for speed and stamina. It was the latter that saved him from the hunter, the one that killed his brother. He ran three long miles back then without stopping.

Here he was under a wintry light, feet crunching through snow and detritus, drifting rather than running. He felt the chill through his shirt, creeping down his spine like a thousand tiny spiders.

Beyond an array of tree stumps where woodsmen had once felled over fifty trees, the ruins of a second cabin loomed ash gray in a clearing. Out of the darkness to the right side, came the girl, walking slowly along the margin of the trees toward the front door. In the windless night he could see the vapors pouring from her mouth and he could almost hear a pounding heart.

Her face was radiant, unearthly, looking on the world with her extraordinary eyes. Nothing could prevent its true nature from sparkling through, a guiltless face well suited to smiles and laughter. He could imagine a face like that painted in the vaulted ceiling of the Sistine Chapel. It was painted in the frescoes of the papal conclave and if you looked hard enough it was in Perugino's painting of Moses, if indeed an angel could ever be a young girl.

As she moved toward the cabin, toward the freakishly black shadows beyond the front door, her chin went up, moving from side to side. If she was a dog, her ears would be flattened against her head, nose quivering at a scent.

The only scent he could sense was old creosote and rotting timbers, and the room was crowded with cobwebs and shadows. He was surprised she even considered going in. But she did, pushing back the door with one hand, bolts grinding in their knuckles.

Ole eased around the back of the cabin and as long as he remained low, he could watch her through the grimy windows, marveling at the icy beam that shone through the hole in the roof. She found the matches he had left over three months ago and the metal lantern.

An orange glow seeped around the abandoned house, bringing the old place alive again, giving it a warmth it hadn't seen for over thirty years. It reminded Ole of Norway with the snow and pine trees, swirling around the house like a snow globe. Only this time, he was on the outside.

He felt a lump in his throat and shook his head, sensing a few cold drops down his nose. The nose she said was the same as God's. Because he was made in His image.

Surely, no man was made in one image. Men were strong and brilliant. Weren't they unique?

Convinced she had spotted him, he took a step back, twigs snapping under foot. He saw her hesitate, but only for a moment, face turned to a fresh shower of snow that fell like a crystalline screen outside the window.

Did she smile? He wasn't sure. And then he heard it, softly at first as her lips moved.

Singing.

His arms were speckled with gooseflesh. The voice wasn't so different from the first time he heard it. A little older, as if Kizzy had come back. Yes, risen from the dead. She twirled in a tumbled down kitchen, arms out, chin snapping around like a ballet dancer. He'd never seen anything so odd.

She should have been terrified, but there wasn't a tremor on those fragile limbs, not even a limp. She was quite beautiful and for a moment he was transfixed, feeling a wrenching in his gut. It wasn't a throw-up wrenching. Something different.

It had to be the drugs he had given her in the car. Not much, just a little chaser before the final dose. He'd never seen one wake up. He'd never seen one survive.

Her gaze slid away from the window, traveling briefly over the furniture before resting on the mantle. She brushed a hand over the old wooden ledge, and those same fingers toyed with a glass bottle, eyes narrowed at the embossed lettering. It gave him a sense of foreboding, a fear he hadn't had since childhood.

She was leaving tracks. Fingerprints.

Holding his breath, he was faced with the mindboggling possibility that this girl might be smarter than most. She had to have known he was there.

Striding through waist high grass to a stone projection, the back side of a fireplace, he saw a second window. Through a single broken pane, he saw her muted figure shimmered against the wall, back pressed against it, face turned toward the front door. In her hand was a rusty knife she must have found on the mantle shelf.

Clever girl, he thought.

She waited.

So did he.

He was invisible in the darkness; that's when he let his mind wander to the past. Many years ago there would have been a fire in the grate, a crackle of blood-red flames and the smell of soot. Tonight he imagined a white-haired father sitting on a three-legged stool, trembling hands cupped around a bowl of soup. On the floor in front of him two little boys, chins turned up, eyes rapt at the legends of Odin and Glidehoof.

He didn't understand this sudden rash of emotions, the sadness, the pleasure, the fear. It must have been the moon shining in his eyes, and while he was puzzling over it he saw a flicker on the opposite wall.

The girl was gone. Quick as spit.

He staggered for the front of the cabin. It was deserted, door half open just as she had left it. He turned for an instant to survey the clearing, throat rougher than a carpenter's bench. He refused to cough. It would only alert her to where he was.

An open stretch of ground led to a knot of trees and a steep downward slope. Adrenalin shot through him and his feet shuffled forward, confused suddenly at the direction she might have taken. He ran full-pelt for the woods until the trees covered him from the moonlight.

Looking left and right, he sniffed the air keeping a sharp eye out for any sign of movement. He knew he could keep going for hours, alternating between walking and jogging, and pausing only to check for tracks.

Then he heard a noise. Sobbing? No. Panting. He saw her a few yards ahead, bent over to catch her breath.

Standing between two young pine trees, he pulled the knife from his belt. Every movement was in his muscle-memory; it was the same every time. A round, smooth swing and he let the knife fly.

THIRTY-THREE

Temeke held Serena in his arms, felt her tears on his neck, felt the warmth from a crackling fire against the back of his legs. He was too tired to talk and there was nothing to say.

Luis was unconscious. Suspected brain damage. With the departure of a friend ended the laughter that echoed in the pubs on Southern Boulevard. Temeke learned for the first time in his life the true meaning of loneliness.

His heart felt like it would burst out of his chest and he wondered how Luis survived with no food, just sucking on a trickle of water for four days. He was particularly partial to a good chicken pie and now all he had was tubes.

"He could have died," she said.

"But he didn't." Temeke buried his face into her thick, black hair, holding back a sob. "And he won't."

"I want to see him."

"They won't let us. Not for another week." Temeke slowly released a deep breath. At least Luis' spirit wasn't climbing into the sky in ever widening circles. At least he wasn't sitting on a cloud in the winter sun. "He's sleeping, my love. Getting his strength back."

"What if he can't feel. What if he can't see, can't hear? What if he never wakes up?"

"He's strong," Temeke said, wiping the tears from her eyes with his thumb. "He'll wake up."

He kissed her mouth and her cheeks, listening to the purr of her voice. And then came the pounding in his chest, a dull roar, a sound so loud that it seemed to fill all his senses. He tried to ignore it, tried to take no notice of the hissing in his veins. Throb, throb, throb, almost drowning in a roll of excitement.

He felt her go rigid, pushing away. She walked up the stairs, a wadded up tissue in those shaking hands. She'd be like that for a time, all nervous and distant. He wanted to call out to her, to follow her. All he could do was open and close his mouth, struggling to find the right words.

That same old feeling again. It never really went away, the need for peace, the need for a smoke. He snapped on a pair of latex gloves and walked outside to the back yard to the downspout. He always felt like a gynecologist when rooting through a knot of rosemary before slipping his fingers in the pipe. Today he felt nothing but an empty space. He tasted a trickle of hot bile in his throat and nearly gagged.

Someone had taken it.

The phone in his pocket began to vibrate and he could see Hackett's name flashing on the screen. "How's Serena?"

Temeke started back toward the house. "Holding up."

"Temeke, if you need—"

"I need to get back out there, sir. That's what I need."

Temeke heard the loud sigh through the earpiece. He wondered if Hackett had had a change of heart, wanted to give him a few days off. Temeke knew how Jarvis and Fowler muttered to themselves in a language exclusive only to them, how they turned their faces to the wall every time he passed. Suspicious of strangers, they turned all outsiders into outcasts. Hackett was no different.

Unless Fowler's team really had missed something

out there at the Shelby ranch. Something they hoped to pin on him…

"Looks like you're stuck with me, sir," Temeke dared, listening to silence on the other end as if Hackett had suddenly choked at the idea.

Hackett wouldn't take him off the case. He couldn't. Someone higher had requested him and there was nothing Hackett could do about it.

"We've got another body," Hackett muttered. "The red-headed realtor. Seems she wasn't on that nice cruise ship after all. You find Tess Williams, I'll deal with this mess. I mean it, Temeke, you foul up on this one and it's your last!"

"Yes, sir. My last, sir."

Hackett blew a chunk of air into the mouthpiece. "I sent Malin over to see Darryl Williams. Seems like he's taking it like a trooper."

"Like a trooper?" Temeke echoed, glad to be back on the case.

"Yeah, he says she's a tough one that Tess. Says she can run faster than a hockey puck. Oh, and just in case you were wondering, no, she never talked about running away and no, she wasn't unhappy at home. Just thought you'd want to know."

"Appreciate it, sir."

Temeke heard a scraping sound from upstairs, the chest of drawers being dragged across the floor. He felt the muscles quivering in his neck, heat flushing through his body. It weighed a ton and how in the hell Serena managed to move it he'd never know.

"The Imaging Specialist called," Hackett continued. "They cleaned up the video outside Cibola High. Our man was wearing a black t-shirt and jeans. He was wearing a full harness. Looked like a cop, probably smelled like a cop. We found the Camaro. It was pulled out of the river just south of Alameda this morning. Had a few holes in the rear side panel. I'll leave you to guess what he's driving now.

"Luis' Charger?"

"He took a whole lot more than that. Stu Anderson remembered seeing a Remington in the trunk. Unfortunately his tiny little brain couldn't tell us what caliber it was."

It was Temeke's turn to sigh. "Least it's not a Mauser, sir. They take stripper clips."

"Listen, I don't care if he's got a dozen hand grenades and a bazooka in there. Find him."

"I will, sir."

"Becky's conscious, by the way. I expect you'll want to see her, but I don't think it's appropriate. So I sent Malin instead."

"Appropriate, sir?"

"Becky described a house on Arroyo Del Oso. Couldn't remember anything else. She did remember a set of golf clubs in the hallway."

"I'll get over there, sir."

"You better get some underpants on over those tights, son. We're dealing with more than just your average bed-wetter."

"Send a car for me, will you?"

"Get your own car," Hackett said. "Oh, I forgot. You don't have one."

The phone was already dead by the time Temeke had formulated an answer sprinkled with a few choice words.

Driving down Alameda toward 2nd Street, he felt a hardening in his stomach and a burning in his chest, especially driving Serena's yellow Scion IQ. He felt somehow cheated, like he'd been sold half a car. But it went like the clappers and that's what mattered.

Where would a guy like Ole Eriksen hang out? He had a working knowledge of the upper-crust lifestyle and gripped a putter on the golf course rather than a jug in the pub.

The phone trilled in his pocket and he almost missed the turn trying to pull it out. It was Malin.

"Sir, we need to talk."

"If it's about Darryl being oddly calm, he's probably been drinking some of that homemade hooch. I smelled it on his breath last time I saw him."

"Can't blame him, sir. But he mentioned life, death, that kind of thing. So I called his doctor. They've put him on suicide watch. Captain Fowler's got a team of officers over there to monitor all incoming calls."

"Well good. Because if he tries to hang himself, they'll book him first."

"Sir..."

He could hear the hesitation in her voice. She was itching to tell him something, only the phone was tapped.

"Still nothing on Tess Williams," she said at last. "They found Kelly Caldwell in the Cerro Colorado Landfill this afternoon. The doctor said she'd been strangled and her lungs were full of chlorinated water. I've already notified the family. Another thing, sir. The Camaro was found in the Rio Grande. There was a briefcase in the trunk full of photos, all young girls."

"Our victims?"

"Yes, sir. And there was one of a redhead said to be Kelly. Looks like she was walking down the street and he took it from behind."

"So she didn't know she was being photographed."

"Right. Thing is, there's a building in the background, pink stucco with blue trim. Looks like the Arroyo Del Oso clubhouse."

"I'm there," said Temeke, taking a screeching right turn on 2nd Street before she could protest.

Twenty minutes later, he was standing in the clubhouse, one hand on the granite reception desk, the other holding his ID. The man behind the counter was well dressed and hungry looking, and the badge on his lapel read Emilio Vargas.

"Looking for a member of yours, a Mr. Ole Eriksen," Temeke said.

Vargas laced his hands together and cracked every knuckle. His fingers hovered over the computer keyboard before tapping in the name. He shook his head. "Don't see an Ol*a* Eriksen," he said, smiling.

"Oliver Eriksen?" Temeke insisted.

Again Vargas shook his head. "Not listed I'm afraid."

"How about Morgan Eriksen?"

This time Vargas hesitated, eyes running down the computer screen and stopping, so Temeke noted, at the halfway point.

"We did have a Morgan Eriksen, only his membership expired last month. Nice man. Great tipper." He grinned until Temeke spoke.

"When did you last see him?"

Vargas scratched his chin, eyes flicking to the floor. "He came in for lunch about a week ago. He was with a woman, well dressed. They left about mid-afternoon just when I finished my shift. Walked up the street to a stone house on the corner. The one with the statue of an angel by the front door."

"How much did he tip you that day?" Temeke had to ask. That's why Vargas watched Eriksen as he walked up the street. Probably stalked him and all.

Vargas splayed ten fingers on the counter, then gave a sly smile and tapped his nose.

"A hundred bucks?" Temeke said loudly. "See what you mean."

He laid the photograph down on the countertop and scooted it toward Vargas' red and sweating face. He heard the man clear his throat, saw him nod.

"Yes, that's him."

Temeke mouthed his thanks and pushed through the clubhouse door and out into the parking lot. Unfortunately, the photograph was of Morgan, but like all the others he had shown it to, it was close enough. His eyes darted in all directions behind dark glasses and he decided to take a stroll up the street to the stone house with the angel.

The statue was large all right, set to the left side of the front door. Lips pursed and cheeks round, it looked as if the poor cherub was about to blow out a mouthful of food.

Temeke pulled on the latex and rang the bell. He waited a few seconds, rang it again and counted to ten. Rang it a third time and took a hike around the back. Heaving himself over a wall, he landed in a courtyard of cherry trees and artificial grass.

Sunlight trickled down between the branches and an edgy wind ruffled cattails, some crowned with shards of glass from a broken window. There was a six-foot chain lying on the ground, equipped with bolt pin shackles.

He cocked his pistol and hesitated for a while behind a tall, skinny spruce, surveying the perimeter. The first thing he noticed was the sliding patio door, blinds closed to the winter sun.

He jogged sideways across the lawn toward the house and pressed his ear to the wooden frame. Jiggling the handle up and down a few times to loosen the lock, he was inside the house in less than four seconds. He parted the blinds with the muzzle of his gun.

To the right was the kitchen and to the left was the sitting room with a high ceiling, running to the front of the house. He froze in the darkness, smelling the tart fragrance of a lighted air freshener. It was the only light there was.

A strong smell of gasoline seeped in from a lit garage and Temeke stared into an empty space. There was no sign of a car, only the imprint of tire treads on a light gray floor. Three cans of gasoline stood against the wall and he saw a set of oily marks where there had been at least seven more.

He inched back into the kitchen and examined the sink. Empty. No dirty plates. There were three take-out boxes in the fridge, a bottle of white wine and a gallon jug of milk. The owner clearly dined out. The knife block was full and there was another of those fat Santa incense burners on the countertop.

In one of the kitchen drawers was a neat stack of closing papers from Desert Sun Properties, all signed by Ole Eriksen.

"Bingo," Temeke muttered, flicking through the first few pages.

Tucked behind the first stack was a buff file labeled *Freedom CSP*. There were photographs of dark girls, laughing girls, dead girls, and a log cabin in a wood. He slipped the picture of the cabin in his jacket pocket and crept around the corner in the direction of the hall.

His confidence seemed to rise with every step. He knew he was alone, felt no other presence. The stairs were partially lit by a picture window, looking out on the golf course and the Sandia Mountains. The blinds were turned downward, letting in only a thin sliver of light.

The master bedroom door was equipped with enough hardware to keep a person prisoner and the back of it appeared to be slightly scuffed where metal scraped against paint. There was a small stain on the carpet, possibly blood, and Temeke visualized a small girl hunched on the floor after banging against the door in the hopes of freeing herself.

The room was smaller than he expected, bedspread drawn back, sheets starched white except for a small smear of blood on the right side of the bed. There were scuffs on the bedhead as if something had been tied there.

He looked out of the window. Trees and streaks of blue sky broke between the branches, and he could see the roofs of other houses. When he thought hard enough a visual came to mind. This was the only view both Patti and Becky had.

The bathroom was devoid of toiletries and the facecloth in the shower was dry. The thermostat had been set at 68 degrees and if Ole showered each day, he had to have been gone more than two days.

Temeke found the rest of the house to be untouched and rushed down the stairs to the front door. He called in the location and told Hackett he was coming back to the station.

It was a lie. He was going north on I-25. *CSP...* the only thing he could think of was Cimarron State Park. It was littered with camping sites and a few dilapidated cabins. He took a deep breath in the driveway, smelling pine needles and fresh exhaust from a passing car.

He called Malin and got her on the first ring. "Where are you?"

"Arroyo Del Oso," she said.

"You don't waste any time, do you?"

"No, sir. I figured you'd be at the clubhouse."

He caught the amusement in her voice and just as he made headway down the street, he saw her car in the parking lot.

"Call Captain Fowler, will you?" he shouted, before snapping his phone shut. "Tell him to pick up my wife's car."

"He's in a meeting with Hackett, sir. So is Jarvis. They're waiting for you."

"I've got better things to do than drink tea and have small talk with Hackett."

"Where are we going, sir?"

Temeke didn't wait to answer. He took off his jacket

CLAIRE STIBBE

and harness, replacing both with a bulletproof vest and a duty belt, and he told Malin to do the same. Checking his gun, he sniffed the air.

"We're going to take a hike, love. And we're going to see exactly what Captain Fowler missed."

THIRTY-FOUR

Ole pulled the knife from a tree. Actually missed. It was a first for him.

He watched her through tired eyes, running with a speed that matched his own. She wasn't yielding. Not yet. And if she knew he was there, she was doing a grand job of hiding it.

And then, an exotic gem of a moment. She paused and looked around at the drab landscape, lost in her own world. She didn't understand she was in his territory, that he could so easily kill her just because she was there.

Such curiosity. Such bravery.

He wanted to capture her, own her. He wanted to wreathe her with the final visions of earth and stars. Take his knife and finish it. All that hovered around this girl was the last struggle of life. Then her soul would be just ashes. And he would feel alive.

Even though he no longer heard Odin's immense voice, he still felt that aching chill reminding him of what he must do.

So why did he hesitate?

Because her body wasn't limp like the others, wasn't drugged and lifeless so that he could whisper the Norse songs as she fell asleep. This one was running through a snarl of branches toward the river.

All of a sudden he was Glidehoof, racing in the

shimmering snow. Faster now, thundering between the trees, seeing a burst of flesh here and there, dark flesh that would very soon meld with the shadows. If he wasn't careful, he would lose her in this riparian woodland.

Whatever she saw on her journey, whatever she felt, she had no idea how precious this moment was. How it would never happen again in quite the same way.

Almost there, almost smelling the sweat on her dark, wet skin. Only a few more seconds and she would be his.

He lost sight of her again, lost track and scent of her. Odd, he had a trace on her a moment ago, caught a distinct sense she was behind that tree, the one with a cloud colored trunk.

When he reached forward, knife poised at her shoulder, she suddenly darted to one side, pushing through the underbrush like a skittish deer. He teetered on the tips of his feet, hand reaching out for that sycamore. In all his years as a hunter, he had never seen quarry move so fast.

A dark chill ran through him as he stood there panting. She was heading for the river, heading for the ice.

For a while he couldn't speak, couldn't think, banishing all thoughts of escape from his mind. It didn't matter that he couldn't see her out there. What mattered more was that he could sense her, searching, hungry for a way out.

He slipped the knife in his belt and started running again, tearing through a far-reaching expanse of grass to the restless river where winter had locked the banks in ice. The ancient fir trees towered over him, dark and sinister against a bleak sky, and the water glinted like an egret's wing.

There she was, thirty feet away, foot tapping away at

a thin layer of ice.

"Don't do it," Ole shouted, holding up both hands.

The water was shallow there, only a trickle and he saw her lift her head, eyeing him with those same mystical eyes.

He threw off the mood, becoming the dispassionate killer once more, edging toward her with a measured step. "Where is your God now, Tessie? Where is he?"

"Right here," she said, finger pointing toward her foot as if someone actually stood there.

Ole narrowed his eyes to the meandering streams, cutting around sandbanks and surging onwards with the current. He couldn't see anyone.

"Come on, Tessie. You can't love a phantom. And I know you're scared. He can't help you with that."

There was a tremor in her lips if he wasn't mistaken, a spasm in her arms. She backed up a few steps, wincing at the icy water around her ankles.

Her head turned toward the river, thinking perhaps how long she had, how she could rush to the other side and be buffeted to death by the cliffs. But the mud would suck her down and those heavy shoes she wore wouldn't help her one bit.

Only ten feet from her now, he reached out, fingers stretched. "Give me your hand," he whispered, tilting his head to one side.

That was the look women couldn't resist. Before they were gouged, broken and shattered, that is.

"You must be a lonely man," she said, panting slightly. "Are you lonely?"

Ole felt a shrinking in his breast, reminding him of the grotesque thing he was, a fading fragment of a man. "Lonely?" he said, feeling a tightening at his temples.

"Afraid then."

Now that was downright stupid. How could he be afraid? He was the one that chased after frightened and hunted things because he had been frightened and hunted himself. It didn't mean he was afraid. Not until she mentioned it.

"I won't be afraid," she said, teeth chattering. "Perfect love drives out fear."

He paused for a moment, wondering how she managed to dredge up these powerful words. Was she in love with him? Was that what she said?

His legs felt suddenly crippled and bent, so cold they would snap if he tried to move them. What was wrong with him? He had once been adept at netting girls to add to Odin's collection. He had once been impervious to the cold. This one was number nine.

The very last one. The one he should have snatched in the first place if it hadn't been for her little sister swapping places in the tent. Morgan hadn't seen that coming.

His knife could slice a grapefruit in half, or a bed sheet blowing on a clothesline. It was sharp enough to slice a branch off a sapling because he polished that blade now and then. He wanted to slide it out of his waistband, but his fingers were so cold they were powerless.

"Who is your god?" she asked.

Death, he wanted to say but his lips were trembling now. The more he thought about it, the more he realized what the change was. Odin wasn't there anymore. Like a migrating bird he had answered the call of the north, returning only with the march of the seasons.

Ole began to feel the gut-aching loneliness the girl talked about. Abandonment.

Hadn't his father abandoned him to a foster home? Hadn't Morgan abandoned him. Even his mother. He wasn't going to be at the mercy of others, wasn't going to be at the mercy of this skinny dark girl in a tartan skirt.

Even though his shirt was soaked in sweat he was cold. He couldn't remember the last time he was cold and he wondered why his bodiless spirit had slumbered all these years. Like it was dead.

He was afraid now, just as he had been after Morgan died, that poor fragile soul who floated around in the darkness because he never knew God.

Don't children go to heaven? He thought they did and suddenly he felt shunned, a thing of ridicule – not infamous, newsworthy. An evil thing that hunkered in an alley wearing a beggar's coat. He weighed it all calmly, never quite sure how his black heart ticked. His father was clothed in a mahogany casket. That's how black Ole's heart must have been.

He gripped that knife and swung in from the right, blade slicing through air and water. He was suddenly head down in the river as if embracing an icy lover. He had miscalculated, heard the tinkle of childish laughter or a shriek of fear, couldn't believe his ears. There she was edging toward the trees, boots crunching in the snow.

A gray northeast wind blew over the land, sighing over the rushing river. He turned his eyes upward just in time to see three geese dropping from the sky, a curious natural rhythm in their pulsing wings. It seemed to mimic the beat of his heart as they raced south, disappearing as mysteriously as they had arrived.

He heard the rustling of the grass as he lifted himself from the icy water, like a cripple rising from the Jordan River. Only he wasn't changed. Not like that.

He was still Ole, misshapen, grotesque Ole. That's why the girl had taken flight from something she wasn't yet able to understand.

He found the knife, felt the cold blade between his fingers, saw the sigh of warm air from his mouth. He staggered through a squelch of mud, heart pounding almost as loud as a base drum. He was excited by what he was about to do, knowing he could never undo it.

THIRTY-FIVE

Malin gripped that steering wheel, sighed and stepped on the gas. She had two choices. Either tell Temeke the car was fitted with a taping device or get her badge taken away. If she didn't bring it up, he'd know. Bound to suspect the procedure, bound to appreciate her loyalty.

They'd been talking about him again – Sarge, Fowler, Hackett, Jarvis. Saying he was a womanizer, a drug dealer. Saying he was having sex with underage girls. Saying he was probably the 9th Hour Killer all along.

Malin began to snigger. She couldn't help it. Temeke wasn't the type to go looking for sex on the Internet. He had a sensual well-bred look about him, somehow wild as if he had come straight off the African plains. Black sweatshirt imprinted with the words *If I don't like you, I'll write about you*, and a black baseball hat that seemed to give him an air of authority. They felt threatened. That's what it was.

His eyes briefly caught hers, eyebrow raised as a slow smile crept across his face. She raised her forefinger and made a wide circle. He would know what it meant.

"Thank you," he mouthed, gazing with focus.

He was probably looking around for anything new in the car, an extra telephone jack, another dial on the dashboard. It had been well over two hours since they left the hospital in Rio Rancho and he'd hardly spoken at all. Seeing Luis wrapped in tubes was bad enough. Seeing Becky and that little bruised body was somehow worse.

He was animated at a large sign to Taos, shifted around in his seat and then checked his phone. He was a shrewd man, been close to death so many times, almost expecting it, and nothing made him nervous. He was used to the dirty tricks and sleaze of law enforcement, and he operated by his own rules.

The GPS told her to bear right on NM68 at Riverside Drive and there were signs to US64 and Eagle Nest. She had no idea where the Shelby Campground Park Office was, only Temeke had called ahead before they left and asked for a ranger to wait at the gate. She reckoned on forty more minutes. Better step on it the rest of the way.

And what was that sign back there?

"Watch your speed, Marl," Temeke muttered, lifting his head up from his phone. "This isn't the Circuit of the Americas."

She eased her foot off the gas and sighed. Sometimes he made her feel inadequate and yet here she was, a raven-haired beauty. Didn't he find her just a teeny bit exquisite?

There was nothing in those black eyes to suggest she was anything at all. That's what bugged her the most. She almost gasped, panicking under her breath. If she wasn't anything to him, she had never really been anything to Hollister except a schoolboy's dare. Maybe she needed to change something. Her hair, clothes, character.

"Did we pass Paseo Del Canon?" he said.

"I think we did, sir."

"Then hang a right on Kit Carson. We'll join 64 in a few."

Malin was nervous, and sitting next to Temeke didn't

help. He hardly looked at her, hardly spoke. Just gave orders like he was a commander in the marines or something. She needed to think, only she'd done a lot of thinking in the past few days. No more men. *No more*.

Instead, she watched the palisade cliffs and the occasional waterfall that trickled down between the crags. Fir trees stood tall on their silvery verges and a full moon shed an eerie light between the branches.

"We're at eight thousand feet," Temeke said. "Want a boiled sweet?"

"Candy," Malin corrected, feeling heat in the back of her neck. She was just plain tired. "No thanks."

It had to have been the bug under the dashboard that made him quiet. He must have known it was there. Hackett could trace them through the GPS, watch their speed, listen to the conversation. Temeke couldn't exactly talk to her about anything if they were listening.

But they wanted her to talk to him, wanted as much information about that weed, or any dirt for that matter.

"You weren't always a detective, were you?" she said.

"I used to be a bell boy at the Sheraton. Multi-tasking, multi-snooping. It got me where I am today."

"So when did you start smoking weed?" she said, staring at a blank face that suddenly lit up.

"I don't smoke weed."

"C'mon, sir, everyone smokes weed."

"Ever rolled a few in your time?"

She grinned at that. "I had a friend once. Never had any money, but she always had a dime bag to sell in the toilets at school. She used to call it her *valuables*."

"As I'm sure they were," Temeke said, "especially valuable to the people she stole it from."

"She used to keep it in her compact and sell it by the lid. It was from Mexico. Burnt your throat, made you wheeze. But she'd sell it to the hard-ups for seventy bucks and pretend it was Thai."

"Sounds like she had a roaring business. Which brings me to the subject of college loans. I read somewhere you paid yours off in six months. Mexican or Thai?"

She ignored the question and changed the subject. "Do you like younger women, sir?"

She saw his body perk up, saw his eyebrows furrow. "You what?"

"Younger women," she repeated for the mic. "Do you like them?"

He stroked his throat and grimaced. "How young?"

"Well you know, sixteen, seventeen."

"Not like that."

"How young would you go?"

Temeke shrugged. "Thirty-nine."

Malin grinned. She knew he was forty-three. "Only a few years, sir?"

"For me, yeah. For Eriksen, anything goes."

Either he was trying to change the subject or he thought she wanted a man's opinion on the case. She watched the landscape changing from arid prairie to chaparral, and then to forest as the elevation increased. And then she thought of Becky. She often stood too close to Temeke in the lobby, sometimes taking him to the water fountain to whisper. Surely someone had seen?

"What about Becky Moran? She's a tight little chick in tight little clothes. Doesn't it make your blood boil?"

Temeke pressed a fist against his mouth and puffed out his cheeks. "You gotta be kidding, right?"

"No," she said, feeling a burning in her throat. "She likes you, I can tell. Wants you even."

"She's just a kid. Probably too scared to look at a man now."

"She's into older men. That's why all this happened. She wanted you, not him."

"I'm married, Marl."

"Even married men, sir. They all look. They all wonder how much they can get away with."

"Not this one. Besides, I won't be kicked out of the department for interfering with a minor. How awful would that be? I'd be homeless, hungry and sleeping down by the lavatories."

Malin felt a bubble of laughter in her belly and saw the friendly grin on his face. He was steaming now, especially for that mic.

"You know, I've always admired Hackett," Temeke said, fingers feeling beneath the dash. "I know he thinks I hate him, that I think he's an impudent swine. But it's not the case. About ten years ago, and I say it was *ten* because you'd never forget a thing like that, there was a photograph going around the department. A girl in thigh length boots, face covered in makeup, breasts covered by nothing at all. It was an old set of buttocks between that young pair of knees. And there was a mole on the left side of those buttocks."

Malin could only giggle at the bug in Temeke's hand, held close to his lips. He was going to lose his badge. There was no other answer.

"Just a little mole, about this big – just about here," Temeke said, leaning to one side and jabbing his rear with the bug. "It was Hackett alright. Dirty old git got a teenager pregnant ten years ago."

He opened the window and flicked it through the gap. That done, he pulled a packet of cigarettes from the glove compartment and placed one in his mouth.

"No one knows how he got off, Marl. I can only suspect he gave up a few pay checks. At his own request."

Malin sniggered, heard the scratch of a match before she could tell him not to light up. "Tell me what you found in that house, sir."

"I found an anchor chain and shackles in the back yard, footprints, broken glass from an upper window. Lucky she escaped. He kept her tied up like a dog. You really can't beat a white Christmas."

Malin could almost hear the clunk of chains and a dog collar around her neck. "I'd hate to be tied up, sir."

"Not into bondage then? No, can't say I would be. Especially if there weren't any slop buckets handy." Temeke tapped a photograph on the steering wheel, cigarette bouncing between his lips. "Do you know where this is?"

Malin stared briefly at the picture of an old cabin surrounded by trees. She shook her head. She hadn't a clue.

"I'm betting it's one of the hunters' cabins near the Shelby Ranch," Temeke said. "Got names like *Lucky* and *Hope*. Let's hope it's the first. Let's hope it's soon."

His last words repeated in Malin's head and she looked at Temeke with a keenness she'd never known before. He was a hunter, skilled at catching the worst of them, unraveling the complexity of an insane mind as easily as a ball of string. But now there was a desperate look on his face, like he was searching for a dark speck against a black sky. She was actually afraid.

The radio suddenly sparked into life. It was Hackett. "I want to see you both in my office tomorrow morning. Seven o'clock sharp!"

"Sorry, can't hear you," Temeke said, blowing out a salvo of smoke rings. "Bad line."

"You're as clear as a bell," Hackett contradicted. "Where are you?"

"Sounds like a crossed line," Temeke shouted. "I can hear a woman laughing in the background."

"I'd appreciate it if you could observe the correct protocols," Hackett shouted back. "You weren't at the briefing meeting this afternoon and I've been hearing complaints. Quite frankly, I'm ashamed."

"Complaints, sir? What complaints?"

"Bawdy comments in front of the female officers, sexual harassment, that kind of thing. I would ask for your resignation if it wasn't for—"

"Did you say sexual harassment, sir?"

"I have witnesses, Temeke. You should have been here, should have had the balls to face the music."

"You forget, sir. You didn't want me in a meeting room. You wanted me out in the field. Those were your orders. I've already gathered you don't want me around and that's because you got passed over by the promotional board last year. Wouldn't want a black foreigner taking over your job now, would you?"

"That's racism!"

"Your words not mine, sir. Bitterness leads to resentment. I've seen it so many times. What's your birth sign?"

"What's my birth sign got to do with anything?"

"December 20th. Sagittarius. Overly expressive, frequent burnouts. That's it, isn't it? You're coming up for retirement."

"That's none of your business, Temeke. Now, where are you? You can't be riding out on your own like John Wayne!"

"Did you say hunting game, sir?" Temeke switched off the radio and pinched out his cigarette. He cracked open the car window and flicked it out as far as he could.

Malin heard the loud sigh, and then a small chuckle. "How cold is it outside?" she said, not daring to look up at the temperature sensor.

"Eighteen degrees. I don't want to tell another father that his daughter was found headless in a garbage bag. There's no way you can tart up stuff like that. Tess won't survive the snow. She won't survive wild animals if they're out there nosing around in the brush."

"What about the hunter's cabins?"

Temeke fumbled in the compartment under the armrest for a flashlight. He unfolded the map and spread it out on his knee. "They're west of here and within a few hundred yards of each other, spread out like an isosceles triangle. The first one borders the river, the second and third form the base. My wife used to camp in the woods when she was a child. Said they were mostly ruins, except for the boathouse. They used to swim from the pier."

"There must be a track somewhere," Malin said, eyelids fluttering in the beam of a passing car.

"Turn off here and douse the lights, Marl," Temeke said, turning off the flashlight and pointing at a pay lodge. "And before you get out of the car make sure you mute your phone. Don't want a stampede of elk every time it rings, do we?"

They approached the turn, tires crunching on gravel, a dirt road that went onward and upward. She turned off the headlights seeing the pallid bark of aspens and the reflecting eyes of elk as they passed between the trees.

There was no sign of the ranger.

THIRTY-SIX

Ole's sense of nothingness had been replaced by something else. An unspoken thing that lay deep down inside. A ghost of a thing he wanted to forget.

Morgan was a fantasy. Like an alter ego deep inside. Nothing could bring him back. No blood. Not even a vat-load of the very best vintage. Ole stood there shivering in a gaining breeze, wondering why he felt so close to the edge.

He ran from the marsh fowl, through giant firs and aspens and back to the tired old lodge by the river. There it was, under a hunter's moon, bright with star glow.

The Charger was just where he left it, hidden behind a screen of trees. He pulled off a coating of broken branches and opened the trunk. Inside was a cable knit sweater, thick and gray and stinking of old man's cologne. He saw the nozzle of the gun peeking beneath a cushion of spare clothes, let his fingers caress the glossy stock and the sling embossed with a stag's head.

It was only a few months ago when he'd tracked an elk, but you never forget how. He'd seen a stag yesterday, four feet in the river, nose sniffing the air. It was a big one. Ole liked the meat. And so would Tess. It was too cold to be out there on her own and she would likely smell that thick gamey gravy and want some.

"I'll fetch you home, Tess," he murmured, checking the spring loaded well, checking the telescopic sights.

He found a yellow and green box of cartridges. There were only six left.

He slammed the trunk and slung the rifle over one shoulder. Replacing a generous camouflage of pine branches over the car, he was out in the cold again, running through the trees. If she kept this up all night he'd be running well into the long golden dawn. But he knew where she was.

He could see the ruins of a small cabin through a break in the trees. The only place where red hot cinders stirred in the wind and dying flames consumed the last of them. Strangely, he felt a stirring of pity. Tess was a storm-driven girl from another land soon to be laid on the sacrificial fire.

He'd done everything Odin asked, hauled the remains up into the trees in their burlap bags and waited for the god to claim them. But they hung there during the summer months and long into the fall, and Odin was silent, taking only the blood offering from a few heads.

The rituals were tiresome and the bodies no more than a stinking mess. Blood pattered on the leaves below and Loki howled and howled until Ole cut them down. It was a week before he saw the animal again, snout crimson with offal.

A door opened in his mind, a memory of another land when he was a child. He was holding a lantern to his chest, windblown and timid on the threshold. The hunter met him there, rifle out before him. Possessed he was, with the face of a demon and the heart of one too. His lips were drawn back over ivory teeth, black eyes peeking beneath blood-matted hair. He had just killed a deer and the buzz of all that butchery was still in him.

Ole was afraid then just as he was now. He was afraid the hunter would find him the same way he found Morgan all because they had been peeking. He called them *stinking little rich boys.* He called them other things, too. Accused them of stealing meat from his fire. It wasn't true. They never stole anything.

But on this day, the hunter had no ordinary visitor in his lodge. A woman with long dark hair and a face like an angel. Ole couldn't work out what they were doing, balanced on that old wooden table, grunting and groaning like two wild hogs. It was hideous to see his mother like that but he had to know. So he watched until it was over, watched until his stomach was all dried out from the vomiting.

She said she would always love him. But she hadn't. He thought she was a beauty queen. But she wasn't.

He woke up crying for months to come. Years even. Whenever he pushed it aside, it came bouncing back like a lost puppy with a wagging tail. He could still see his mother, the color of her eyes and the tilt of her head. He hated what she had done.

That's when he learned to shoot a gun. That's when he learned to track men.

Standing at the door of the cabin now in this cold quiet wood, he saw a table turned over on its side and tattered curtains trembling in the breeze. And through the window on the far side of the room he saw something move by the corral fence and the trees.

Tessie, he thought, lifting the rifle and sighting in on his target.

There was enough moonlight to see her, a dark shadow about five feet tall. It could have just been an old coat draped over a fence post or an animal locked in fright. He was suddenly overwhelmed by the thought that she might already be dead, stiff and staring against that fence.

She must have heard him, knew he was there. That's why she stood rigid like a child in the throes of playing Grandma's Footsteps.

He lifted the rifle and fired one round at 100 yards,

watched her stagger and reel about. The trees were alive with night creatures, some skittering through the trees, some howling and hooting.

To his amazement she seemed to lift herself up, body stretched out now like a wild horse. He rubbed his eyes and changed the elevation of the scope. Before he fired again, she fell and all he could see was an open space.

Calling her name, he ran to the back of the cabin, down the steps and out into the gray night world. There on the ground between an old drinking trough and the horse corral was a young elk, ears twitching, nostrils a plume of steam. One leg was caught in a twist of barbed wire, and there was a hole in the side of her face where he'd shot her.

Hardly trophy-worthy, he thought, looking at the mess he'd made.

Ole blinked, felt a throbbing in his chest. He could see perfectly in the dark, but he hadn't seen this. The animal's head flopped to one side, body rolling after it. He thought he heard whimpering but he knew elk didn't whimper and he lifted his chin and sniffed.

Tess was out there watching him, listening for his footsteps in the crunchy earth. He would never see her from the ground, but perched in a tree he could see everything. That's when he picked a lookout. A white fir with tiers of branches and a belly full of bluish-green needles. It offered enough concealment for a few hours and he could scan the ground from his high tower and pick off anything that moved.

He slung the gun over one shoulder and began to climb, keeping to the thicker branches against the trunk. He found a sturdy limb reaching out at a 45 degree angle, easy to perch on and with his back pressed against the trunk, he could nurse the gun on his lap, legs dangling on either side.

All he could see were trees running deeper and

deeper into the endless shadows and directly beneath was a dusty floor barely covered with snow. Holding his breath for a moment, he listened for the modulating song of the cicadas, but the snow had silenced them. Only the pulsing hoot of an owl and the whisper of wind as it rushed between the trees. Closing his eyes, he allowed his muscles to relax and the last thing he remembered was how cold it was.

Snap!

The crunch of dried leaves. A twig perhaps. How long had he been asleep? He never slept more than twenty minutes at a stretch and he looked up through the canopy above. Darkness.

When he looked down he saw a gradual slope heading to the left leading to a game trail. To the right was the small cabin and the horse corral, and a few feet in front of the fence was the dead doe. It was the shadow that lay beside the animal that fascinated him, brought a gradual smile to his face. Keeping warm within those soft flanks was a leggy girl in hiking boots, head tilted upwards and staring right at him.

"Tess," he whispered, raising his gun. "You clever girl."

THIRTY-SEVEN

Darryl saw the silver cross against Pastor Razz's sweater, flickering like a blazing hearth. "I never knew you lost your father. You never talk about it."

Razz's eyes reflected a dipping candle wreathed in holly on the table between them. "He was loving one minute and savage the next. Pushed me down the cellar steps when I was seven. Didn't mean to. I hid for hours in the garden shed. Wasn't afraid of the shadows except when I thought of life without him. When I found him sobbing in the kitchen he put out his arms and of course I ran to him. I really thought if I held him tight the demon inside would never come out again. The next day he was dead."

"I'm so sorry," Darryl heard himself utter. He winced as he tried to swallow, hand covering his throat.

"Suicide isn't all it's cracked up to be. He missed the first time and shot the bulb out of the hall chandelier. Second time he was lucky. Used a razor. Doctor said he bled out all over the bathroom floor," Razz said with a shallow sigh. "Tess isn't dead. She's got too much spit and spirit."

Darryl felt the rise and fall of his chest, felt like he was floating in a space without limits. He knew when to trust Razz and he nodded. "I've lost everything. I didn't ask to be born. In fact—"

"Yes, we've already had the *in fact*. That's why this

place is crawling with cops. Stupid thing to do. And with a neck tie. You just don't get it, do you?"

Darryl rubbed his neck and began to sob. "I tried it twice just to see if it would hurt. Even looked it up on the Internet. Just give me a chance, will you?"

"I've given you many chances. Although not quite as many as the Almighty." Razz nodded at Captain Fowler a few feet away in the kitchen. He seemed to give officer Jarvis a squinty stare as he dug into Darryl's cookie jar.

"I wish the cops would leave."

"They're only doing their job." Razz's eyes seemed to run along the wires to the tape recorder and he pinched his lip with a finger. "She still might call you know."

"She won't call. He's probably taken her phone. I should have killed him when I had the chance."

"Then why didn't you?"

Darryl had to think about that for a moment. "I just wanted to disable the car. You know, keep him there for the cops."

"You know that's a lie. You just said you wanted to kill him."

"I said I *should* have killed him."

Darryl didn't see Tess like a spirit far above the clouds, rising like a swallow into the firmament. She wasn't dead. Couldn't be. "It's never really dark in the woods, is it? It's never really quiet."

Razz looked over the rim of his glasses. "I know what you're thinking. He's probably got a gun. Probably got a knife. No doubt he's stacked. But she can run fast. Like a deer."

Darryl smiled at that. He could almost see her feet pattering against the leaves and he could almost smell the musty odor of the burrow where he imagined she lay. "I told the girls what to do if they ever got lost. Told them to find a place."

Razz nodded along, face shining as it always did. "A little more faith, son."

Darryl gently bit his lip. He never liked to talk about God, never knew what to say. It was all fluff and stuff, something to make young people behave and old people happy. "He's taken everything."

Razz flicked a look at Jarvis as he walked to the front door. "He hasn't taken your cookies."

Darryl watched the two officers, heads down and deep in conversation. "Why didn't God just let me die?"

"Because those heavenly mansions need a good cleaning. Probably haven't made our beds yet."

"I want to die."

"So do I. Can't wait. But it's not my time yet. Not yours either. How would I know you were hanging like a pheasant in your garage? I was called, that's why. And not on the phone in case you were wondering."

Darryl looked at Razz long and hard. He had a point. How would he have known? It felt like a dream to him afterwards, the tie, the rafter, the drafty old garage.

"Had to have been a miracle," Razz said, scratching food off a front tooth with a fingernail.

Darryl felt his hands tremble, felt his foot jitter under the table. Couldn't sift through his thoughts fast enough to understand what Razz had just said. Couldn't quite get over that miracle either.

"Family," Razz said, tapping Darryl's arm. "Like the Dad we never had."

The trilling of the phone gave them a start. That's when the officers came running in. The Captain checked the caller ID and nodded at the number. "It's him."

Jarvis tapped out a rhythm with his fingers. "Three, two, one," he whispered, signaling for Darryl to pick up the phone.

"Tess... Tess!" Darryl said. A dull excitement coursed through his veins just as the flame of the candle danced in a sudden draft.

"Tell me something, Darryl," said a voice between short breaths. "Did you really think I was in your house on Sunday?"

"Who is this?"

"We've never been formally introduced. I'm Ole Eriksen. And I have your daughter."

"Where is she? What have you done with her?"

"I know the police are listening so I wanted to get something straight. Tell them to bring Morgan outside the front gates. Straight exchange. Morgan for Tess."

Silence.

"Hello, hello!" Darryl squeezed the phone in his sweaty palm, felt his fingers being prized from the receiver. He heard one of the officers telling him the line was dead and he snatched his hand away, drawing it back to his body in a protective flinch. "He could have killed her—"

"Nah, he couldn't have," Razz said. "Can't make a fair exchange with a dead body."

THIRTY-EIGHT

The wind slashed at Malin's cheeks as they left the warmth of the car. She wound her scarf tighter, burying one hand into her pocket, the other gripping the strap of her backpack. The woods were bright with moon glow and she could see almost as far as sixty feet between the trees.

Temeke checked his radio and turned up his collar. "What did you put in these backpacks, Marl?"

"First aid, water, knives, spare batteries, energy bars. A few rounds. An extra sweater for Tess." She knew he would be impressed even if he didn't say so. She was prepared.

"A woolly hat might have come in handy. It's bloody freezing out here."

She looked up at a telegraph pole, cable running parallel to the river. "They must have electricity," she said.

"They? No one lives out here. Not anymore."

Temeke walked ahead, nose twitching as if he tracked a scent. She watched his long limbs gliding down the slope with catlike ease, turning occasionally as if there was some telepathic link between them. That was the African in him.

Then she saw the cloudy vapors curling between his lips and the trace of a smile as he waited for her, a dark shadow beneath the palisade cliffs and a glossy river.

"Thought there was supposed to be a ranger up here," he whispered, hand reaching for hers as she stumbled over a tree root. Only it wasn't a tree root. It was a wooden stake, sharpened to a point.

"Someone's building a fence," she said, pointing.

Temeke grunted and made no reply.

"Maybe the ranger's here somewhere," she said, feeling the warmth of his fingers as he steadied her. But only for a second. He kept his distance, polite to the point of honor. It was a side of him she had never seen.

"Hope he didn't flatten the grass around our crime scene."

"Crime scene, sir?"

"Every scene's a crime scene. Even my desk at work. And quit making so much bloody noise."

"Sorry, sir," she said, flushing with blood and color. She crunched through another pile of dead twigs, wincing all the way down the slope. The moon shed enough light on the aspens that their hoary trunks seemed to stab upwards like knives out of the black earth. Tiny flakes drifted like a rain of pollen and it wasn't as cold as it was before.

Temeke stopped again and lifted his chin. He blew out another swirl of steam which the wind caught and split into shreds. "What's that smell?"

"What smell?"

"That," he whispered, lifting a finger and pointing toward the dense blackness of the trees. His eyes skirted the fringes for a moment and then narrowed at a flicker of light so distant it could have been a spark from a cigarette. "Methane."

Malin smelled the faint odor of charcoal and what reminded her of burnt hair. It was both nauseating and sweet.

"Must be close to the first cabin," Temeke murmured, neck craning back for a moment.

She felt the cold sweat oozing between her shirt and the bulletproof vest, felt the weight of her pack as she ducked beneath the branches. The path twisted and turned, and it was nearly twenty minutes before they saw another flicker of light through the trees.

Situated in front of the river and dwarfed by the cliffs, the cabin nestled in a large clearing. Tendrils of smoke danced above the chimney, and light seeped through a dilapidated door. It would have been idyllic in the summer, a shallow cove to tie up a raft and a wide ledge far out at the base of the cliffs to jump from.

Temeke waved a hand in a downward motion and crouched beside a gnarled juniper bush. "Make sure your phone's off. It's been vibrating in your pocket like a sex toy."

Malin hunkered beside him and took out her phone. She half covered it with her scarf and nodded. "It is off, sir."

"And don't go waving it around like a flashlight."

She was about to open her mouth when he placed a finger against her lips.

"If he's a good hunter, he already knows we're here. I'll take the front. You go round the back. And don't go inside, OK? If you see anything move give me the signal."

"What signal, sir?"

"The signal, you know. Middle finger. In the air. Like this."

She felt the rising giggle and suppressed it with a snort. Temeke always made light of things, always positive in a dangerous situation. She smelled the fragrance of his polished black skin that plunged her briefly into an erotic yearning. There was no time to play it out in her mind, so she stood when he did, barely hearing him slip between tall tufts of buffalo grass on those silent feet of his.

She chose a downhill slope parallel to the back of the cabin and where a faint beam of light illuminated a track cut between dense patches of snake grass and cattails. She felt sleek and nameless in the shadows, a reedy speck that could suddenly take to the air like one of the many migratory birds that came to roost each year.

A loud snap caused her to stop and her leg felt as if it had been gripped in a vice. Bending down, she untangled the trailing vine that had somehow caught around her calf, and she ripped it away with a single tug.

It wasn't a vine. Too cold for that. Too thin. A rabbit trap strung across the path.

Steadying herself against a young aspen about fifteen feet from the house, she saw the perfect example of a Scandinavian male, solidly built, roaming gracefully about the room until he came to a stop by the window. It was his profile she saw, skin a yellowish tan in the candlelight and chin turned upwards as if he was studying the ceiling.

Ole Eriksen, the man in the drawing.

A cable knit sweater hung from a chair and all he wore was a dark t-shirt and pale jeans. She wasn't expecting to see him at such close range, neck longer than she imagined, face angular and maddeningly striking. Sliding the gun from her waistband, she took a deep breath and aimed.

It was then he turned and stared right at her, finger wagging as if scolding an unruly child. It threw her off guard and her mind went blank. She saw the smile, head cocked sideways as if sizing her up, measuring her mood.

He couldn't possibly see her. She had been too careful for that. So what could he see? A shadow, a shape against the pale bark of the aspen.

She dared to look behind, seeing only a mangled thicket in the darkness. When she looked back at the house he was gone.

"No, no, no!" Breath caught in her throat, grip tightening on the gun.

She didn't know whether to throw up or be ashamed. He could only have left through the front door, striding out toward a pointed muzzle. Temeke was waiting for him. Hell, he'd probably already cuffed him.

It was the silence that told her otherwise and she knew better than to stand like a sitting duck in the beam of a guttering candle.

Idiot! she said to herself, feeling her legs jerk as she leapt along the back of the cabin, crouching beneath a second window. The odds said run a mile, only she felt like she was going nowhere fast. Gun muzzle pointing down, she stood slowly and pressed her cheek against the window frame. All she could see was a wooden table and a chair and the remains of a round braided rug on the floor. A candle flickering on the mantelshelf, flame bobbing in a downward breeze.

She slipped past the window and flattened herself against the stone wall. Gripping the gun even tighter, she heard the rustle of the crisp dead leaves in a gentle breeze. Stepping forward, her foot caught beneath a thick gray limb. She squatted and patted the snow, feeling the silky fabric of a ski jacket before she gripped a man's arm.

She gasped, felt the backpack slip from her shoulder, felt a scream rise in her throat.

Temeke…

A surge of anger brought her to her senses. Fumbling for the zipper, she no longer cared if the flashlight shot upwards through the trees like a strobe. Directing the light toward the ground, she saw the wide staring eyes all puffy and red. His nose was a swollen mess, clotted blood streaking from both nostrils into a blackened mouth. His neck was covered in livid bruises and the wreckage of his chest revealed a crater where his heart had once been.

She placed the gun on the ground beside her and felt for a pulse in his neck. There wasn't the slightest whisper of life in that body. Only the word *Ranger* on his sleeve that indicated who he was.

She radioed Temeke. Heard no response.

A snapping twig urged her to turn off the flashlight and she slipped it into her coat pocket. It seemed to come from the shadows about fifteen feet in front of her. Again, she was plunged into darkness, eyes adjusting slowly to the darkness and ears pricked to the surrounding sounds. A stream trickled nearby and the yipping chime of a coyote tore through her thoughts.

She fumbled for the gun, heart racing in her chest. It wasn't behind her. It wasn't in front.

Snap… snap!

Backing up against the wall, she tasted a fresh tumble of snow on her lips and she turned back toward the window to see if he was there. Couldn't see much, couldn't hear much. But she could smell a scent that reminded her of freshly mown grass. Somewhere inside she knew it was wrong and it took several minutes to assemble her thoughts.

Go back to the car, radio Hackett, Fowler, Sarge, anyone.

No, she'd never make it.

Climb a tree…

She looked up at the trees and almost choked. A warm hand reached around from behind and tucked itself beneath her chin. She felt a sturdy body pressing against her spine and towering over her as she cowered.

"I won't hurt you," he whispered. "Not unless you scream."

She could hear the upward inflection, the *w* to *v* transition. It was musical and disgustingly warm against

275

her ear. She would have lifted her knee and kicked back, but her legs were anchored by one of his.

"You should never leave a gun on the ground. Didn't they teach you that at the academy?"

She knew he didn't expect a response, knew the snapping sound was a lobbed rock in the bushes to divert her attention. She was humiliated all the same.

"I don't mind trespassers. No, not at all. It's a new way of hunting. That's what I love to do."

She did the only thing she could think of and that was to settle against him, letting him take the whole weight of her body. He sensed the shift, sensed her dependence. Whether he believed it was another matter.

"The wind is cruel tonight. So is the snow. It's warmer inside."

Malin didn't dare move. She didn't dare think he might not be human behind that seductive voice. It was the only thing that kept her focused.

"I'll keep you warm if you tell me where your partner is."

So he didn't know where Temeke was. That was worth something. Malin almost let out an audible sigh but she caught it just in time. He would have sensed her intake of breath, sensed the sudden flinch.

"I don't know," she stammered.

"Storm's coming. Better get inside."

Malin felt the gun muzzle against the small of her back. *Her* gun. She only wished she could stop panting out large clouds of breath, only wished she could scream at the top of her lungs without being shot.

The cabin stank of rotting wood and years of dust, and several candles flickered on a wooden table, some dripping wax on the surface and oozing into a ball of nylon rope. It was the fire in the grate that gave out that bold flicker of light through the windows, the light that shone in her face when he first saw her.

She saw a large dog, a wolf perhaps, lying on a circular mat, nose resting between its paws. Its fur was not just gray in the moonlight, but brown and black and beige. Golden eyes, rimmed in black, seemed to follow Ole as he pushed her inside and there was the hint of a snarl when she resisted.

"Loki," Ole scolded, flicking his fingers at the wolf before closing the door with his foot.

"You're cold," he said as if he truly cared, hands resting on her shoulders now.

She felt him watching her, felt his eyes looking almost lovingly as if she needed that assurance. He pressed her down onto the seat of an old wooden chair. Taking her hands, he gently tied them to the back rails. She felt him behind her, felt his breath on the back of her neck, felt her toes curl inside her boots.

Then he knelt on the floor in front of her, hands resting on her knees. Ginger eyebrows arched over oval eyes giving the impression of an inquiring gaze. It was a face younger than she imagined, a smile broader than she would have liked. The well-developed physique was honed from weight training and savage hunting in the woods. This man was no lightweight and it would take hours to take him down.

Words. That's all she had.

When he opened her knees she caught the sparkle in those blue eyes, caught the slight widening of his nostrils. It was offensive and he knew it. Taking one foot at a time, he slowly tied them both to the chair legs, fingers moving with grace and deliberation, bonds firm but not too tight.

"You have to know I nearly sold my soul for a woman like you. I won't do that again," he said, hesitating briefly before standing.

She felt no anger. She felt no fear. It was the remote courtesy she couldn't understand.

"You know who I am, don't you?" He stared down at her with a fire in his eyes, waiting for some kind of response. When she nodded, he nodded too. "Ole," he said so softly she almost failed to catch it over the wind. "And you are Malin. Such a beautiful name."

This was the man they called the 9th Hour Killer and yet here he was walking toward the hearth, giving the wolf a cursory pat. He stoked those flames and set a pot on top of a three-legged stand. She could smell twigs and pine cones and very soon a bubbling chicken broth. The wind whistled in the chimney above the hearth and that's when she noticed tiny specks of snow whirling down into the flames.

"Where's Tess?" she asked.

He ladled enough to fill a wooden bowl and pressed it against her lips. He told her to drink and she did, and then he wiped her mouth with his finger.

"She was hiding beside a kill when I found her."

"A kill?"

"Yes, a kill. A dead elk. Very smart, don't you think?"

Malin took another sip, smelling man scent. His eyes narrowed and his mouth tilted into a secretive smile.

"Sit still now. Don't fret."

She tasted something bitter in the back of her throat and she knew what it was.

"Little Tess was fast," Ole said, tilting the bowl toward her lips again, "Faster than I thought she'd be. She jumped when she saw me and ran through the trees. I was very impressed. If there was a way out she would have found it by now. But there isn't. She broke the rules and now she's paying for it."

He became blurry and indistinct, and that's when Malin closed her eyes and felt her head snap forward onto a muscular shoulder.

THIRTY-NINE

Temeke crested the hill after about fifteen minutes, already feeling the strain in his thighs. There were trees all over the place, some denser than others and he hoped Tess was sheltered somewhere beneath a canopy of branches.

The acrid smell was stronger and he looked east and west and didn't see anything moving. He couldn't feel his feet and if it wasn't for his scarf he wouldn't have been able to feel his ears. How could he possibly do any surveillance with Hackett butting in every five minutes. The radio vibrated into life and he fumbled to switch it off.

"Old misery guts," he mouthed as he paced the edge of the clearing. Hackett was probably sitting at home with his feet up drinking a full-bodied glass of ale.

Where was Malin? She should have seen something by now. Probably tripped over another gnarly root and knocked herself out.

He was about thirty feet from the cabin and all he could hear was the dull rattle of dead leaves in the wind. Before getting to the edge of the deck, he noticed a narrow shaft of light that fell through a crack in the door mullion. In front, a wire stretched about three inches above the deck boards secured around the porch columns.

An alarm.

That's the trouble, thought Temeke, pinching his eyelids together as he peered into the gloom. There might have been a few in the woods. *I'll never see the sod. He'll jump me from behind.*

He trained his eye on a shudder of movement to the right of the cabin, slipped the gun out of his holster and crept forward. He learned very quickly in his life that it was one thing to read body language from a distance and another thing to see it close up. He barely recognized the slip of a girl, arms crossed and wrapped around her waist. Out of her mouth came a stammer and a violent shake of the head and she tried to hold up a hand.

He lifted the chain around his neck and pulled out his badge. Slipping the gun back into the holster, she flinched, and then ran into a thicket of spruce. He followed her, followed that strong smell of ammonia that only confirmed she had been tied up for days. Racing under a canopy of fir trees, he lost her for a moment and he waited, listened, measuring the density of his hiding place. He couldn't see her but he knew she was there.

"Tess," he said. "It's Detective Temeke with the DCPD. You're safe."

She came out from behind the tree trunk, eyes wide and glistening. The moonlight was enchanting on her oval face and the bones of her cheeks, and he could see she had been crying. How to explain the clear evidence of African and Spanish blood in all of them, the petite frame and the brightness of the eye against a tan colored face. Yet it was there.

"Are you OK?" he said, peeling off his backpack.

It was a stupid question. She couldn't answer through the sobs, the incoherent stutter. He wanted to keep her warm and the car was at least a twenty minute hike. He'd make it in ten if he ran.

He felt it in his chest and in the pit of his stomach, a terrible gut-wrenching pity that wouldn't go away. He covered her in his jacket, held her close. He felt that age old stirring in his gut, felt his tongue sticking to the roof of his mouth. He had to ask. He had to know.

"Are there any others?" Through the chatter of teeth he heard the word *pit*. He asked her where it was.

Her finger pointed at a dark mass about thirty feet from the cabin, much closer than he had expected. Through an overhanging branch he could see an old chimney surrounded by a low brick wall. It was the glowing embers that made his stomach pitch.

Bloaters, he thought, the familiar stench of decomposition. He pulled a bottle of water from the backpack and held it against her lips. She struggled to swallow.

A scraping sound and the squeal of neglected hinges brought his attention back to the cabin. The front door was open now like it held some kind of supernatural power. There was no sign of Ole Eriksen, at least not that he could see.

Tess looked up at him again with those large searching eyes. She must have heard it, too. "Don't go in there," she said.

Going in there was the last thing he intended to do, not with a flickering light in the background. He'd appear larger than an elk within twelve yards of a rifle bore. It was exactly what Ole wanted.

There was the possibility – the extremely remote possibility – that it was Malin. But he didn't believe it for a moment.

He took out his phone and partially covered it with his scarf. Dialing Hackett's number, he pressed the phone face-down in Tess's hand. "No need to talk," he whispered, curling her fingers around it. "The police are on their way."

She began to shake her head, looking up into the thick limbs of the tree above them. "He's coming. I can hear him."

"Easy, love, easy…" Temeke pressed a hand on her shoulder. He wasn't giving up, even as he shivered and rubbed his arms. "It's warm in the car. Safe, too. You've been so brave. Just a little longer."

He took the sweater from the backpack and pulled it over his head. He heard the sound of boots against bark and turned to see Tess was already half-way up the tree and nestled in the fulcrum of two branches.

It was the gunshot that made him hit the ground, made him shudder. Tess was hidden in a thick spiny canopy without a bullet-proof vest.

To the right, he could see a downhill slope leading to an icy stream at the foot of the palisades. To the left was the old chimney looming like an ancient monolith against the night sky. He could smell that stench again.

He pulled out his gun and aimed beneath the low hanging branches, watching every shadow. The chimney was old, glowing embers streaking through the cracks and he could see a trail of pale roots amongst the soot.

Not roots. Human limbs, naked and white like wax dolls. Bones were stacked against a low wall, arranged in size and displayed like a row of trophies.

His stomach began to heave and his eyes snapped back and forth in the darkness. Panting, lungs searing from lack of water, he wanted to call out to Tess, wanted to reassure her. But the snap of a loading port warned him that Ole was out there, rifle pointing right at him.

Something moved from behind the chimney, a head, an arm perhaps. It seemed to slink forward, not like a relieved hostage running into the arms of a savior, but like a hunter dropping to the ground to take aim.

Temeke lay there under the trees, both hands gripping his weapon.

FORTY

Malin took a deep breath as cold air rushed at her cheeks through the open door. She could see the trees and smell the snow, but she couldn't see Eriksen. She couldn't see the wolf.

She had no coat and no scarf. When had he taken them off? She couldn't remember.

It was too quiet in the cabin, just the crackling of the fire in the hearth, a wooden bowl on the floor and two large jerry cans under the window. The cabin was a large open room and to her left was a mantelshelf thick with years of dust. There were a few thin lines drawn in that dust, angled forward like cursive script. She squinted and held her breath. *TW*.

Tess Williams.

Malin wondered if Ole had written the name immortalizing the girl in some sick way, or if it had been written by Tess. Perhaps Tess wanted someone to know she was there, to know she was still alive.

Malin curled her toes and flexed the muscles in her arms. She hadn't swallowed much of that soup, letting three small sips settle behind her bottom teeth. It had all spilled out of her mouth when she fell forward on his shoulder, a trick she had learned as a child.

There was another stench, a familiar one that made her study the hearth and the rising flames in the grate. Gasoline. Glossy puddles of it everywhere.

Malin began to rock frantically in the chair without taking her eyes from the front door. Straining against the ropes again and again, she heard one of the chair rails squeal. The structure was rotten just like the rest of the house and if she didn't get out soon, she wouldn't get out at all.

Leaning forward and taking the weight of the chair on her back, she made for the door in six lumbering steps. That's when she heard the gunshot ricocheting against the cliffs. That's when she heard a man's laugh and the whoosh of flames behind her.

Get out! her mind screamed.

Flexing her arm muscles one last time, the chair back split away from the seat. The heat was terrible, flames licking the chimney and the walls. In a matter of seconds, her throat was burning and her lungs were filling with smoke. Holding her breath, she struggled for the deck just as the floorboards disintegrated under her feet, forcing her down into the darkness. She groaned as she lay beneath the house, wrists no longer bound to the chair.

The pain in her right thigh was so intense she squealed in horror. A large splinter of wood poked out a few inches below her right hip, blood glistening from the open wound. Sobbing, she turned on her left side, one hand clawing through clods of earth, the other hand covering her nose. Heat seared through her back and all she could think about was staying low as black smoke began to settle on the ground.

One last breath. That was all she had.

Splintering wood indicated she was directly below the front deck, only it was on fire above her. Kicking and dragging a leg she could no longer feel, she punched through a clump of grass and out into the clearing.

Move!

She couldn't determine where that last shot came

from, couldn't measure how close it was. She crawled faster now toward the trees.

Trembling, she lay in a small hollow, taking shallow breaths and wincing at the pain. The sliver of wood was no small splinter. It was about two feet long and sewn into the flesh at her hip. Gripping one end of it, she counted to three. The pain was too intense and she knew she couldn't shift it without passing out. Coughing made her retch, burning her nose and throat, and she was too thirsty to go on.

It was fear that brought her to a stand, made her limp for high ground. There was no water now, no backpack, no gun. Ole had seen to that. But there was the river behind the burning cabin and she suddenly longed for it, no matter how cold, how contaminated.

Working her way back along the trail where she found the ranger, she saw embers swirling in the sky. It would only take a few of them to light up the rest of the forest and it would become a burning grave. She would have to swim out as far as the ledge below the cliffs if she wanted to survive. It was the safest place to be.

Energized by the knowledge that someone had fired that shot, Malin knew she had to run. Her thigh burned at every step and she panted through gritted teeth.

If he's a good hunter, he already knows we're here.

The snag around her ankle when she first arrived at the cabin was no rabbit trap. It was an alarm to alert Ole at any sign of movement. She prayed his mind wasn't smart enough to build bigger traps.

The fire made the woods hotter than the summer months, searing heat that made you sweat behind the knees. She began to wonder if the wound was charred and bruised, toxins already eating their way into her veins. She needed ice. She needed water.

Sometimes she dragged that leg and sometimes she just reached out to the nearest tree to catch her breath.

Then she heard it – a low rumbling sound. A growl. It was coming from the foliage behind her.

Glancing back and listening to the sound, she saw a shadow loping between the grasses toward a boulder. Long tail, sloping shoulders, snout as long as her hand. It was the wolf, although what breed or size it was, she didn't know.

It doesn't matter what it is, she thought irritably. A wolf's better than Ole, isn't it?

She wasn't sure. Either way, the animal could smell blood and that's what it was tracking. She went rigid, tried to hold her breath, tried to force her knees to stop trembling. The occasional snap of a twig from all sides confirmed her worst fear. The animal was circling her.

Five minutes, ten minutes. She had no idea how long it was. Silence one minute, chuffing the next. She saw a shaggy coat and head rising above the boulder, settling on the summit. Bathed in a soft reddish glow from the flames around the cabin, it gave a long snuffling breath as if weighing the threat.

Something deep inside told her to keep perfectly still. She saw the eyes, the tilt of the head, the oddly smiling face. There was the faint sound of the wind rustling through the long grass and the fur at the wolf's flank rippled in response. It was the most frightening thing she had ever seen.

It was also the most beautiful.

The mournful howl took her by surprise as did the razor-sharp jaws. The wolf looked up and down, nostrils working in the breeze. Two shiny eyes stared over her left shoulder at some distant object and she heard claws clacking against rock as the animal launched into the air and streaked like a cheetah into the wilderness.

Sucking in breath, she gave a long sigh of relief. What it had seen or heard she had no idea. Stretching her leg made her gasp, took her breath away. The pain was followed by a dull throbbing and she knew she had to keep walking.

Taking off down the slope, the trail curved back and forth through deep canopied trees and a musty smell took away the stench of burning timbers. She saw the Charger then, tucked behind a screen of broken branches. It wasn't easy to crouch by the tires, to break off a stout twig and press it against the top of the metal pin. A loud hissing of air escaped from each valve and twice she stopped and listened, hearing the sound of water lapping against wood. The river was ahead of her now and if she was lucky, she would reach the bank just as a low hanging cloud covered the moon.

Flames flickered from the river bank and she could almost see the veins in the nearest leaves. About fifteen feet downriver, she saw a pitched roof through a break in the trees, a simple wooden structure astride a pier. She couldn't get to it without walking down an open path and the thought of meeting Ole half-way was unthinkable.

She was wading almost knee deep in water before she realized it, flinching at the bite of icy water against her skin. A boat bobbed in a mild current, mooring line tied to a wooden stake.

An escape. It was all she needed.

Taking the rope, she looped it around one shoulder and waded out into the river. Her legs were almost numb with cold and she knew what she had to do. Gripping her pants leg, she tore a hole big enough to see flesh covered in blisters and half blackened with soot. The point of the splinter ran through the top of her buttock, tip visible at the curve of her thigh.

She took a deep breath, gripped the blunt end with both hands, and pulled.

FORTY-ONE

Temeke heard the scream. He took a breath and froze. Malin. He wasn't sure where it came from, possibly the game trail near the cabin. At least that was his hope.

He looked up into the canopy of the tree above him. Tess was lying against the branch, body trembling with fear. He tried to get her attention, tried to tell her it would be OK.

He saw the flames as they broke between the thinning rafters in what was once the roof of the cabin. There was an overhead cable behind the trees, promising a round of fireworks, and he heard the unmistakable sound of someone extracting a spent cartridge casing before chambering a new round.

Crack!

Temeke mashed his face into the dirt, hugging the ground as close as he could. It was a snapping twig about a hundred yards from where he lay. Eriksen couldn't have seen him camouflaged amongst the shadows, dark clothes, black face, unless...

Temeke didn't want to think of the *unless* – the night vision goggles he hoped Eriksen didn't have. Luis almost always carried a box of twenty cartridges in the back of his car. This could go on all night, Temeke thought.

He lay there on the leaf-strewn ground, staring through blades of grass at the fire pit. He could see at least twenty feet in every direction because of that bright round moon and the fire that blazed behind him. Trouble was, he couldn't see a sniper amongst the ashes.

But what he could see was a metal frame with steel springs about ten feet to his right and partially hidden behind a clump of grass. The frame was armed with teeth, and he knew exactly what it was.

A man trap.

He began to shiver, elbows pressed into a bed of pine needles. How many were scattered about the perimeter he had no idea, but there were likely to be more in the shadows if he didn't watch out. It was the acrid smell that made his throat sore and he worked up a glob of spit to stifle a cough. Easing up slowly, he peered cautiously over a branch and glimpsed something powering through the trees. It couldn't have been Eriksen. It was too fast for that.

A coyote, or something bigger.

Another gunshot, only this time something whistled about ten feet to his left, popping as it struck a tree.

Too close. Much too close.

He rolled sideways, plunging into a soft crater of earth and barreling into the corky tree trunk. If it wasn't for the backpack he would have surely bruised his spine. The lower branches only reached out to a maximum of five feet, but it gave him the cover he needed.

He peered up at Tess again and signaled for her to stay down.

Another snap, and then another. Footsteps. He reckoned this one was about a hundred yards to his right and looping toward the river. At least Eriksen was heading away from him. He wasn't about to shoot what he couldn't see and besides, he didn't want the bugger knowing where he was.

Lifting his head, he plucked a few pine needles from his cheeks. His eyes streaked up through the branches at

Tess. She was sitting astride a thick branch, back nestled against the trunk. Torn tights ripped to a mesh and barely covering those long dark legs. Eyes blinked down at him, finger stabbing at the ground. He saw the flashing light flickering about in the detritus and realized she'd dropped the cell phone.

It took him a few seconds to find it, hearing the soft purr of a female voice on the other end. He left it open so the police could hear them and slipped it in his trouser pocket. "Climb down, love. I'm right here," he whispered, urging Tess with a flapping hand.

He wanted to add, *and make it snappy,* only the kid would probably start bawling and fall. She shook her head, shoulders back, chin high. He couldn't blame her, not after what she'd been through.

"Tess, we have to get out of here."

Tess shook her head, hand flapping in front of her face. He had seen that gesture before, the jitters, the defeat. The gunshots had been loud and he was already preparing for another round.

"Don't give up. Not now." Drawing a deep breath through his nose, he was aware of a churning stomach and tingling legs. "Blimey, girl. You're going to make me come up there, aren't you?"

She nodded, wrapping her arms around her waist. There was only one thing for it. Climb up there and get her down, only he was feeling a tad sick just thinking about it. She looked safe enough to him, couldn't really fall between the branches. After all, she'd probably been up there a good twenty minutes, and the flames from the cabin would keep her warm.

Get up there, you sissy. It was his father's voice with its thick Amharic accent. The man had climbed enough palm trees in his poaching days and would never understand vertigo even if it slapped him in the ribs.

Temeke holstered his gun and reached up to the first

snag, keeping his eyes on the weathered bark. He was sure it wouldn't hold his weight and he began to feel that familiar dizziness and the tightening in his chest.

"Just look up," Tess said.

Temeke wondered how she knew he was a first-time climber. "Tell me if you can see anything," he said. He was almost a hair breath from breaking point and he was only six inches off the bloody ground.

She must have had a good view of the cabin and the river, with the chimney stack to her right. "Just trees."

"Anything else? A man perhaps?"

"Nothing."

Temeke heaved up to the third branch and wondered if it was high enough.

"He shot an elk," she said. "This big."

Temeke didn't look up to see how wide her hands were. He was too busy deciding if all this bother was worth the fuss. If she had scurried up, she could surely scurry down. "Sure you don't feel like coming down here, love? It'd be a darn sight quicker."

"So I hid behind it," she said, voice quivering. "I stayed there until the thing went cold. Until he found me. Then I ran."

Temeke pulled himself up to the fourth branch and listened to her voice.

"I found the fire pit. I had to keep warm. Only there's bones in it. And legs. It's awful."

That's when the panting started. "All right, I'm coming up. Don't do anything daft," he said.

"The world's so big up here. I feel lost. I won't cry," Tess sobbed. "I don't believe in crying."

Temeke stretched a hand toward her. This is what he could understand. Action. "Good girl. Now tell me what you can see besides trees."

"The cabin's all burnt up. It smells really bad up here. Have you got any water?"

"Plenty," he said, bending one knee and pressing down on a branch. It was then he realized the wind had changed because all that thick black smoke was starting to get in his eyes. "Do me a favor, love. Cover your nose."

He hoped she had. He could no longer see. And he was beginning to feel a little smoke sick himself.

"I can see something," she whispered, voice quieter now. "Over there."

"Over where?" Temeke said, blinking repeatedly and stopping to hug the trunk. The smoke wasn't as thick as he thought and he strained to see what she saw.

He parked his butt on a branch perpendicular to Tess, feet resting on another below. He ripped off his bulletproof vest and handed it up to her.

"I'll help you put this on. Under that jacket."

Facing the fire pit, Temeke had no view of the cabin and the clearing behind him. The smoke swung back around, drifting across the river like a heavy fog and all he could hear was snapping flames and the bark of that coyote. A pebble rattling against stone.

He looked up at Tess and realized she had heard it, too. Her eyes were big and round, fixed on an object behind him, an object he couldn't see.

She stayed perfectly still.

So did he.

No matter how bad things get, he thought, they can only get worse. And what could be worse than having your back to the target?

They waited a few moments and then Tess tugged off her jacket. He told her how to tie the vest, but he couldn't for the life of him get up there to help her.

He was lusting for a whiff of tobacco and tried to get comfortable on that prickly branch. Hiding up trees was hell and so was screwing up his eyes to see in the dark. The moon was hidden by clouds now and he couldn't see a bloody thing.

He leaned against the bark, hearing the creak of the limb beneath him. It wasn't a soft creak, more like a loud groaning which increased every time he moved. There was something poking at the crown jewels and he reached down to his crotch and snapped off the offending twig.

"Let's hope the bastard's deaf," he muttered.

Tess looked down, mouth widening just a little. "I think I can climb down now," she whispered.

Temeke held a finger to his lips and shook his head. He wanted to listen to the forest murmurs and measure the wind. Something was sniffing around down there, feet scuffling through fallen leaves. Probably the wolf he saw earlier, chewing its way through his crime scene.

Then he saw the figure walking toward the tree, face brilliant with the light of the flames from the cabin, rifle balanced in his right hand. Temeke glanced around the area as he quietly slid the gun from his belt. He saw no one else, just the man. Sighting his target, he aimed. And fired.

The man staggered back a couple of feet, before falling to his knees. He was a blurred image amongst branches, head bowed, rifle discarded by his side.

It was the night vision goggles on the man's head that got Temeke moving. His brain was working faster now and he began to plead with God that Malin was out there with a loaded gun. Tempting Tess down from the upper branch, he reached the ground first, easing her down with a steady arm.

He felt a hand on his shoulder as he was jerked around. Felt his cheek explode, felt the gun ripped from his holster. Tess was right beside him, screaming, cheek pressed against his arm.

Temeke felt the sting of that punch. That's when he realized Ole was wearing a bullet-proof vest. He had thought of death in the past three days, wondering what it would be like to go in one's sleep. Luxury. And here he was in a forest staring at a man with movie star looks and a gun pointed right at him. It just didn't seem real.

Whatever the outcome, it would be a violent death, over in a second, no farewells and a ton of questions. His wife would wonder if he suffered, what were his last thoughts and were they of her. He wondered if she was still hiding in their bedroom behind the chest of drawers. That all seemed so silly now.

Temeke didn't much care for himself. It was Tess he was worried about. If she didn't die, she would watch him die. And if she survived two more days, she would be in a place of permanent terror. Ole wouldn't let them go. Not after Becky ran away.

"You forget," Ole whispered, "I'm immortal. Now move."

Temeke felt the cold nudge of a rifle bore against his right arm while hugging Tess in his left. Bushes clutched and pulled at their legs, and in the harsh glare of the fire he could see the leaves were a pale shade of green. From a long way off was the scrunch of something dragging through dirt.

A car? He hoped so.

Ole heard it too and urged them on with a shout. They walked toward the river's edge and stood about twenty feet from the rear of the cabin and a row of boulders. Temeke saw a twitch of movement across the river, a figure cowering in a boat at the foot of the cliffs. It was Malin.

He started as he heard the shot behind him, so loud it hurt his ears. Pushing Tess to the ground, he covered her body with his. "Are you hurt?"

"No." Tess shuddered under his weight.

He looked out at the river. Malin was still standing. Ole had missed.

"Want to see real fireworks?" Ole shouted, chin high, eyes flicking toward the river. "Then watch this."

Temeke looked back and saw the gun in Ole's hand, raised upwards toward the utility pole. It was then he heard a loud boom and the popping of electrical wires like a bursting corset. The cross-arm snapped clean from the horizontal bar and a cable bounced downward like a bungee line, sweeping out to the middle of the river and toward the rocky ledge.

FORTY-TWO

The cable grazed the surface of the water until it reached the middle. Through the intermittent sparks, Temeke could just make out a small sandy island about ten feet beyond its path, crowned with tall clumps of grass.

Around him the forest was silent. The moon was full. The wind was still. He heard only the steady hammering of his heart in the darkness and a sharp intake of breath from Tess beneath him. Out of the corner of his eye he could see Ole standing five feet to his right, aiming the rifle right at him.

"Get up," he said.

Temeke pulled Tess up with him and stood in front of her. He hoped Ole couldn't see the blinking light in his trouser pocket and he hoped the female officer on the other end wasn't about to break into song.

The cable stuck fast to the grass, sparks and flames leaping up the stems. It shuddered for a time as if trying to decide which way to go and then, slowly, very slowly, it began its journey back toward them, this time carrying a bundle of burning brush and dead leaves.

It must have taken Ole by surprise because Temeke heard the moan of disappointment. He was glad Malin was spared a nightmare from which he couldn't have saved her, and he was glad he didn't have to watch her die.

He heard the unmistakable sound of coughing. Tess

needed water and instinct drove her toward the river's edge and away from the smoke. She didn't get far before Ole began to laugh, taunting and shouting a warning.

"Kid's got guts," Ole said, lowering the rifle and aiming Temeke's pistol. "Let's see them spill all over the rocks."

Tess turned toward the loaded gun, face blanched mouth slack. Temeke took a chance and swung toward her, hearing the sharp crack, knowing the bullet had hit her. The knock-back threw her three feet into the water and the spray slapped him in the face.

The growl took him by surprise, so did the large cage of teeth and hot fetid breath. It was a wolf, a coyote, some such beast, front legs splayed, head lowered. It took him a second or two to realize that it was now standing in the water directly in the path of the cable.

He saw sparks and flames and streaks of red. The wolf was lifted from the ground, a burning mass of hair and teeth, a stench that would cling to Temeke's nostrils for days.

He pulled Tess from the water, held her against him to keep her warm. She wasn't moving, wasn't breathing and then a twitch at the corner of her mouth, a long loud breath, hands reaching for the center of her chest. She tried to wriggle to one side, wheezing and panting.

He heard Malin scream his name, saw her wading toward him waist-deep in the water, face pinched in pain. Her voice sounded out of breath the third time she spoke.

"Go after him!" she shouted, hand pointing to his right. "Run!" She had to have been freezing in that icy water to make her voice resonate like that.

All Temeke saw was the tremor of leaves and the sound of snapping twigs as Ole darted along the water's edge and into the shadows. The rifle had to have been empty. That's why Ole had used the handgun. And the scraping of gravel earlier? Cars halting at the crest of the trail from the open phone in his pocket. Now police officers were bursting through the foliage.

Hackett took a quick head count and nodded at all those stacked up near the burning house and ready to go. Forty officers fanned out in different directions, two came forward to take Tess.

"What's the situation?" Hackett said, handing Temeke a vest.

"The situation," said Temeke, wiping the blood from his lip. "Tess has been hit, but the vest took most of it."

"And Malin? Because if anything's happened to Malin—"

"I'm here, sir," said a trembling voice behind them, hand pressed against the top of her leg. "He can't get far. Not without the boat. And I let the air out of his tires."

Temeke wanted to hug her, wanted to tell her how grateful he was. Instead, he reached out and took her cold, trembling hands and helped her out of the water. "I want you to call Darryl Williams," he whispered. "Tell him Tess is safe. Tell him she's coming home."

Temeke watched those dark glossy eyes, saw the quivering chin. She nodded just enough to let him know she would.

"Lucky your phone was open," Hackett interrupted. "We've got most of it on tape. Good job." He swung his arm at Fowler who was shining his flashlight along the water's edge. "Stop paddling and get a blanket!"

Temeke couldn't resist a final jab and Hackett was the perfect victim. "He's threatening to kill us all, sir, if we don't meet his demands – a spitfire to take him to PNM to pick up Morgan or some such rubbish."

"Don't be ridiculous. Next you'll be telling me he wants a car and we have to promise not to go after him." Hackett delegated a task to Officer Jarvis and then scowled at Captain Fowler. "Make sure the marksmen are positioned exactly where I indicated. They are not, repeat *not*, to fire a single round unless I give the signal. Is that clear?"

Fowler nodded. "Yes, sir."

"But, sir," Temeke said, seeing the officers trailing off toward the road. "He's run off into the woods. That way. And you might want to radio your officers about the mantraps."

"Mantraps? What mantraps?"

"Well that's the thing, sir. I don't know—"

"He's not going back in the woods, Temeke. He'll go toward the road. Any smart man would figure that out. Well don't just stand there."

"Do I still have a badge? Has my name been cleared?"

Hackett handed him a .40 caliber Smith & Wesson and one magazine. He jerked his chin toward the trees. "Find him and I'll make it worth your while."

Temeke wouldn't be surprised if his annual review was outstanding. He gripped the stocky frame of the Smith & Wesson and checked the magazine. Ten rounds.

His left eye felt numb and he could smell blood in his nose. He was suddenly achy and stiff as he walked beside the river under the canopy of trees. There was no cascade of water from the palisade cliffs, just a smooth channel where a summer waterfall had once been. It reminded him of his wife's childhood, how she loved to come to the park and camp. It reminded him of her black hair, her faraway smile.

A soft rustling under the pine trees told him to keep alert, to listen to the wind against the cliffs and the occasional whisper of the grasses. And under all those sounds he could hear something else, a scraping sound, like a boot against bark.

He paused, holding the gun in his right hand, sensing a slight shake in his support hand. He turned a half circle, first one way and then the other. Looking into the gloom he could see twisted gray limbs and a gnarled old tree trunk that had been struck by lightning. Beyond it was a pit of blackness he didn't want to explore. There were mantraps in the long grass. He couldn't see them but he sensed they were there.

Somewhere to his left he heard the soft gurgle of a stream that had cut away from the main body of water, and to his right the occasional flutter of a night bird lifting high into the sky.

A night bird lifting into the sky. There was someone out there. Hunting. Tracking. Smelling the scent of the woods, nose twitching with every current of air.

Temeke was baffled. Why hadn't Ole run deeper into the woods when he had the chance? He didn't have any attachment to the dead girls and there was nothing in that burnt out cabin.

What was he waiting for?

Ole was an ambusher, not a hunter. He could wait in parking lots hidden in dark colored cars and stalk innocent girls. He was good at waiting, good at watching. And he was probably watching the police fanning out in all directions and making a heck of a racket. A man like Ole enjoyed soaking up the media hype of his latest kill, took pleasure in the excitement and pain.

That's when Temeke knew. Ole was smarter than the rest. He wasn't camouflaged in the underbrush like most hunters were. He was perched in a lofty roost, watching as he always did. In the trees. Morgan's trees.

As the path curved off to the right away from the river and the hoary moon, Temeke could see splinters of light shining through the branches, only he could hardly see the path underfoot. He started down the sloping hillside and away from the cabin, moving silently in the darkness, boots tapping on the hard, dry earth.

He paused often to consult his wrist compass. He was heading west along rugged terrain where tree roots and craters were treacherous, and the sense of isolation was getting worse by the minute.

His heart pounded as he continued across a slushy stretch of mud, and then up again. At the top of the next ridge there was a break in the trees. To his left was a rim of bluish cliffs bordering the river and to his right, he saw a clearing where intermittent shafts of light pooled onto the ground and there, leaning up against a tree, was a rifle.

His eyes followed the line of the trunk up into the foliage. There was nothing up there that would indicate a human shape, nothing perched on an upper branch.

He began to wonder why it was suddenly so quiet.

Ole was out there, waiting to take out a few cops. And let's face it, he'd already used three of those eight rounds in his pistol. So it couldn't be cops he was waiting for.

Something kept nagging in the back of Temeke's mind, something important.

My wife used to camp in the woods when she was a child. Said they were mostly ruins, except for the boathouse.

The boathouse.

FORTY-THREE

Ole felt a shiver down his spine. For a second he couldn't move, couldn't swallow. The boat was gone. He didn't know how long he stood there, absorbing the shock. The musty walls began to throb and there was an air of menace in the place as if he had suddenly stumbled across his own tomb.

Releasing the tension with long shuddering breaths, his legs burned from all that running. There weren't enough rounds in his gun to finish off forty men in the dark, let alone the detective he wanted to break. Loki was dead now, and that foul rotten stench coated his tongue.

Ole leaned against a wooden support, tongue dry with thirst. There had been patches of snow in the woods to suck on but the boathouse offered no such relief. He listened in the darkness, waited for the patter of FBI feet. He was the prey now and none of it made any sense.

He focused on the only ugly thing that had turned his whole world upside down. His mother.

She had been little more than a girl herself, too young for his father, too naïve. He hadn't known that then. But he knew it now. Brown slanted eyes still brimming with tears and olive skin soft against his own. She couldn't have wanted to leave him behind. He was her favorite.

He remembered her voice and the hymns she would sing. *Take the veil from our faces, the vile from our heart.*

Was it something inside of him or was it outside? Did he have a broken soul?

"You don't have a soul," she said. "Your kind never does."

He cast his mind back to an image of candles guttering against an open door, and he saw her standing there against a moonlit forest, gripping a suitcase. A night just like tonight.

"Do you love me?" she said.

When he nodded and ran to her, she held him so tight it hurt. She kissed his nose, his blond curls, his neck. It used to make him laugh when he was a boy. He could still smell her perfumed hair on spring nights when the honeysuckle bloomed, and he could smell her now.

"Mamma," he wanted to whisper, "I've killed you eight times."

Snap!

The sound took him out of his trance and he stood in that boathouse listening to water lapping against the pillars. The walkway was half rotten, timbers creaking under his weight. But if he edged closer to the perimeter where the soil was packed and damp, no one could hear him, and through the gaps in the clinker-built framing, no one could see him.

Ole raced around the inside like a caged animal, but all he could see was dried leaves and silver-gray branches. Sometimes he could hear the hollow sound of wind through the pine trees and the longer he stood there, the longer he felt the agony of loneliness.

Silent as light.

He listened to the sound of the wind, the scuttle of leaves. And then he heard another sound, like the cry of a bird, but sharper.

Fear shot through him and he had enough sense to stay still. His eyes tried to penetrate through grooves in the tree trunks, tried to imagine a face in the bark like the ones he had carved near the Tolby barn. Just as he was about to take a breath, he saw a shape between two trees. It seemed to drift on a gust of wind, moving sideways and forwards at the same time. He couldn't remember where he had seen that movement before, but it was similar to the gait of a dressage horse.

He felt a catch in his throat and for a second he couldn't move. It was too late to run only he couldn't afford to wait any longer. The way out was along the pier and he didn't feel much like swimming. Not tonight. Not in the cold.

Dry leaves scuttled across the path and there was a keening in the wind. He thought he heard footsteps through the underbrush, coming closer and he knew why he couldn't see this particular marksman. He was black, eagle-eyed and as determined as a sniper.

Ole was surrounded on three sides by sturdy wooden walls and he could see only a few yards ahead on two sides, the third gave him a view of approximately fifty yards back up the hill toward the burning lodge. He hoped that was the direction the detective had chosen.

He was silent, but he knew his eyes were wide. He stayed very still, hardly daring to breathe.

The shape came out of the shadows, armed with a gun, nozzle tilted downward, back against a tree. He was staring at the boathouse, hesitating, moonlight sheering off one side of his face, skin blacker than pitch.

Ole recognized the gun. Great striker fire action, great recoil. He gave it a high rating, promising himself the very same one as a side carry. He also recognized the man, enormous and sleek, muscular neck thrust forward and almost as broad as the tree he leaned against.

Ole couldn't take his eyes off him, knowing he had never been close enough to study him. He raised his gun and waited until the sniper swung around slowly, chest directly in his line of fire.

There was something odd about him, standing frozen, staring right ahead, eyes blank. His head lowered and Ole heard him sniff repeatedly, head moving from side to side with each inhalation.

He had the distinct impression the sniper was sniffing like a Massai tracker and if he didn't do something soon, his life would be lost. Not knowing whether he was up or down wind, he pushed that gun quietly between two slats of wood and fired.

For such a buff man, the sniper moved with surprising grace. His reflexes could never have been that fast had the bullet surprised him. Ole knew, with absolute certainty, the sniper had sensed him in the boathouse and hunkered to the ground before the bullet had even been discharged.

He stared, felt his mouth drop, gripped his gun in two sweating hands. The foliage shuddered and rustled, and the man was gone.

There was only one way out. And that was to swim. Ole listened first to the wind and the occasional cry of a bird. He heard the flutter of wings and saw a heron speeding across the surface of the river, feet kicking up a spray. He placed a hand on the side of the boathouse and edged his way forward along the pier.

He could smell the wind on the water and he knew it was cold. Cold? I don't feel the cold, he told himself. But he felt it now.

He felt other things he hadn't felt in a long time, things he thought he couldn't feel. Despair, fear, dread. When he came to the edge of the pier, he looked down in the icy water, saw bubbles rising to the surface.

He realized that despite all his planning, despite all his skill, things had gone terribly wrong. He didn't see the shape standing like a shadow between two aspens, gun aimed right at him.

He heard the voice… "Police! Drop the gun. Step away from the water."

Ole's gun arm twitched and he raised it just a little. There was a flash of light before a resounding crack.

Like mountains, high soaring above.

He never felt the pain as he fell backwards on the rotting boards.

Oh help us to see.

It was so silent in the woods. That's how he was able to hear the faraway thump of a helicopter.

FORTY-FOUR

Temeke stared out of the hospital window. The landscape was lightly dusted in snow and bloated clouds threatened to spill more rain.

He remembered a time when he hid out in an arroyo armed with a bow. Between the silvery heads of Apache plume, he watched the coyote as it scavenged on the dry river bed, vulnerable, unsuspecting. Pulling the drawstring to his cheek, he watched the arrow as it cambered and fell, striking the animal in the throat. He wasn't afraid then, and here he was dreading the moment when Ole would open his eyes.

He looked over at the bed and saw pale blond eyelashes flickering in sleep and a large bandage wound around the left shoulder. It would be so easy to take out his gun out and finish it, only Jarvis was sitting outside, ear pressed to the glass.

Temeke sat on the couch and flicked open the file turning to a photocopy of the little red notebook. He read the tiny scrawl as a deep and gnawing sadness began to build inside. He saw a vision through the wooden slats of a barn wall, a vision Kizzy had the day she died.

When I am afraid, I put my trust in you.

Her writing stopped there because the little pencil ran out of lead. A little pencil tied to the spine of an old milking journal the farmers once used. The field investigators found the room where Kizzy had been held. It was six feet by four, an old henhouse.

A groan and a clinking of chains brought him back to the present. Ole opened his eyes and gave Temeke a long hard stare.

"Are you sleeping okay?" Temeke said, hoping it wasn't as much as Sarge was getting. He still felt a twinge of fear like a cudgel in his ribs.

"There're demons in the Pen. Morgan says he can hear them screaming at night. He's in Level VI. Death Row."

"Supermax," Temeke said, nodding. Ole was dreaming up all kinds of guff in that comfy hospital bed. "It's to be expected. All those ghosts. You know, the ones after the riots."

"You say it like you don't care, Detective."

"I cared enough to find you, didn't I?"

"Took you long enough."

"And I cared enough to sit in the helicopter all the way to the hospital. Never heard such whining. Anyone would think you'd been shot in the head."

Ole half smiled at that. "You missed."

"Aimed for your shoulder, son. Could have been lower. You'd have a squeaky voice then, wouldn't you?"

Temeke leaned back, hands laced behind his head. It made him feel superior since Ole couldn't move his hands at all. He was proud of himself after that helicopter ride back to Albuquerque and he'd even climbed a tree, hadn't he? "You'll be in Supermax for a week or two over the holidays. Must be nice to have your best friend in the next cell. Because that would never happen in a hotel."

"We're brothers, detective. Always. Stick. Together."

"Not for long. Looks like California wants you more than we do. So you'll be going to San Quentin where every syringe is a cringe."

Ole leaned forward, eyes glaring. "Odin wanted nine heads. *Nine*. What was I supposed to do? Ignore him?"

"So you kidnapped nine girls. Nine beautiful girls. Jaelyn Gains, Lavonne Jackson, Mikaela May Ortega, Lyana Durgins, Elizabeth Moya, Mandy Guzman, Kizzy Williams, Patti Lucero and Becky Moran. Becky Moran got away so you took Tess Williams instead. And you killed Jack Reynolds."

"He was following me. He shouldn't have done that."

Temeke bit his lip to stifle the lump in his throat. "We found most of the girls' remains by the fire pit but we never found Kizzy Williams."

"I didn't want Loki to have her."

"Your wolf?"

Ole winced and laid his head back down on the pillow. "He made a meal out of the rest."

Temeke remembered the bones. When the animal had chewed them down to the gristle they had been set apart and arranged in order of size.

"It wasn't quite nine though, was it? Becky is a resourceful young woman. She found a way. And Tess Williams is a mystery. Do you know what I learned today? I learned she ran four hundred meters cross country for her school last year. She clocked the fastest time ever for track and field in New Mexico. She's going to meet the Governor tomorrow. Next year, the Olympics. And you would have killed my partner had it not been for her tenacity and dedication to find Tess. None of these women are like your mother, Ole. Remember that."

Ole gave a curt nod, muscles tight around his jaw. "Morgan thought he and Patti could run off with three million dollars."

"That's a tidy sum."

"I sold stocks and shares in the Bergenposten six

years ago. A multi-million dollar business. So I challenged him to a game of poker. Put a gun to his head. Made him agree to offer Patti up as a reward. He lost, of course. So I got Patti and the money."

"And he got time." It was all beginning to make sense to Temeke now.

"I took her with me, gave her a home. She was afraid. I didn't want her to be afraid."

"And that bothered you?"

"Yes. I look after my friends."

Friends? There was nothing *friendly* in a good kidnapping. "Did you rape her, Ole?"

"No. Patti wanted me. Loved me. She was the only one who did."

Temeke didn't want to ask about Becky. "What did you talk about?"

"Her mother. My mother."

"That was a scary thing wasn't it. Your mother. She became a crack addict after the real Morgan died. That's when her hunter boyfriend was put in jail. But she was found some years later hanging from a roller towel in a truck-stop bathroom. I never understood how she did it, roller towels being so close to the ground and all."

Ole seemed to go quiet. Seemed to frown at the memory. "Patti looked more like my mother than the rest. Same eyes, same smile. I loved her. I hated her."

"Tell me about Kizzy. Who did she remind you of?"

Ole shook his head. "No one I've ever known. She said there was a voice in the wind, a still, small voice. I don't believe in that stuff. I believe in other things."

"What kind of things?"

"Wings and voices." Ole's voice was smoother than a shrink. "You can hear them if you listen."

Temeke shook his head. It was all beginning to sound like a ghostly freak show.

"The demons of the nine worlds, Detective, half-animal, half-man. Odin's horde."

Temeke wasted no time in researching Odin, a Norse god, hanged from the world tree for nine days and nights. Only this *Odin* was beginning to sound like a real person and that was the part that bothered him.

"Kizzy wanted to go to the river," Ole murmured with a loud sigh. We went to the beaver ponds to catch fish."

"What kind of fish?"

"Trout. There are loads of them behind the boulders. She told me to close my eyes so I could listen to the trees. God's music she called it."

Pity she hadn't run away when your eyes were closed. Temeke had a vision of a little girl sitting on a rock like one of those woodland fairies he had seen in a book. She was a little person once. She was a little person still.

"We caught three and put them on the coals. It was her last supper."

Last supper... The words seemed to linger in Temeke's ears like a sad song.

"Then it was Wednesday, Odin's day. That's when it happened."

Wednesday, October 29th... Temeke felt a sliver of terror. He imagined a hunter's knife slicing through skin and bone and he had to clamp his lips together to stop from heaving.

"What happened?" Temeke said, clearing his throat.

"I was carving her face on a tree."

Temeke flexed the muscles in his legs. So Ole was the face-carver.

"They're like headstones you see," Ole said. "In memoriam."

"But there were no graves there."

"No." Ole looked out of the window for a moment and then back at Temeke. "I saw Patti running for the

311

road. She was dragging the little one by the hand. I wanted to shoot them. But I hesitated."

"Why? Why didn't you shoot them?" Temeke said.

"Kizzy treated me with respect. She called me *sir*." Ole's gaze drifted to the window again. "I liked her. But I am what I am."

"What are you?"

"Immortal. She wasn't scared of me until she knew."

The drone of Ole's voice was more than Temeke could stand. He hardly listened to the details and he hoped there were enough drugs in that cocktail to have knocked Kizzy out cold.

"Where's she buried?" he said, at last. "Can you at least tell me that?"

Temeke thought of the upright stones at the ranch. From the sky they would have appeared as two elliptical shapes joined together like a Norse funeral ship. Burial places. Only there was nothing buried there.

Ole looked down at his hands, the cuffs and the chains. His eyes were moist, but not enough for tears. "I… I carried her to the barn, to the table."

Temeke couldn't listen to the foul things Ole did with that axe. He tuned his mind to a pair of round cheeks, a slightly crooked front tooth, two pigtails and a smile that made him feel like he was floating. A face on the cork board in his office, a face in his mind.

Nothing seemed to scare him anymore.

"I covered her body with a bag," Ole murmured. "Tied her high up in the trees. This is where the great spirits are. The wolf spirits. I did it for them."

Temeke realized her body would have been well hidden when the leaves were still on the trees. The smell of creosote and paint on the tree trunks would have deterred the dogs from sniffing any higher and nobody had seen fit to check again. Captain Fowler missed the evidence and he would likely receive a disciplinary letter or suspension.

The room began to spin and Temeke couldn't breathe. A detective too emotional to control his feelings was like a doctor operating on his own child. It just wasn't allowed.

"You can hate me all you want," Ole murmured, "but I did what I was told to do."

"Who told you?"

"Odin."

"But you know he doesn't exist. What did your mother tell you in those early days? Do you remember?"

Temeke saw the curling lip and eyes that flicked around the room. "I remember the day I strangled the cat. I was six. She hated me then. I could see it in her eyes."

"Her cat?"

"Yes."

"Why did you kill it?"

"To punish her." Ole opened his mouth slightly, tongue pushed forward. "I saw her with the huntsman, saw her kissing him. I knew it was wrong. I told papa. That's when it all started. She slapped me. Told me I was a liar. She locked me in the outhouse. I was so cold I thought I was going to die."

"Who came to let you out?"

"Papa."

"Do you know how long you were in there?"

"Two days."

"He left soon after that, didn't he? Your father."

"The day Morgan died. The day I lost everything."

"Why Morgan?" Temeke asked. "Why did Johannes Elgar kill Morgan?"

Ole stared down at his hands, voice breaking. "He should have killed me…"

Temeke heard the sob in that tormented voice, began to replay the scene in agonizing detail. A little blond boy streaking through the woods, laughing, chasing rabbits. The huntsman couldn't possibly tell the twins apart. He wasn't to know the boy he caught at the cabin that day had been Ole, not Morgan.

Temeke studied the flat gaze. "So you inherited the Bergenposten."

"It gave me a future."

"It gave you something to barter with. A carrot to dangle. Morgan Eriksen was an athlete, a well-known swimmer in his class. Got himself in the local newspapers. That's how you found him. Same age, same build, same color hair. Same shaped face. Job done. Only Morgan was a sucker for money. Liked that lifestyle, didn't he? Patti was a corker and all. Only, she fell for you, for your charisma. Until she found out what you really are."

"She loved me," Ole said. "The only one."

"You took her by force."

"I never forced her."

"If the scars on her hands and feet are anything to go by, I'd say she was forced. And Morgan? How do you think he feels? Like a right prat I should imagine. You used him." Temeke closed the file and stared at those dead eyes. "Did you really believe the blood from nine heads would resurrect your dead brother?"

"The mead of poetry."

Temeke could almost taste the bile in his throat and he forced it down with a swallow. "And your mother? She died as many times as you strangled those girls. You won't be seeing me again. But I'll think of you on that last day. You'll be lying on a bed in agony and I'll be saluting your passing with a glass of whisky. And when you get to hell, they'll burn you good and well just to make sure there's nothing left."

FORTY-FIVE

Temeke closed the door and stood in the corridor. He looked down at Jarvis half asleep in his chair. "Think you can handle him?"

Jarvis frowned. "He's tied up, isn't he?"

"That's the problem. They had to take the cuffs off on account of the pain killers. You'll give him a hand if he wants to take a leak?" Temeke permitted himself a brief smile of satisfaction. "Must be off. Can't hang about."

He walked down the corridor to a tall oblong window, took out his phone and dialed Serena. *Your call cannot be completed as dialed. Please check the number and try again...* He listened to the intercept message before hanging up a second time. And when his phone did ring, it made him jump.

"Serena!" he was happy to hear her voice. "The case? Yes. We've got him. I tried to call you a few moments ago."

She mumbled something about a new number, thought it was time. Temeke felt lightheaded, thoughts scrambling to understand. "I'd like to take you to Ruidoso for a few days. Just you and me. Would you like that?"

He paused when he heard the sobs, the rasp in her voice. It was a sixth sense, something he could smell on the wind, and he tried not to hear her words, tried not to feel the aching in his chest.

"Why?" he asked.

It was no use running home. She had withdrawn to a distant place, far beyond his reach now. It was hard for him to imagine the house without her, an empty closet, an empty bed.

"I know it's hard for you to say these things. But not over the phone, love. Please not on the phone. We could meet. We could talk—"

She didn't want to talk, didn't want to hear another false promise. She was tired of the endless days waiting for him to come home, terrified he was lying face-down in a ditch like Luis. He had nearly died, hadn't he?

"But he didn't die, love. He's awake, talking. He even gave me his car keys."

That should have made her laugh, but instead there was a tremor to her voice, the sound of soft panting. Then she mentioned the weed, the smoking, the lying.

"Yes, I have lied to you. I've lied about the smoking because I'm an addict. I'm not perfect, Serena."

She wanted him to stop, wanted him to love her enough to stop. Did he love her?

"Of course I love you," he said. "You know I do. It's agony for me. All of this."

What was this thing about Becky? If he was lying about the smoking, then what else was he lying about?

"Oh, love, no. She's a *child*."

But there was talk in the department about women. They all gave her strange looks at parties, like she was the last to know.

"I wouldn't dream—"

He was left with that infernal dialing tone and for a long time he didn't move. He looked at his caller ID and saw the words *Private*, a message that told him she didn't want to be found. A small intake of breath, a hardening of the stomach and he raged inwardly at his own stupidity. Too late, he realized. He should have seen the signs.

He stared out at a speckled wilderness regimented with green piñon trees and cone-shaped hills. He began to debate with himself whether to trace the number or leave her in peace. It wouldn't be fair to run after her, he thought, seeing the remains of a white fir tree that lay embedded by the side of a hillock, bark calcified like the bones of some prehistoric animal. The relationship was dead. It had been dying for years.

There was one thing that gave him hope. Serena wouldn't go far, not with Luis in the hospital. He pictured himself standing in the hospital lobby wearing a dark suit and starched white shirt. He'd have his back to the front door, of course, so she wouldn't see the flowers.

He pressed the heel of his hands into both eyes, determined not to descend into that black mass of misery. What good would it do?

"Sir?"

Malin hobbled toward him, hand nursing her hip. He ignored her open mouth and the torrent of questions she was obviously itching to ask. "Does it hurt?" he asked.

Her hand signaled a so-so reply, golden skin radiant as if age would never touch her. "Doctor said I'd be fine in a day or two. Have you seen the papers?"

Temeke shook his head. It must have been good if she was smiling.

"The headline read *Two Albuquerque detectives hailed as heroes when they rescued a fourteen-year-old girl from the 9th Hour killer*. We've already got six thousands likes. Seems our photo went viral."

Temeke chuckled. He curled an arm around her waist. She was smaller than he expected, warmer too. He helped that strong, slender body to the parking lot, half-lifting her over the concrete parking blocks.

They found the Charger rammed between two trucks, cleaned and smelling of pine, judging by a small green tree that dangled from the rearview mirror. Malin eased herself into the passenger seat, face cringing with pain.

He started the car, keeping his eyes straight ahead, knowing she was savvy enough to have sensed a change in him. He was lonely. She must have sensed that.

"How's Eriksen?" she asked.

"Grumpy. I doubt he'll apologize in court. The jury will deliberate for less than three hours and give him the death penalty. No one will feel sorry for him. Except a few horny girls. He'll get his fair share of fan mail."

"How did he ever get into the United States?"

"Apparently, he boarded a fishing vessel at a port in Norway called Svelgen, gave the captain $40,000 in cash and kept him and his crew in beer for six weeks. He landed near Biddeford, Maine and stayed with a man called Mike Salthouse, a dab hand at forging ID's. Eriksen bought a truck and drove across land to California. Got residency there."

"That easy?"

"Afraid so."

"Morgan didn't kill the girls then?"

"He's an accessory." Temeke blew out a lungful of hot air. "He'll fry in California if I have anything to do with it."

Malin nodded. "I want to understand. I want to know why."

The question took him back to his rookie days in a finger snap. He'd asked his sergeant the very same question. "There's nothing to understand. A killer is a killer, a creature of incredible appetite. He blends in so you would never know. Alone, he isolates himself from humanity and all the while he lives in a valium-filled trance, pretending he is more than he is. A conqueror. But they all have one thing in common. They're unable to control their inner monster."

Temeke knew how flippant it all sounded. He blamed himself for the way it came out, tumbling from his mouth like a gush of words he was too numb to feel.

"Why did Ole keep the heads?" she asked.

"Souvenirs… it serves to refuel the fantasy. He'll waste away in a jail cell until he dies alone. Something every killer fears."

Ten minutes later, Temeke pulled up in front of her apartment, powered down the window and let the car suck in the cold air. There were no clusters of swirling snowflakes now, just a glaze of sunlight on a bed of dried leaves.

Malin grimaced, until she dropped her gaze. "Will you keep me on, sir?"

Temeke lifted his chin, realizing he was looking at her with unrestrained approval. She was strangely beautiful in the harsh glare of sunlight. "You're my partner, aren't you? Oh, and just call me Temeke."

She nodded and then smiled. He could smell her perfume now, stronger at the curve of her neck. He was painfully conscious that he had no right to touch her and he paused for a breathless second to look down at those large sympathetic eyes. "I'm proud of you," he said.

Malin scraped one hand through her glossy, black hair and took a calming breath. "Want to come in?"

He swiveled his eyes toward the parking lot, feeling her straighten just as he had. He almost buckled on account of his loneliness and shook his head. "You better get some sleep, Marl. I better go home."

ABOUT THE AUTHOR

Originally from England, Claire is a world traveler and makes her home in New Mexico, USA. She began writing as a child and received school awards for English literature. A former medical and executive assistant, she has helped lead workshops and has spoken at various literary events across the Southwest. Her interest in archaeology has inspired and informed all her writing from historical fiction to thrillers, and she is the author of two ancient Egyptian novels, *Chasing Pharaohs* and *The Fowler's Snare*.

She has published short stories and once ran a newspaper for two local businesses in Albuquerque. She has completed the second book in the Detective Temeke series, *Night Eyes*, in which she explores how even in the darkness of criminal depravity the light of faith is never entirely extinguished. She is currently working on the third novel, *Past Rites*.

To learn more about Claire, visit www.cmtstibbe.com. For news of her books, reviews, blogs and free eBooks, sign up for her newsletter at http://eepurl.com/bqCQhv.

Thank you for reading *The 9th Hour*. I sincerely hope you loved reading this novel as much as I loved writing it. If you liked it please consider posting a short review as genuine feedback is what makes all the lonely hours writers spend producing their work worthwhile.

An Excerpt from NIGHT EYES.

The second in the Detective Temeke series.

NIGHT EYES

Claire Stibbe

United States of America

ONE

He struggled alone in that deep, dark place, head tilted back as far as it would go. Water plugged his ears and the sharp pain between his ribs reminded him to take small breaths to preserve what little oxygen he had left.

It was some kind of urban runoff, a sewer that had become filled with sea water from one of the worst storms Long Beach had ever seen.

All because he'd kissed the girl.

He drew a bite of oxygen into his lungs and sunk slowly to the bottom. He tried to see something in those murky waters, pushed off again, broke through the surface and gasped for air. No way out, not that he could see.

During Basic Underwater Demolition Training, the instructors wouldn't allow a twenty-one-year-old SEAL to die in a watery grave, not with their shark eyes. He had been in the first group for drownproofing, all that bobbing and swimming and somersaults, hands tied behind his back. Only today, his hands weren't tied, nor were his feet.

Where am I? He tried to remember.

They had been on the beach that morning, shivering in the darkness. He couldn't see the ocean behind him, but he could hear the waves. It took one hundred push-ups to get warm, body sagging in the front leaning rest, waiting for permission to recover.

He remembered the instructor, a cold hulk of a man who did the PT with them, voice piercing through the early dawn. "Run with your thighs. Keep your arms loose. And breathe!" If they looked sleepy, they did it all over again.

He kept up with the pack, never looked back, didn't even blink when one of his team 'rang the bell.' He wouldn't quit. He'd never see her again if he did.

And here he was in a storm drain, a torrent of sea water gushing in through a cement pipe and large enough to stand in. Screaming to get out, screaming to be free and every part of him craved air. *Where were the rest of his class?*

They were gone, that's what. Him against the instructor, him against that terrible accusation. He hated everything. Everyone. It started when he saw the girl, frail like a little brown bird. He knew she wanted him, eyes following his every move. If felt good. It felt wrong. And he had fought it with every muscle in his head.

Now that same head felt tender on the left side and he thought he could smell blood, thought he could hear shouting. Another test perhaps, where the instructors watched from an observation chamber? Goosebumps pricked his flesh and his mind began to focus on his heart rate and the sudden peace he felt.

Be calm. Block the negative. Slow each breath, control the rhythm.

He had done more pushups than he could count, sit-ups, chin-ups and runs. Tried to get into shape, tried to be like the best of them. A friend persuaded him to take the PST, pushed him to swim five hundred yards in eight-and-a-half minutes. Called him Dingo. Because he could run.

It seemed so long ago when he swam in that wide ocean, waves breaking about his face and blurring his vision. A large bird flew overhead, a winged shadow in a dark sky. It blocked out the sun for a time, a climbing spec breasting the morning wind.

He had a fast crawl stroke, faster than the rest of them until he felt the vicious stab of cramp in his right calf. Kick-and-breathe... kick-and-breathe. He switched to sidestroke, had no technique whatsoever, except the will to finish as fast as he could. And he did finish. Eight minutes and twenty-seven seconds with three seconds to spare.

He barely remembered six pull-ups from a dead hang. He did eleven. Some did twelve. He ran eight-and-a-half miles in eight minutes and out of the twenty-nine who started, he was one of the six who passed. Trained to ensure that all muscles had adequate strength, a split body routine, no muscle left out. He should have been proud of himself.

His inner voice told him to give up, told him to look forward to a steaming cup of coffee. What it didn't tell him was that he would drink it in front of his teammates, watch them persevere, watch them become heroes. If he didn't survive the trials to go on to BUD/S, he would never become a SEAL, an unstoppable force, an elite group that the United States of America sends to do the impossible during times of war.

He gripped even harder then, got past the chaffing of sand on raw skin, the burning of salt water, the lack of sleep. He always looked past the fierce blue eyes of his instructor, through them, around them, anywhere but straight at them. He passed the underwater swim on the first try, his run times were good and he held the record in the obstacle course.

If only he hadn't seen the girl in the surf that Friday night all alone, cheeks spattered with tears. Looked like she'd been slapped around a bit. Looked like she wanted some comfort. He did a lot more than comfort her. Rolled in the sand for a while, held her close, loved her until the morning.

June… the year 2000, he thought. Blood poured down his face and the slit above his eye yawned wider than a crater. He'd need stitches when he got out. If he got out.

Something different. His feet touched bottom and he felt the final catch in his breath.

Hell Week. That was the last thing he remembered.

16871976R00195

Printed in Poland
by Amazon Fulfillment
Poland Sp. z o.o., Wrocław